A VISION OF SHADOWS

WARRIORS

RIVER OF FIRE

WARRIORS

THE PROPHECIES BEGIN

THE NEW PROPHECY

POWER OF THREE

OMEN OF THE STARS

EXPLORE THE WARRIORS WORLD

Warriors: Enter the Clans
Warriors: The Ultimate Guide
Warriors: The Untold Stories
Warriors: Tales from the Clans
Warriors: Shadows of the Clans
Warriors: Legends of the Clans

MANGA

The Lost Warrior
Warrior's Refuge
Warrior's Return
The Rise of Scourge
Tigerstar and Sasha #1: Into the Woods
Tigerstar and Sasha #2: Escape from the Forest
Tigerstar and Sasha #3: Return to the Clans
Ravenpaw's Path #1: Shattered Peace
Ravenpaw's Path #2: A Clan in Need
Ravenpaw's Path #3: The Heart of a Warrior
SkyClan and the Stranger #1: The Rescue
SkyClan and the Stranger #2: Beyond the Code
SkyClan and the Stranger #3: After the Flood

NOVELLAS

Hollyleaf's Story
Mistystar's Omen
Cloudstar's Journey
Tigerclaw's Fury
Leafpool's Wish
Dovewing's Silence

Mapleshade's Vengeance
Goosefeather's Curse
Ravenpaw's Farewell
Spottedleaf's Heart
Pinestar's Choice
Thunderstar's Echo

Also by Erin Hunter

SEEKERS

Book One: The Quest Begins
Book Two: Great Bear Lake
Book Three: Smoke Mountain
Book Four: The Last Wilderness
Book Five: Fire in the Sky
Book Six: Spirits in the Stars

RETURN TO THE WILD

Book One: Island of Shadows
Book Two: The Melting Sea
Book Three: River of Lost Bears
Book Four: Forest of Wolves
Book Five: The Burning Horizon
Book Six: The Longest Day

MANGA

Toklo's Story
Kallik's Adventure

SURVIVORS

Book One: *The Empty City*
Book Two: *A Hidden Enemy*
Book Three: *Darkness Falls*
Book Four: *The Broken Path*
Book Five: *The Endless Lake*
Book Six: *Storm of Dogs*

THE GATHERING DARKNESS

Book One: *A Pack Divided*
Book Two: *Dead of Night*
Book Three: *Into the Shadows*
Book Four: *Red Moon Rising*

Survivors: Tales from the Packs

NOVELLAS

Alpha's Tale
Sweet's Journey
Moon's Choice

BRAVELANDS

Book One: *Broken Pride*
Book Two: *Code of Honor*

A VISION OF SHADOWS

WARRIORS

RIVER OF FIRE

ERIN HUNTER

HARPER

An Imprint of HarperCollinsPublishers

Special thanks to Cherith Baldry

River of Fire

Copyright © 2018 by Working Partners Limited

Series created by Working Partners Limited

Map art © 2018 by Dave Stevenson

Interior art © 2018 by Owen Richardson

www.harpercollinschildrens.com

Library of Congress Control Number: 2017951334

ISBN 978-0-06-238653-3 (trade bdg.) — ISBN 978-0-06-238654-0 (lib. bdg.)

Typography by Ellice M. Lee

18 19 20 21 22   CG/LSCH   10 9 8 7 6 5 4 3 2 1

❖

First Edition

ALLEGIANGES

THUNDERCLAN

LEADER

BRAMBLESTAR—dark brown tabby tom with amber eyes

DEPUTY

SQUIRRELFLIGHT—dark ginger she-cat with green eyes and one white paw

MEDIGINE GATS

LEAFPOOL—light brown tabby she-cat with amber eyes, white paws and chest

JAYFEATHER—gray tabby tom with blind blue eyes

ALDERHEART—dark ginger tom with amber eyes

WARRIORS

(toms and she-cats without kits)

BRACKENFUR—golden-brown tabby tom

CLOUDTAIL—long-haired white tom with blue eyes

BRIGHTHEART—white she-cat with ginger patches

THORNCLAW—golden-brown tabby tom

WHITEWING—white she-cat with green eyes

BIRCHFALL—light brown tabby tom

BERRYNOSE—cream-colored tom with a stump for a tail

MOUSEWHISKER—gray-and-white tom

POPPYFROST—pale tortoiseshell-and-white she-cat

LIONBLAZE—golden tabby tom with amber eyes

ROSEPETAL—dark cream she-cat

BRIARLIGHT—dark brown she-cat, paralyzed in her hindquarters

LILYHEART—small, dark tabby she-cat with white patches and blue eyes

BUMBLESTRIPE—very pale gray tom with black stripes

CHERRYFALL—ginger she-cat

MOLEWHISKER—brown-and-cream tom

AMBERMOON—pale ginger she-cat

DEWNOSE—gray-and-white tom

STORMCLOUD—gray tabby tom

HOLLYTUFT—black she-cat

FERNSONG—yellow tabby tom

SORRELSTRIPE—dark brown she-cat

LEAFSHADE—tortoiseshell she-cat

LARKSONG—black tom

HONEYFUR—white she-cat with yellow splotches

SPARKPELT—orange tabby she-cat

QUEENS

(she-cats expecting or nursing kits)

DAISY—cream long-furred cat from the horseplace

CINDERHEART—gray tabby she-cat (mother to Snapkit, a golden tabby tom-kit; Spotkit, a spotted tabby she-kit; and Flykit, a striped tabby she-kit)

BLOSSOMFALL—tortoiseshell-and-white she-cat with petal-shaped white patches (mother to Stemkit, a white and orange tom-kit; Eaglekit, a ginger she-kit; Plumkit, a black-and-ginger she-kit; and Shellkit, a tortoiseshell tom-kit)

IVYPOOL—silver-and-white tabby she-cat with dark blue eyes

ELDERS (former warriors and queens, now retired)

GRAYSTRIPE—long-haired gray tom

MILLIE—striped silver tabby she-cat with blue eyes

SKYCLAN

LEADER **LEAFSTAR**—brown-and-cream tabby she-cat with amber eyes

DEPUTY **HAWKWING**—dark gray tom with yellow eyes

MEDICINE CATS **FRECKLEWISH**—mottled light brown tabby she-cat with spotted legs
APPRENTICE, FIDGETPAW (black-and-white tom)

PUDDLESHINE—brown tom with white splotches

WARRIORS **SPARROWPELT**—dark brown tabby tom
APPRENTICE, NECTARPAW (brown she-cat)

MACGYVER—black-and-white tom
APPRENTICE, DEWPAW (sturdy gray tom)

PLUMWILLOW—dark gray she-cat

SAGENOSE—pale gray tom
APPRENTICE, GRAVELPAW (tan tom)

HARRYBROOK—gray tom
APPRENTICE, FRINGEPAW (white she-cat with brown splotches)

BLOSSOMHEART—ginger-and-white she-cat
APPRENTICE, FINPAW (brown tom)

SANDYNOSE—stocky light brown tom with ginger legs
APPRENTICE, TWIGPAW (gray she-cat with green eyes)

RABBITLEAP—brown tom
APPRENTICE, PALEPAW (black-and-white she-cat)

BELLALEAF—pale orange she-cat with green eyes
APPRENTICE, REEDPAW

ROWANCLAW—ginger tom

TAWNYPELT—tortoiseshell she-cat with green eyes
APPRENTICE, SNAKEPAW (honey-colored tabby she-cat)

JUNIPERCLAW—black tom
APPRENTICE, WHORLPAW (gray-and-white tom)

STRIKESTONE—brown tabby tom

STONEWING—white tom

GRASSHEART—pale brown tabby she-cat

SCORCHFUR—dark gray tom with slashed ears
APPRENTICE, FLOWERPAW (silver she-cat)

VIOLETSHINE—black-and-white she-cat with yellow eyes

MINTFUR—gray tabby she-cat with blue eyes

NETTLESPLASH—pale brown tom

QUEENS　　**TINYCLOUD**—small white she-cat (mother to Quailkit, a tom with crow-black ears; Pigeonkit, a gray-and-white she-kit; and Sunnykit, a ginger she-kit)

SNOWBIRD—pure white she-cat with green eyes (mother to Gullkit, a white she-kit; Conekit, a white-and-gray tom; and Frondkit, a gray tabby she-kit)

ELDERS　　**FALLOWFERN**—pale brown she-cat who has lost her hearing

OAKFUR—small brown tom

RATSCAR—scarred, skinny dark brown tom

WINDCLAN

LEADER　　**HARESTAR**—brown-and-white tom

DEPUTY　　**CROWFEATHER**—dark gray tom

MEDICINE CAT　　**KESTRELFLIGHT**—mottled gray tom with white splotches like kestrel feathers

WARRIORS　　**NIGHTCLOUD**—black she-cat
APPRENTICE, BRINDLEPAW (mottled brown she-cat)

GORSETAIL—very pale gray-and-white she-cat with blue eyes

LEAFTAIL—dark tabby tom with amber eyes

EMBERFOOT—gray tom with two dark paws
APPRENTICE, SMOKEPAW (gray she-cat)

BREEZEPELT—black tom with amber eyes

LARKWING—pale brown tabby she-cat

SEDGEWHISKER—light brown tabby she-cat

SLIGHTFOOT—black tom with white flash on his chest

OATCLAW—pale brown tabby tom

FEATHERPELT—gray tabby she-cat

HOOTWHISKER—dark gray tom

HEATHERTAIL—light brown tabby she-cat with blue eyes

FERNSTRIPE—gray tabby she-cat

ELDERS   **WHITETAIL**—small white she-cat

RIVERCLAN

LEADER   **MISTYSTAR**—gray she-cat with blue eyes

DEPUTY   **REEDWHISKER**—black tom

MEDICINE CATS   **MOTHWING**—dappled golden she-cat
WILLOWSHINE—gray tabby she-cat

WARRIORS   **MINTFUR**—light gray tabby tom
APPRENTICE, SOFTPAW (gray she-cat)

DUSKFUR—brown tabby she-cat
APPRENTICE, DAPPLEPAW (gray-and-white tom)

MINNOWTAIL—dark gray-and-white she-cat
APPRENTICE, BREEZEPAW (brown-and-white she-cat)

MALLOWNOSE—light brown tabby tom

BEETLEWHISKER—brown-and-white tabby tom
APPRENTICE, HAREPAW (white tom)

CURLFEATHER—pale brown she-cat

PODLIGHT—gray-and-white tom

HERONWING—dark gray-and-black tom

SHIMMERPELT—silver she-cat

    APPRENTICE, NIGHTPAW (dark gray she-cat with blue eyes)

LIZARDTAIL—light brown tom

HAVENPELT—black-and-white she-cat

SNEEZECLOUD—gray-and-white tom

BRACKENPELT—tortoiseshell she-cat

    APPRENTICE, GORSEPAW (white tom with gray ears)

JAYCLAW—gray tom

OWLNOSE—brown tabby tom

LAKEHEART—gray tabby she-cat

ICEWING—white she-cat with blue eyes

ELDERS

MOSSPELT—tortoiseshell-and-white she-cat

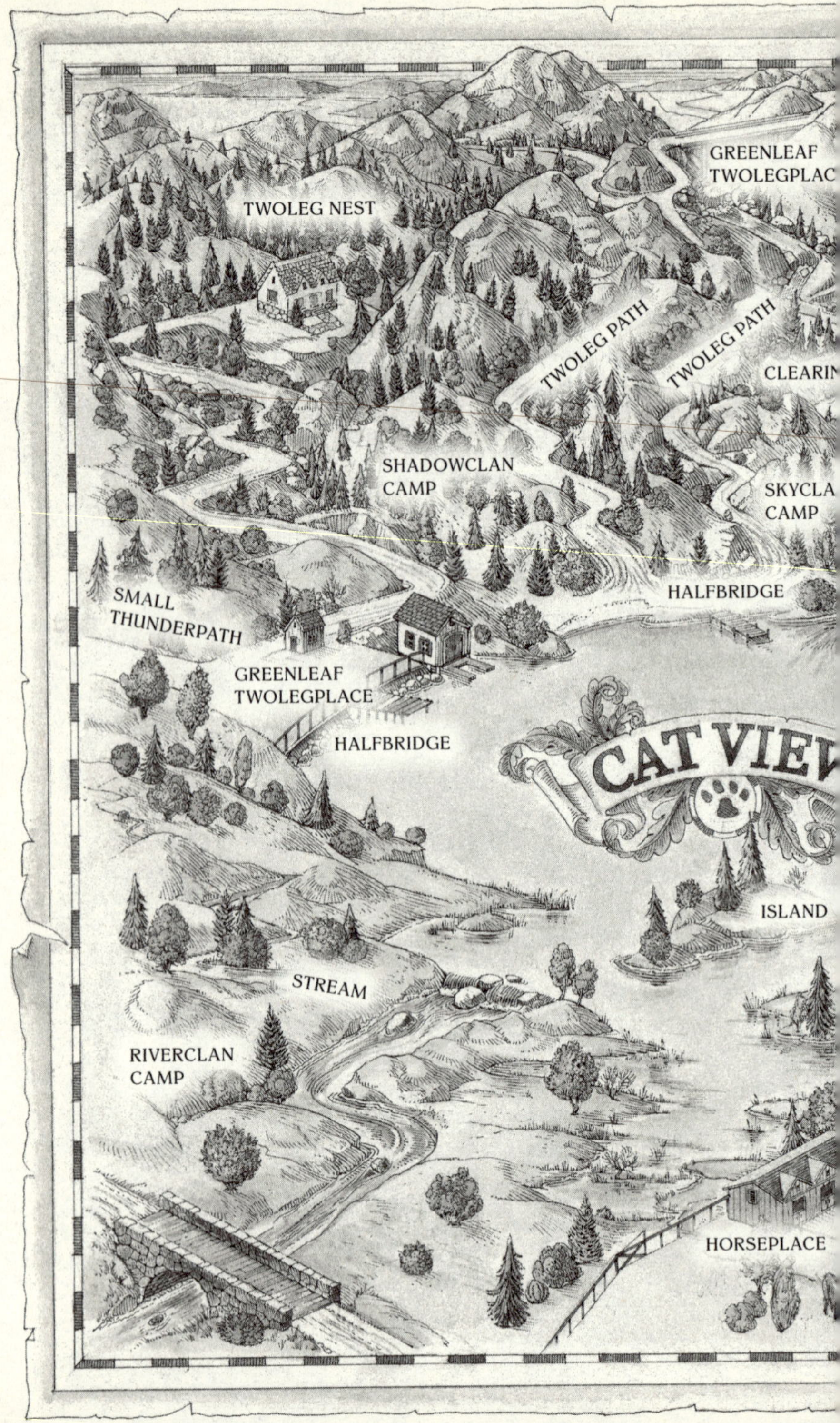
GREENLEAF
TWOLEGPLAC
TWOLEG NEST
TWOLEG PATH
TWOLEG PATH
CLEARIN
SHADOWCLAN
CAMP
SKYCLA
CAMP
HALFBRIDGE
SMALL
THUNDERPATH
GREENLEAF
TWOLEGPLACE
HALFBRIDGE
CAT VIEW
ISLAND
STREAM
RIVERCLAN
CAMP
HORSEPLACE

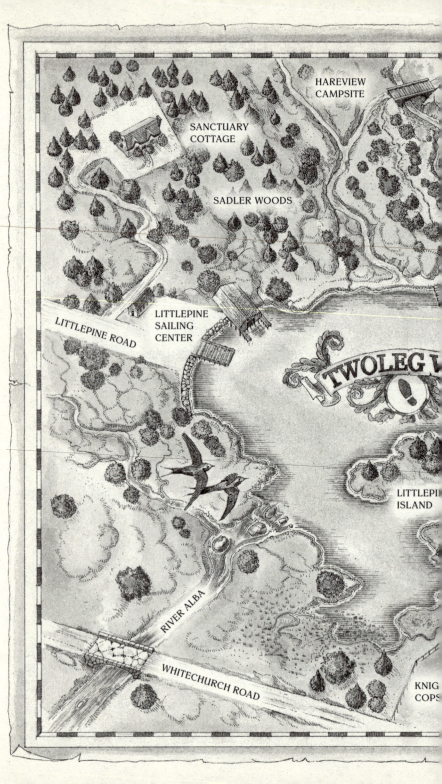

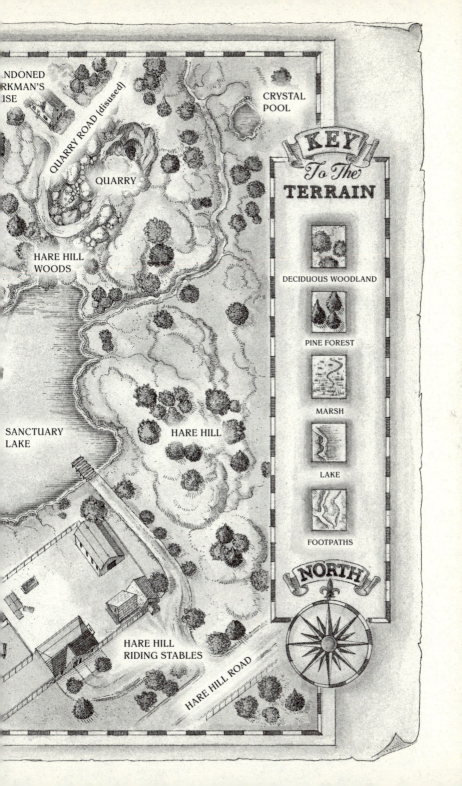

PROLOGUE

A warm breeze wafted over the grass, carrying with it the scents of prey and the fresh green growth of newleaf. The sun shone from a blue sky crossed by scudding white clouds. A small stream gurgled its way down a gentle slope, then widened out into a pool fringed with rushes.

A group of cats sat beside the pool, while others stalked up and down along the bank. Frost shimmered in their fur, and starlight glittered at their paws and in their eyes.

"I can't believe this has happened!" a cream-furred she-cat lamented. "I gave up my life trying to get back to Shadow-Clan." Her voice shook as she went on. "I never thought there would be a time when ShadowClan didn't exist!"

A plump white she-cat nuzzled her shoulder briefly, her black ears quivering. "I know, Dawnpelt," she murmured with a sorrowful glance around at her Clanmates. "Maybe it's our fault. Maybe we didn't fight hard enough for ShadowClan while we were alive."

A disdainful hiss came from a slim, silver-pelted cat, who had been pacing restlessly near the water's edge. She halted and rounded on the others, her front claws tearing angrily at the grass. "You're wrong, Beenose," she snarled. "We couldn't have saved a Clan that didn't want to be saved. We have to place the blame where it belongs: on Rowanstar. Rowan*claw*, as he's calling himself now."

"That's easily said, Needletail." The rasping voice came from an old gray she-cat with rumpled fur and glaring amber eyes, who sat on top of a boulder a couple of tail-lengths away. "But Rowanstar wasn't the only cat who misunderstood Darktail's true intentions. Did some of you not call yourselves Darktail's Kin?"

"Of course, Yellowfang, you always know everything," Needletail retorted, her tone edged with sarcasm.

"I've seen more in my time than you young cats." Yellowfang's voice rumbled from deep within her chest. "I thought once that nothing worse than Brokenstar's leadership could happen to my Clan. But I was wrong."

"I trusted Rowanstar," a white tom added from where he sat at the base of Yellowfang's rock. He swiped his tongue over one black forepaw and used it to wash his ears. "I thought he would make a fine leader after me. But what was he to do when half his Clan betrayed him and followed Darktail?"

Dawnpelt nodded sadly. "You're right, Blackstar. I know we also made mistakes."

"And now the ShadowClan cats who are left have joined SkyClan," Beenose murmured. "But will Leafstar and the rest of SkyClan ever really trust them? We should all have tried harder when we had the chance."

"That's a load of mouse droppings!" Needletail meowed,

her green eyes narrowing. "A strong leader could have held the Clan together, Darktail or no Darktail. We were only tempted by Darktail because of Rowanclaw's weakness. And now that Darktail is dead, a strong leader would already be rebuilding the Clan. Rowanclaw accepted nine lives from StarClan, and now he's all, 'Thank you very much, I don't want them anymore.' What cat *does* that?"

Blackstar puffed out a sigh and shook his head. "No cat . . or at least, no cat *should*," he admitted.

"And now the whole Clan is suffering," Needletail hissed. "That mange-pelt—"

"Enough!" A new voice rang out.

They all turned to see a cat standing at the top of the slope, outlined against the sky. As they watched, she headed toward them, brushing her way through the grass with neat, purposeful paw steps. Stars streamed through her thick black fur like water.

"Who's that?" Needletail muttered, glaring at the newcomer.

"No idea," Blackstar replied, looking puzzled. "She's no ShadowClan cat I've ever seen."

The strange cat halted in front of the group of cats, seemingly undaunted by their bristling neck fur and twitching tail-tips.

"You may not have seen me," she mewed calmly to Blackstar, "but I have seen you, many times. I am Shadowstar, the first leader of your Clan."

Every cat instinctively took a step back. Dawnpelt let out a gasp, while murmurs of astonishment rose from the other cats. Yellowfang dipped her head respectfully, and even Needletail looked awed.

"You should not pass blame along so casually," Shadowstar went on, fixing Needletail with a stern gaze. "The end of ShadowClan is about much more than Rowanclaw's failure or the loss of your territory. Since the beginning, ShadowClan was destined to be one of the five Clans."

The ShadowClan cats glanced uncertainly at one another.

"Why have you come to tell us this?" Yellowfang asked at last.

"The other first leaders and I led groups of cats, each group finding the place—moor, forest, river, or marsh—best suited to those cats' characters and abilities. These groups, which would become the five Clans, then united in purpose for all our survival," Shadowstar explained. "Only by working together, five separate but connected groups, like the petals of the blazing star, could we survive. Now you—not just ShadowClan, but the ancestors of all the Clans—*must* send a message to the living cats." Her eyes glowed, the color of sunlight on fresh leaves, as she added, "There *must* be five Clans! ShadowClan *must* be saved!"

"But it's too late," Dawnpelt mewed wretchedly.

"We've already given the Clans a prophecy," Blackstar pointed out. "But they're ignoring it."

Shadowstar lashed her tail. "If the fifth Clan is not saved, worse things will come than a storm," she meowed. "Eventually it will mean the end of all the remaining Clans. And if we have no living cats to guide, it will mean the end of StarClan itself."

A shocked silence fell over the group of starry warriors. None of them had ever imagined a time when there would be no StarClan.

It was Needletail who broke the silence. "In that case," she responded, raising a paw to smooth her whiskers, "we'd better get working on the right message to send. . . ."

Chapter 1

"Look at this tree!" Finpaw exclaimed. "It's *huge*! Do you think there are squirrels up there?"

Twigpaw halted, suppressing a sigh of exasperation as she watched Finpaw scamper over to a massive oak tree and balance precariously on a thick, gnarled root. Her paws were tingling with anxiety and anticipation. She didn't want to stop *again*; she wanted to be at ThunderClan's camp.

What if they don't want us?

"I wouldn't be surprised," Twigpaw responded, firmly pushing her nervousness away. "But we're not hunting now. Remember, we have to reach the ThunderClan camp before it gets dark."

Already the sun was starting to go down, flooding the forest floor with scarlet light, barred with the long, dark shadows of trees. Twigpaw and Finpaw had spent most of the afternoon traveling from the SkyClan camp, slowed down by Finpaw's irrepressible urge to explore.

"I can't wait!" Finpaw leaped off the root and raced across the grass to rejoin Twigpaw. She had to step back abruptly to save herself from being knocked over. Finpaw's tail flipped into her face.

"Hey, watch it!" she exclaimed with a glare.

"Sorry." Finpaw veered in front of Twigpaw, and she almost fell over her own paws trying to avoid him. "Do you think they'll be pleased to see us?"

A flutter of anticipation woke inside Twigpaw's belly at the thought of meeting her old Clanmates again. *I tried so hard to be a SkyClan warrior,* she thought. *But my heart is in ThunderClan. I'm so glad I made the decision to come back . . . and even happier that Finpaw decided to come with me. Surely they'll welcome us. ThunderClan is my home.*

"I'm sure they will," she replied to Finpaw.

"Is it true what they say about ThunderClan?" Finpaw asked as the two young cats walked on side by side. He stretched his jaws into an enormous yawn. "Are they really so bossy, always telling other cats what to do?"

Twigpaw wasn't sure how to reply. She knew that was exactly the way the other Clans sometimes viewed Bramblestar's cats, but she had lived with ThunderClan for many moons, and she knew there was no simple answer.

Besides, she had more important things on her mind. Even though she had told Finpaw she was sure ThunderClan would be pleased to see them, she couldn't help wondering how they would really react when she and her friend walked into their camp. *They will be happy, right? Surely they've missed me since I chose to go with my father?*

Twigpaw's father, Hawkwing, was the deputy of SkyClan, and every cat had expected she would stay in the newly settled Clan with him and her sister, Violetshine.

But I wasn't raised *there,* she told herself. *It took me a while to realize how big a part ThunderClan has played in my life, right from when I was a kit.*

As they rounded a bramble thicket, a familiar scent drifted over Twigpaw; she opened her jaws to taste the air more carefully.

"What is it?" Finpaw asked. "Is it prey? I'm starving!"

"No," Twigpaw replied. "It's the ThunderClan border scent markers. We're almost home! Come on!"

She bounded forward, with Finpaw pelting along enthusiastically at her side. The ThunderClan scent grew stronger as they approached the border, and as they reached the line of scent markers, Twigpaw began to distinguish another familiar scent, this one of a single cat.

"That's Sparkpelt!" she exclaimed. "You must have met her when SkyClan was living in the ThunderClan camp. She's Alderheart's sister. She must be somewhere around here. Sparkpelt!" she yowled, leaping up onto a small boulder that lay on the border line. "Hey, Sparkpelt!"

A clump of ferns rustled, and the fronds parted as Sparkpelt charged into the open. To Twigpaw's amazement, her orange tabby pelt was bristling, and when she halted at the border, she arched her back and slid out her claws as if she was facing an enemy.

"Twigpaw! What's going on here?" she demanded. "Why

are you so far away from your camp, without your mentors? Has SkyClan been attacked? Is it more rogues?"

"No, no, everything's fine," Twigpaw meowed reassuringly, feeling almost amused at Sparkpelt's urgent questions. "There's no trouble in SkyClan."

Sparkpelt relaxed slightly, her fluffed-out fur lying flat once more. But her eyes narrowed in suspicion as she glanced from Twigpaw to Finpaw and back again. "So what *are* you doing here?" she asked.

Once again Twigpaw felt the enormity of what she was doing, like a huge cloud gathering over her head, ready to release a storm. *There's no going back,* she thought. *Leafstar would never take me in again, after this. What will happen if ThunderClan sends me away?*

"I've come home," she replied, leaping down from her boulder. It was hard to form the words, as if her mouth were full of prey that she couldn't spit out. "I want to be part of Thunder-Clan again."

"And I've come with her," Finpaw added cheerfully.

Sparkpelt's ears twitched. "Just like that?" she meowed scornfully. "Cats can't just defect to whichever Clan they feel like, whenever they want. That isn't how it works. You made your decision, Twigpaw, and now you have to stick to it. And this SkyClan cat—he has no relationship to ThunderClan, so what does he think he's doing here?"

Pain slashed deep inside Twigpaw like a massive claw. Whatever she had expected, it wasn't this outright rejection. *I thought Sparkpelt was my friend!* Her head drooped, and she struggled to keep her voice steady as she responded.

"I know I must have hurt and upset some of you when I chose to go with my kin to SkyClan," she began, praying that she would find the right words. "It was a huge mistake, and I shouldn't have left the way I did. But surely you can understand that I was mixed up at the time?"

Sparkpelt made no reply, but the tip of her tail twitched once, then back again.

"Living with SkyClan showed me that I really *am* a ThunderClan cat," Twigpaw went on desperately. "This is where I belong."

"I'm not sure Bramblestar will see it that way," Sparkpelt growled.

"I need to talk to him," Twigpaw assured her. "I just want the chance to tell him how I feel. If Bramblestar doesn't allow me back, then I'll accept his decision."

But what in StarClan will I do if that happens? she asked herself.

"There's no way Bramblestar will turn away a cat like Twigpaw!" Finpaw mewed, bright and full of spirit as he always was. "Twigpaw is great!"

Sparkpelt fixed the small brown tom with a glare. "And who are you again, and what exactly are you doing here?"

"I'm Finpaw." Sparkpelt's aggressive stance didn't seem to bother him at all; he faced the ThunderClan warrior with his head raised and his short tail stuck in the air. "We met when SkyClan first came to the lake—remember?"

"Now I do." Sparkpelt's eyes narrowed again. "That still doesn't tell me why you're here."

"I'm here to be part of ThunderClan with Twigpaw," Finpaw asserted confidently. "All the cats in ThunderClan are heroes—every cat around the lake knows that. You're the best! I want to join you and have adventures!"

Sparkpelt seemed unmoved by Finpaw's praise. "Well, all right," she meowed, flicking her ears irritably. "I'll take you to our camp. Walk a tail-length ahead of me, so I can keep an eye on you. And don't think of putting a single *whisker* out of line."

"We're not enemies!" Twigpaw's pelt bristled indignantly. "What do you think we're going to do?"

"Keep your fur on!" Sparkpelt retorted. "I'm just taking the proper precautions."

And hedgehogs fly! Twigpaw thought resentfully.

With Finpaw at her side, she crossed the border and headed in the familiar direction of the stone hollow, feeling awkward under Sparkpelt's suspicious gaze. She was trying hard to ignore the growing heaviness in her belly, but Sparkpelt's hostility had come as a nasty shock.

It'll be fine once we get to the camp, she reassured herself. *Bramblestar will understand. He* has *to!*

The sun had gone down by the time the cats reached the thorn barrier that stretched across the entrance to the hollow, and twilight brought the chill of early leaf-fall. Sparkpelt pushed past the apprentices to lead the way down the tunnel.

"Follow me," she mewed curtly.

When Twigpaw emerged into the stone hollow, the whole of ThunderClan seemed to be there. Her heart warmed as she saw so many familiar faces: Cherryfall and Molewhisker sharing a piece of prey beside the fresh-kill pile; Blossomfall sitting with Cinderheart at the entrance to the nursery while their kits frisked and play wrestled around their paws; Graystripe and Millie stretched out drowsily side by side in front of the hazel bush where they slept; Leafpool and Jayfeather earnestly discussing something beside the bramble screen that shielded their den.

With a swish of her tail Sparkpelt beckoned the two apprentices a few paces farther into the camp, then signaled for them to halt. "Wait here," she ordered.

Twigpaw watched her as she bounded across the hollow and scrambled up the tumbled rocks to the Highledge, where she disappeared into Bramblestar's den.

"I hope everything's going to be okay," Twigpaw murmured.

"Of course it will." Finpaw nuzzled her shoulder briefly. "Bramblestar would have to have bees in his brain not to want you in his Clan."

Before Twigpaw could reply, Sorrelstripe slid out of the warriors' den and headed toward the thorn tunnel, only to come to an abrupt stop as she spotted Twigpaw and Finpaw.

"Hey!" she exclaimed. "Twigpaw's here!"

Her surprised yowl alerted every cat in the camp. Cats in the open sprang to their paws, while more pushed their way out of the warriors' den. All of them crowded around Twigpaw and Finpaw, until Twigpaw felt that she could hardly breathe in the midst of so many bright, questioning eyes and twitching whiskers.

"I thought I caught a familiar scent." Brackenfur gave Twigpaw a friendly nod. "It's good to see you, Twigpaw."

"Why are you here?" Fernsong asked.

"Is there trouble in SkyClan?" Lionblaze slid out his claws. "Do you need our help?"

Twigpaw swallowed hard, her pelt prickling with nervousness. Every cat was looking at her expectantly. "No, SkyClan is fine," Twigpaw replied. "But I've left them. I've come home to live in ThunderClan."

Utter silence greeted her announcement for a couple of heartbeats, followed by an outbreak of astonished yowling.

"Coming *home*? Your home is in SkyClan now."

"What about your kin?"

"Who is this SkyClan cat with you?"

Berrynose, at the front of the crowd, looked down at Twigpaw with a disdainful twitch of his whiskers. "You chose to leave, and now you want back in?" he demanded. "Can we ever trust you again?"

Murmurs of agreement came from several other cats.

Twigpaw wished that the ground would open up and swallow her, until she spotted movement from the medicine cats' den. With a gasp of relief she recognized Alderheart pushing his way through the cluster of cats to stand at her side.

Thank StarClan! Alderheart practically raised me. He'll understand.

"Of course we can trust her," Alderheart meowed, his dark

ginger pelt beginning to bristle as he faced Berrynose. "Of course we want her back! She was raised in ThunderClan, so she's one of us." His amber eyes were warm and supportive as he gazed at her.

Twigpaw felt as if the sun had just come out from behind a cloud when she heard Alderheart call her "one of us." Aware that some of her former Clanmates were still hostile, she tried to hide her sudden happiness by bowing her head and studying her paws. But Alderheart's praise made her feel warm from her ears to her tail-tip.

I've missed Alderheart so much since I left ThunderClan!

"Twigpaw!"

A commanding yowl rang out across the camp. Twigpaw looked up to see Bramblestar standing on the Highledge with Sparkpelt by his side. He beckoned Twigpaw with his tail. "Come up here," he ordered. "You and I must talk."

Twigpaw exchanged an uncertain glance with Finpaw. *Will he be okay if I leave him here by himself?*

Then Alderheart gave her a gentle push. "Go on," he meowed. "I'll look after Finpaw. Let's find you some prey," he added to the young tom. "You must be hungry."

"Starving!" Finpaw agreed fervently.

Reassured, Twigpaw hurried across the camp and began to climb the tumbled rocks. Sparkpelt passed her heading downward; she said nothing, but gave Twigpaw an unfriendly stare.

"Come into my den," Bramblestar invited Twigpaw when she reached the Highledge.

Following him inside, Twigpaw felt uncomfortable, almost

unworthy, to be having a private conversation with the ThunderClan leader. To her relief, Bramblestar didn't seem angry, but there was concern in his eyes as he stood looking down at her.

"Sparkpelt reported to me that you say you want to rejoin ThunderClan," he said. "You must realize, Twigpaw, that it's not usual for a cat to be so confused about where they belong."

Something in his words woke a spark of defiance inside Twigpaw. "How many cats have grown up the way I did?" she challenged Bramblestar. "Has any other cat lost her parents and her entire Clan, been separated from her sister, and then found a father she thought was dead? I admit I was confused, but I know where I belong now. Haven't I proved my loyalty to ThunderClan by coming back? I'm ready to become a ThunderClan warrior."

Bramblestar's voice was quiet as he responded. "I don't doubt that loyalty to ThunderClan is in your heart today," he mewed. "But it's not always that simple. The warrior code requires us to be loyal to *one* Clan. If you're moving back and forth between Clans, where does your heart really lie?"

Pausing, he settled himself in his nest and motioned with one paw for Twigpaw to sit opposite him.

"I remember when I was an apprentice, back in the old forest," he began. "Something similar happened: Graystripe left ThunderClan for RiverClan because he had kits with a River-Clan cat named Silverstream. She died, and when RiverClan claimed the kits, Graystripe thought it was his duty to go with them and raise them."

"Graystripe . . . ," Twigpaw breathed out, hardly able to imagine that the sturdy, loyal elder would ever have mated with a cat from another Clan.

Bramblestar nodded. "Then, when RiverClan invaded and tried to take Sunningrocks from ThunderClan, Graystripe couldn't fight for them against us. RiverClan drove him into exile. Bluestar, who was leader then, took him back, but it was a tense and confusing time, and no cat knew who could be trusted."

"But it worked out in the end, right?" Twigpaw pointed out. "Every cat trusts Graystripe now. Besides," she added, her neck fur beginning to bristle in spite of her efforts to stay calm, "SkyClan isn't going to *attack* us! That's mouse-brained!"

The words were hardly out before Twigpaw realized that a mere apprentice shouldn't call her Clan leader mouse-brained. *I've probably ruined my chances of getting back in!*

But Bramblestar's only response was to twitch his ears. "I know they won't—but when you get so indignant at the very idea, it shows that you still hold some loyalty to your kin's Clan. SkyClan is in your blood."

"But I've already tried SkyClan!" Twigpaw protested. "Now I *know* I don't belong there."

Bramblestar hesitated, letting out a thoughtful sigh. "I can see you really mean it," he mewed at last. "And I would be happy to welcome you back into ThunderClan, but . . ." His voice trailed off.

Twigpaw's sudden flash of optimism at the Clan leader's

first words faded into uncertainty. "But?"

"This is where your story is different from Graystripe's," Bramblestar told her. "He was a grown *warrior* when he switched Clans, not an apprentice. You chose to leave ThunderClan right before your warrior ceremony rather than become a ThunderClan warrior. Twigpaw, I want to believe that you will be loyal to ThunderClan, but I think it will be the right thing for you to complete a short apprenticeship here . . . a kind of probation, to make sure you really want to be a ThunderClan warrior."

At first Twigpaw felt hot anger gathering in her belly. She had already completed a ThunderClan apprenticeship, and then another after she left to join SkyClan. She had assumed that Bramblestar would make her a warrior right away.

More apprentice work? she thought. *I bet that no cat who ever lived has ever shifted as many ticks off the elders' pelts!*

But Twigpaw knew she had to control her anger. She was too grateful for the chance that the Clan leader was offering her, and she knew that she had no choice. Leafstar would never welcome her back.

Besides, she reflected, *what's a few more moons of apprenticeship, compared to the whole of the rest of my life in ThunderClan?*

"Okay, Bramblestar," she agreed. "It'll be good to work with Ivypool again." Relief was spreading through her—even if she had to be an apprentice again, at least Bramblestar wasn't going to send her away.

"Oh, no, Ivypool can't be your mentor," Bramblestar

meowed. "She's in the nursery now, about to have the kits she's expecting with Fernsong. No, I'll have to find a different cat for you. . . ."

Twigpaw waited, her paws itching with impatience. *Cherryfall might be a good mentor. Or maybe Whitewing . . .*

"Yes . . ." Bramblestar let out a purr of satisfaction. "I think you'll do very well with Sparkpelt."

Oh, StarClan, no! Twigpaw barely stopped herself from speaking the words aloud. *I know Sparkpelt doesn't want me here.* Then she realized that Bramblestar might already be testing her. "Fine," she mewed, trying to sound enthusiastic. "I promise I'll try my hardest."

"Good." Bramblestar rose to his paws and beckoned with his tail for Twigpaw to follow him out onto the Highledge and down the tumbled rocks into the camp. Most of the Clan was still waiting, and a murmur of anticipation rose from them as their leader appeared with Twigpaw behind him. They gathered around in a wide circle with Bramblestar and Twigpaw at the center; then Bramblestar called for Finpaw to join them.

"Cats of ThunderClan," their leader began. "As you can see, Twigpaw has returned to us. I have decided that she should continue her apprenticeship here in ThunderClan."

Glancing around, Twigpaw was relieved to see that most of her Clanmates looked happy to welcome her back, though she could see uncertainty in the eyes of some of them.

"She'll still be an apprentice?" Dewnose muttered.

Meanwhile, Bramblestar turned to Finpaw. "What are we to do with you, Finpaw?" he asked, half to himself.

Twigpaw realized guiltily that she hadn't even asked Bramblestar about Finpaw. *But surely Bramblestar won't send him away?*

Finpaw stood boldly in front of the Clan leader and met his gaze. "I want to be a ThunderClan warrior," he declared. "I've heard so many tales about Firestar, and how brave and honorable you all are. This is the best Clan in the forest, and I can't wait to be part of it." He gave an excited little jump. "*Please* let me join!"

Twigpaw could hear murmurs of appreciation at the young tom's enthusiastic words.

"Let him in, Bramblestar," Graystripe called out. "We need eager young cats like him."

"Yes, we can't afford to turn any promising cat away," Squirrelflight added; her green gaze rested on Finpaw, half amused and half admiring.

"I don't know . . ." Thornclaw looked doubtful. "Should we really be taking in just any cat? Not every cat is right for ThunderClan, after all."

"True," Cloudtail meowed with a flick of his tail. "Look at what's been happening since the Clans started taking in every cat that happens to stroll into camp."

Listening to the senior warrior, Twigpaw couldn't help thinking about the destruction Darktail and his rogues had caused—but also the chaos *she* had caused when she'd led the remains of SkyClan into the ThunderClan camp. She wondered whether Cloudtail was aiming the sly remark at her, though the white tom's gaze was firmly fixed on his leader.

"Maybe SkyClan cats don't understand that they can't just jump from one Clan to another," Brightheart said sternly. "Finpaw, you have to be sure."

Finpaw's eyes widened. "I *am* sure," he said earnestly. "I want to be part of ThunderClan."

"These are unusual times," Bramblestar said thoughtfully. "With so many changes in the Clans, we have to consider making changes as well. It's possible that StarClan has some reason to want us to welcome Finpaw to ThunderClan. . . And he does seem convinced that this is where he belongs."

"We should keep him for now." Cherryfall spoke up. "Let's give him a trial and see if he shapes up."

"Oh, I will!" Finpaw's eyes stretched wide as his confident gaze swept around the group of cats. "I promise!"

Bramblestar nodded. "Very well. Finpaw, we'll welcome you as an apprentice for now, but you must show loyalty to ThunderClan. Can you do that?"

Too overwhelmed to speak, Finpaw nodded eagerly.

"Then, Finpaw, from this time forward you will be a ThunderClan apprentice," Bramblestar announced. "Larksong, you are a loyal and committed cat. You will be his mentor and pass on your skills and experience to him."

The young black tom, looking stunned at his leader's praise and the honor of being chosen as a mentor, took a pace forward and dipped his head respectfully. "I won't let you down, Bramblestar."

Finpaw skipped across the circle of cats to stand in front of Larksong, and reached up to touch noses with him. "This is going to be *great!*" he announced.

"Finpaw! Finpaw!" the ThunderClan cats acclaimed him. Twigpaw could see that he was going to be popular, and she couldn't repress a tiny twinge of jealousy. *Are they more excited to have Finpaw join the Clan than they are to have me back?*

Her heart lurched as Bramblestar turned to her. "Do I need a ceremony?" she asked him. "I mean, what's the point. I've already had one. Twice," she added, the last word under her breath.

"You should do as you're told," Sparkpelt snapped at her from where she stood a couple of tail-lengths away.

Uh-oh, Twigpaw thought. *She's not going to be pleased when she finds out what Bramblestar has in mind.*

"Yes, you had a ceremony with Ivypool," Bramblestar meowed, his voice even. "And now you need one with your new mentor."

"It's so exciting!" Finpaw piped up. "We'll be apprentices together."

"Sure we will," Twigpaw responded, wishing she could share her friend's enthusiasm. She turned and nodded to Bramblestar, wishing too that she hadn't protested in the first place. *I don't want to start out by being difficult.*

"Then from this time forward," Bramblestar began, "Twigpaw will be a ThunderClan apprentice. Sparkpelt," Bramblestar continued, "you are a brave and loyal Thunder-Clan cat, and I know that you will pass on all you have learned to Twigpaw."

"What?" Sparkpelt's eyes widened and her neck fur began

to fluff up as she gazed at Twigpaw. But she had enough sense not to protest her Clan leader's decision, even though he was her father. "I'll do my best, Bramblestar," she added with a sigh.

Twigpaw padded over to Sparkpelt and made herself touch noses with her as she met her new mentor's irritated gaze. *I'll show you!* she resolved. *I'll be the best apprentice any cat ever had.*

Once the ceremony was over, Bramblestar returned to his den, and the rest of the Clan began to disperse. Most of them headed for the warriors' den to settle into their nests for the night.

Twigpaw found herself alone in the middle of the camp, suddenly feeling a little lost, as if she didn't belong there after all.

I'm sure I made the right decision to come back, she insisted to herself. *But I never thought it would be like this. I thought it would be better. . . .*

A few tail-lengths away, Larksong was talking to Finpaw, making arrangements to take him on a tour of the territory the following day. Finpaw was bouncing up and down, hardly able to contain his excitement.

Somehow her friend's enthusiasm made Twigpaw feel even more uncertain. Staring at him, she waited for the swell of excitement to come back to her. Instead she felt strangely flat.

Oh, StarClan! This is my home now. So why don't I feel happier to be back among my Clan?

CHAPTER 2

Violetshine clamped the fern stems more firmly in her jaws and began dragging the bundle of fronds into the SkyClan camp, through the tunnel between the brambles that reinforced the fern walls. It was almost sunhigh, and she had been gathering bedding for the new ShadowClan nests since just after dawn.

This is an apprentice task, she grumbled to herself. *But there's so much to do, and the new apprentices are so young. . . .*

She had never imagined that fitting the ShadowClan cats into SkyClan would be so difficult. Expanding the cave where the warriors slept to make room for the new arrivals was only one of the things that had to be dealt with. Her father, Hawkwing, was up to his ears in problems, encouraging the cats from SkyClan and ShadowClan to work together, and they were all tripping over one another's paws.

I'd complain, she thought gloomily, *but who am I going to complain to? No cat listens anymore!*

Sometimes she wanted to blame ShadowClan for all this extra work, but then Violetshine would remember that it wasn't just ShadowClan or SkyClan alone, but the strength of all the cats around the lake that had finally defeated Darktail and his rogues. She knew she should do everything she could to help the ShadowClan cats adjust to their new life, because the lake territory needed *all* the good and honorable warriors who had survived.

But it's kind of weird to be so close to ShadowClan cats again, she thought, giving her bundle of fern fronds another tug. It reminded her of the time when she had been a lost kit and then a ShadowClan apprentice, with a sister who lived in ThunderClan.

It wasn't our choice back then. The cats who found us decided we should be divided between their Clans. . . .

Once, when they were young, Rowanstar had held Twigpaw at ShadowClan's camp for a few days, and Violetshine had been so happy to share a den with her sister, to be together at last. She had thought Twigpaw felt the same. But then Twigpaw had chosen to go back to ThunderClan. And just recently, after they had joined SkyClan together, she had decided to return to ThunderClan yet again, instead of taking her warrior name in SkyClan.

Twigpaw made her choice. . . .

Violetshine didn't want to think about Twigpaw. It made her sad that her littermate had twice chosen ThunderClan over her.

Shaking her head, Violetshine resolved not to give in to these dark thoughts. Instead she concentrated on dragging her burden of ferns across the camp. But annoyance rose inside her again when she spotted Tree, lounging on a flat rock beside the stream. Sunlight shimmered on his yellow fur as he stared drowsily into space.

I don't think he's moved all morning!

Too tired to be tactful, Violetshine dropped the fern fronds. "Anytime you want to get off your hindquarters and pitch in," she hissed at Tree, "you'll be more than welcome!"

Tree turned his head to look at her. At once Violetshine felt a little guilty for being so harsh; Tree's amber eyes were fraught with indecision.

He still doesn't know what he wants to do, she realized. *Stay with SkyClan, or go off on his own again.*

"Look, Tree—" she began awkwardly, not sure what she wanted to say.

To Violetshine's relief, Leafstar's voice interrupted her. "Tree—over here, please. I want a word with you."

Violetshine turned to see Leafstar standing outside her den in the hollow of the old cedar tree at the far end of the camp. As Tree rose to his paws, Violetshine abandoned her bundle of bedding and followed him across to the Clan leader. She was careful to stay a respectful distance behind the loner, not wanting him to think she was putting pressure on him, or Leafstar to think she was nosy.

Even if I am! she admitted to herself.

As she approached, Violetshine noticed that a few other cats were also hovering, including Frecklewish, the SkyClan medicine cat. She could see her own curiosity reflected in their eyes.

"Well, Tree," Leafstar began. "You've had time to think about whether you want to make SkyClan your home. *Plenty* of time. Have you made a decision yet?"

Tree shook his head. "I'm really not sure if this life is for me," he replied; Violetshine could detect an edge of strain in his voice. "Sure, I like you SkyClan cats"—he broke off briefly to flick a glance at Violetshine—"but I've been a loner for my whole life. Who can say whether I'd be able to adjust to life as a Clan cat?"

Disappointment pricked Violetshine, as if she had set her paw down on an unexpected thorn.

She watched Leafstar closely, wondering if the Clan leader's face would betray irritation or, worse, a complete loss of patience with Tree.

But Leafstar remained calm. "We are grateful to you for your help, but we can't let you stay here as a visitor forever. You need to make a choice. Maybe you should try out as a warrior's apprentice," she suggested. "See if you like it. If you do, then maybe you can join SkyClan for real."

Tree gave his chest fur a couple of quick licks. "I'm not sure I want to do that," he meowed. "Being an apprentice doesn't sound like much fun."

We're not here to have fun, Violetshine thought.

From the look of her, the same response was going through Leafstar's mind. Though there was understanding in her expression, Violetshine could see frustration in her twitching whiskers and the way her claws kept sliding in and out.

"As much as we like you, Tree," she told him, "it's not fair to other cats if you live in camp without contributing as a member of the Clan. I hope you understand that."

Violetshine couldn't account for the sudden clenching she felt in her chest. *Why should I feel so tense and agitated when Leafstar suggests that Tree might have to leave the camp? I hardly know him.* But she knew that she *did* care, even if it might be smarter not to.

Before Tree could respond, Frecklewish stepped forward with a respectful dip of her head to Leafstar. "Remember that Tree has had visions," she mewed to her Clan leader. "Maybe his destiny is as a medicine cat?"

Though maybe we already have enough medicine cats around the lake, Violetshine thought.

Leafstar looked uncertain, then turned to Tree with a shrug. "Perhaps Frecklewish is right. StarClan chooses some cats to be medicine cats, and, since you see visions, maybe they have chosen you. Would you like to spend some time working with her, to see if you might find a home here as a medicine-cat apprentice? I'm sure StarClan will let you know if that is what they intend for you."

"Okay, I'll give it a try," Tree responded, though Violetshine didn't think he sounded particularly eager. "Honestly, Leafstar," he went on, "I really don't mean to take advantage of SkyClan's kindness."

His words earned him an approving nod from Leafstar, who waved her tail to dismiss him.

Tree turned away, heading for his den, and Violetshine padded alongside him to retrieve her bunch of ferns.

"Do you think Frecklewish is right? Could StarClan intend for you to become a medicine cat?" she asked him.

Tree shook his head. "I'm not sure," he admitted. "Medicine

cats talk about *weird* stuff. Besides, I'd have to memorize all the herbs and remedies, and get really close to sick cats." His nose wrinkled. "It's kind of gross. . . . I'm not sure that sort of life is for me. I'd rather be sunning myself on a rock."

Wouldn't we all? Violetshine wondered, though at the same time she felt an odd wash of relief, like the first cool lap of water on a hot day.

She half turned toward where she had left the ferns, then turned back. "Tree," she mewed, "I want to ask you something about your visions."

"Ask away," Tree responded amiably.

"Do you ever see Needletail these days?" Violetshine waited eagerly for his response. Tree had helped the cats of Shadow-Clan see and speak to their Clanmates who had died because of Darktail, and Violetshine had at last been able to let go of her guilt over Needletail's death. Needletail didn't blame her, had never blamed her, and that was a weight off Violetshine's mind, but she still missed her friend. Tree's ability to see dead cats made her feel that she still had some connection to Needletail.

Tree thought for a moment, then shook his head. "No, I haven't seen her for a while. Perhaps she's in StarClan."

As she said good-bye to Tree and began dragging the bundle of fern fronds over to the warriors' den, Violetshine wondered if that was true. *I hope it is; I like the idea of Needletail watching over me. Maybe Pebbleshine is watching too.*

The idea was comforting, as if her mother and her friend were still close to her, as if they were still a part of her life.

Then her tail drooped as another thought crept into her mind.

Can Pebbleshine watch over both me and Twigpaw, if we live in different Clans?

"You lay out herbs on boulders to dry," Frecklewish meowed. "How else would you do it?"

"Hang them on twigs and leaves, of course," Puddleshine replied.

Violetshine was lingering at the edge of the medicine-cat den in the cave under the roots of the old cedar. Morning sunshine flowed into the camp, and a fresh, invigorating breeze ruffled her fur. Watching her Clanmates, she saw Frecklewish's whiskers twitch in exasperation.

"Well, this is the way *we* do it," Frecklewish insisted.

Puddleshine looked confused. "I don't see why I can't do it my own way. That's how Yellowfang taught me, and she's a StarClan cat. It's the way we've always done it by the lake, for moons upon moons."

Frecklewish's neck fur began to bristle. "You don't always know better just because you were taught by Yellowfang," she hissed. "You're a *SkyClan* cat now, and you'll do things the SkyClan way."

Violetshine spotted Tree, sitting a tail-length away from Frecklewish. He had been training with her for a quarter moon now, though Violetshine didn't think he was enjoying himself much.

"Hang on a moment," he meowed, interrupting the two medicine cats, who were glaring at each other in mutual irritation. "Does it really matter, if you get the same result?"

Both medicine cats transferred their glares to Tree, who looked completely relaxed, his fur flat and his tail still, as if he really had no idea what the fuss was about. Did he really not care that Frecklewish and Puddleshine were arguing? Even if Tree's visions meant that he was a natural medicine cat, maybe he still wasn't cut out to be a Clan cat.

He'll probably decide to move on, she told herself, trying to ignore the hollow feeling in her chest. *Just one more cat who leaves me behind, whether he means to or not.*

Puddleshine and Frecklewish had resumed their argument, making Violetshine's fur prickle with annoyance. Since she didn't want to listen anymore, she turned away, wondering if there was a hunting patrol she might join. As she headed toward the warriors' den to see who was around, she was intercepted by her father, Hawkwing.

"Is everything okay with you?" he asked her, looking concerned and even a little suspicious.

"Yes, I'm fine," Violetshine assured him. "I'm just tired. There's a lot going on in camp just now. I'm sure you've noticed that too!"

Hawkwing glanced toward the medicine-cat den and nodded. "Making one Clan out of two isn't as simple as moving all the cats into the same camp."

At that moment Leafstar slid through the lichen that screened her den and took up a position on the tangle of cedar roots outside the entrance. "Let all cats old enough to catch their own prey join here beneath the Highroot for a

Clan meeting!" she yowled.

Cats appeared from the warriors' den and sat in a ragged semicircle around the rock. They were joined a few heart-beats later by the apprentices, scampering over from their den under the low-growing juniper boughs. Frecklewish and Puddleshine gave up their argument and moved away from their den entrance to sit next to the elders. Last of all, Tree strolled over to join Hawkwing and Violetshine.

When the cats were assembled, Leafstar let her gaze travel over the combined Clan until it rested on the former Shadow-Clan leader. "Rowanstar, do you want to stand up here with me?" she asked.

Nearly as one, all the Clan cats turned their heads toward Rowanclaw, waiting to find out how he would respond.

The ginger tom dipped his head. "I wouldn't want to tread on your tail, Leafstar," he meowed. "I'm just a SkyClan warrior now. And I'm not Rowanstar anymore—just Rowan*claw*."

At his words, a deep groan of dismay came from one of the former ShadowClan cats, but when Violetshine turned her head, trying to work out which cat it had come from, she couldn't be sure.

With a nod of appreciation to Rowanclaw, Leafstar began to assign the day's duties. Violetshine wondered why she didn't leave that task to her deputy, then realized that maybe with so much confusion it was better for orders to come from the Clan leader.

"Rowanclaw," she mewed, "I'd like you to lead a patrol down to the old ShadowClan camp. And while you're there, maybe you could collect some of the material for nests that was left there."

"What?" Tawnypelt, Rowanclaw's mate, sprang to her paws, her tortoiseshell fur fluffed up and her green eyes glittering with fury. "That's an apprentice job. Rowanclaw is a former leader!"

"It's not a slight on Rowanclaw," Leafstar assured her. "It's just that you both know your old camp really well."

"I'm okay with it," Rowanclaw added, resting his tail on Tawnypelt's shoulder. "I'm not a leader anymore, and I want to pitch in and help, just like any cat."

Violetshine noticed that even while he spoke to Tawnypelt, Rowanclaw was avoiding her gaze with a faint look of guilt. She wondered whether disappointing his mate was the worst part of his decision to disband ShadowClan.

"Thank you, Rowanclaw," Leafstar mewed. "I'm grateful that you feel that way. Tawnypelt, you can go with him. And Violetshine, too," she went on, turning toward her. "You know ShadowClan territory from the time you lived with them."

"Sure, Leafstar," Violetshine replied.

"May I go too?" Hawkwing asked.

Violetshine glanced at her father with narrowed eyes. *I'm a warrior now! I can go on a patrol without any cat to watch over me.*

But she said nothing, and after a brief hesitation Leafstar nodded. "Of course, Hawkwing. It'll be good for you to learn every paw step of our new territory."

Rowanclaw raised his tail to gather his patrol together, and

all four cats headed out of the camp, leaving Leafstar to orga-
nize the other patrols.

As soon as they were out in the forest, Hawkwing slowed
his pace a little, angling his ears at Violetshine to draw her to
his side.

"Let Rowanclaw and Tawnypelt go on ahead," he murmured.

"Don't you want to patrol with them?" Violetshine asked,
surprised that her father would show hostility toward his new
Clanmates.

"No, it's not that at all," Hawkwing replied. "But they're
mates, so they might want to speak together privately." He
hesitated, then added, "You'll understand when you're older."

Violetshine tensed. *The last cat I want to talk about* mates *with
is my father!*

But Hawkwing said nothing more. Distracted by a scuf-
fling sound in the debris underneath a beech tree, he sprang
forward, then straightened up again with a mouse in his jaws.

"Good catch!" Violetshine exclaimed, glad to talk about
something else.

Letting Rowanclaw and Tawnypelt draw ahead, Violetshine waited while Hawkwing buried the mouse to collect
later. Afterward they picked up the pace, until the former
ShadowClan cats were in sight again.

As they crossed into ShadowClan's old territory, Violetshine drifted closer, several paces ahead of her father, wanting
to hear what they were saying. She realized that she didn't

entirely trust them; she wouldn't have been surprised to hear them complaining about Leafstar, or even plotting against her.

Rowanclaw and Tawnypelt were padding along side by side, talking together and clearly unaware that any cat could overhear them. Violetshine stayed as far back as she could, not wanting to be caught eavesdropping. The pine trees grew close together here, and her paws made no sound on the thick layer of needles that covered the ground.

"Is this what you really want?" Tawnypelt was asking Rowanclaw as Violetshine crept into earshot. "To end Shadow-Clan forever? We're one of the *five* Clans, remember. I'm sure the rest of our Clan would support you if you decided you'd made a mistake."

Rowanclaw looked as if he could barely meet her gaze. "Without Tigerheart, there's no point," he responded, his voice full of grief. "I wasn't a strong sun. Puddleshine told me he saw in it in a vision, before Tigerheart left. . . . So I don't see how ShadowClan *can* go on."

Glad that neither cat seemed hostile to Leafstar, Violetshine twitched her tail, torn between wanting to hear what they said and feeling reluctant to intrude. Rowanclaw's words had brought her own ShadowClan roots vividly back to her mind. She wanted nothing more than to be a SkyClan warrior, and yet she couldn't pretend she didn't feel deep sadness at the loss of ShadowClan. She knew too that some of the younger ShadowClan cats felt even worse: at least Violetshine had kin in SkyClan.

But what can any of them do if Rowanclaw doesn't want to lead?

Violetshine could sense clouds gathering on the horizon, and she felt a sudden chill, like claws of frost probing through her pelt. It gave her a weird feeling that something was wrong, but she couldn't put her paw on what that might be. The forest suddenly seemed strange and foreboding.

Turning back, she spotted Hawkwing rounding the trunk of a pine tree. "We've patrolled, so we can head back to camp, right?" she meowed as he padded up to her. "Rowanclaw and Tawnypelt can find the bedding from their old camp, if there's any left."

Hawkwing gave her a curious look. "We're not finished with the patrol," he said. "Leafstar wanted us to go to the old ShadowClan camp with Rowanclaw and Tawnypelt, remember?"

Violetshine's pelt prickled with embarrassment. "Right," she meowed. "It's just . . ."

She was aware of her father's gaze resting on her. "So why are you in such a hurry?" he asked.

Somehow Violetshine couldn't raise her head to look at him. She didn't reply to his question, even though she knew the answer. When she thought about how unsettled life was in SkyClan, and how uneasy some cats seemed, she was suddenly nervous about the idea of Tree leaving SkyClan.

Suppose I get back to camp and he's gone?

CHAPTER 3

Alderheart brushed through the long grass on his way to the stream that marked the border with WindClan, his pelt growing heavy from water droplets left by the recent rain. He barely noticed the forest sounds around him, because he was worrying about the belly sickness that was spreading through the ThunderClan camp. Several cats had become ill over the last quarter moon, and last night they had been joined by Brackenfur, Whitewing, and Plumkit. Alderheart was especially anxious about the sturdy little kit; she was strong, but too small to fight the sickness for long.

He was also worried about Cinderheart's kits, Snapkit, Spotkit, and Flykit. They had just begun to venture out of the nursery during the day, and they were all keen to explore the camp. But if they caught the sickness, like Plumkit, they might not have the strength to fight off the illness.

StarClan, let me find watermint today, Alderheart prayed. *We really need it.*

But when he reached the border stream, it looked as though there was no watermint left at all. Perhaps WindClan was also suffering from the illness. He tried not to feel resentful that Kestrelflight had taken so much, instead of going to the border they shared with RiverClan, where it also grew.

Harestar won't want to start any trouble with RiverClan. Since RiverClan had closed its borders and abandoned contact with the other Clans, no cat knew what Mistystar and her cats might be thinking.

Alderheart padded along the bank, heading upstream, and finally spotted a few stems of the precious herb. They were growing close to the water's edge, and he had to lean precariously over the stream before he could manage to pick them.

After scrambling back to safety, he headed back to camp with the scant bundle. Overhead, dark clouds were massing again, and Alderheart felt a tingle of unease as he glanced up at them. The first drops of rain splashed onto his head.

It feels like half a moon at least since I really saw the sun, he thought. *I've never seen anything like this before.*

His medicine-cat awareness told him that these clouds were more than just the promise of rain. *The dark sky must not herald a storm.* Could the darkening sky be a literal sign of the prophecy coming true? The clouds seemed darker and denser than any he had seen before, bulging with rain, and Alderheart couldn't shake a sense of impending doom, disaster hanging over the Clans just as the clouds were looming over the forest.

Something is coming. I can feel it. . . .

"Why are you chewing up that chervil root?" Jayfeather demanded, giving Alderheart a sharp prod in his shoulder with one paw. "The sick cats need watermint! Are you still an apprentice?"

Alderheart spat the chervil-root chunks onto a dock leaf and suppressed a sigh. Since so many cats had come down with the sickness, Jayfeather had become crankier than ever. But Alderheart knew him well enough not to be offended.

"We don't *have* watermint," he pointed out calmly. He had given the few scraps he had managed to find to Plumkit. "Do you expect me to pull it out of my ears?"

"No," Jayfeather grumbled. "I expect you to stay out there until you find some."

Alderheart cast a glance at the bramble screen that covered the entrance to the medicine-cat den. Outside, the rain was hissing down; still, Alderheart would willingly get soaked to the skin if it meant he could find the herb they so desperately needed.

"Don't act like such a kit," Alderheart mewed teasingly to Jayfeather, "just because we have a lot to do!" Alderheart thought for a moment. "You know there's hardly any watermint left in the border stream. We might have to find another supply," he added.

"And you need to chew that chervil root more thoroughly," Jayfeather added irritably, prodding at the pulp with one paw. "The chunks are far too big. How do you think you can force that down Whitewing's muzzle? Any apprentice knows that!"

Alderheart stopped himself from pointing out that it was Jayfeather who had interrupted his chewing. "We ought to talk about the prophecy," he meowed instead, hoping that with so many cats to treat, Jayfeather wouldn't be likely to wander off, and at last they could have a useful discussion. "Without ShadowClan and with RiverClan closing its borders . . ." StarClan had made it clear that they needed all five Clans.

But Jayfeather waved his tail dismissively. "I don't care about that right now," he responded. "It's more important to get all these cats better, so that they can get back to their duties."

Leafpool was lying beside Plumkit, licking her gently when she whimpered from the bellyache.

Now the medicine cat raised her head. "Alderheart, this sickness spreads so quickly, I think we should move Briarlight into the nursery. It could be especially dangerous for her, if she catches it."

Briarlight, who was drowsing in her own nest, roused at Leafpool's words. "Don't worry about me," she mewed. "I'll be fine."

"No, Leafpool's right," Alderheart declared. "It's a good idea."

Even while he spoke, he couldn't help thinking of Whitewing, the most seriously ill of the cats. She seemed to be missing her daughter Dovewing, who had disappeared more than a moon ago, so much that she hadn't the will or the strength to fight the sickness. Day after day, Alderheart had to encourage her to eat her herbs.

"It's going to be pretty crowded in the nursery," Jayfeather pointed out.

Since there was no room in the medicine-cat den for all the

sick cats, Alderheart had sent all of them except Plumkit into the apprentices' den, and moved Twigpaw and Finpaw into the nursery.

"There's room," he murmured. "The apprentices are helping over there, after all. And if we move Briarlight, we'll have space over here for Whitewing. I'd like to keep a closer eye on her."

Jayfeather's only response was a grunt.

Alderheart stuck his head out through the bramble screen, wincing at the cold rain that showered down on him. Glancing around, he spotted Lionblaze padding past, his golden pelt darkened and plastered to his sides, a squirrel dangling from his jaws.

"Hey, Lionblaze!" Alderheart yowled. "I need your help."

"Okay," Lionblaze mumbled around the mouthful of prey. "Whatever it is, I can't get any wetter. Let me just drop this on the fresh-kill pile."

"Find another cat to help too," Alderheart called after him.

A few moments later, Lionblaze returned with Bumblestripe, Briarlight's brother; Alderheart guessed he had been on the same hunting patrol, because he looked just as wet as Lionblaze.

"Don't even *think* about shaking your pelts in here," Jayfeather snapped.

"How can we help you?" Lionblaze asked Alderheart, ignoring Jayfeather's irritable tone.

Alderheart explained about needing to move Briarlight to the nursery. Immediately Bumblestripe's eyes stretched wide with alarm.

"You mean she's in serious danger?" he asked, then went on rapidly without waiting for an answer. "Yes, of course she shouldn't be around sick cats. Let's get her out of here right now!"

"For StarClan's sake!" Briarlight hissed at her brother. "There's no need to get your whiskers in a twist. Maybe my back legs don't work, but I'm still a strong cat. It'll take more than a bit of sickness to finish me off!"

"We're going to move you anyway," Alderheart meowed, hoping to calm both cats down. "Better safe than sorry."

With Lionblaze's help, Alderheart hoisted Briarlight onto Bumblestripe's back. Then, with the other two toms steadying her on either side, Bumblestripe padded out of the den and splashed through the puddles to the nursery on the far side of the camp.

"You should thank me," Briarlight murmured into her brother's ear. "I'm keeping the rain off you!"

It did look fairly crowded in the nursery, Alderheart thought, as he and the others maneuvered Briarlight down the tunnel into the heart of the bramble thicket. Blossomfall and Cinderheart were there with their kits, along with Ivypool, her belly bulging as she drew close to giving birth, and Daisy, who always stayed in the nursery to help the queens with their litters. The two apprentices weren't there; Alderheart guessed they were away somewhere, training with their mentors.

"Of course she must stay with us!" Daisy responded when Alderheart had explained. "Briarlight, you're very welcome.

Look, there's a nest for you over here. The moss is nice and thick."

"Yes, it's great to have you here," Blossomfall, who was Briarlight's sister, meowed. "Our kits can help you with your exercises."

"Yes, we will!" Eaglekit squealed excitedly.

"We'll be good at it!" Flykit agreed.

All the kits hurled themselves at Briarlight; Daisy reached out with her tail to stop them before they scrambled all over her. "Gently, kits," she mewed. "All of you at once will be a bit much for Briarlight."

"No, they'll be fine," Briarlight told her. "Come on, kits. Who can play moss ball?"

"Me!"

"Me!"

"And me!"

This might be the best idea Leafpool has had in moons, Alderheart thought, with a *mrrow* of amusement.

Since Briarlight was clearly settled, Alderheart was about to follow Bumblestripe and Lionblaze out of the nursery when Blossomfall reached out a paw to stop him.

"How is Plumkit?" she asked.

"Doing fine," Alderheart told her, hoping that was true. "She was sleeping when I left."

Blossomfall shifted uneasily in her nest. "I should be with her."

"No, that's the last thing you should do," Alderheart mewed gently. "Suppose you caught the sickness and brought it back here to the nursery?"

Blossomfall shuddered. "That would be terrible. You're right, Alderheart," she added with a sigh. "But it's hard."

"I know. But she's getting the best care possible," Alderheart reassured her.

Heading back to the medicine cat den, Alderheart wasn't sure that was true, either. The best care meant giving the sick kit watermint, and now they didn't have so much as a leaf left.

"Alderheart," Leafpool meowed as soon as he reached the medicine cat den. "We could *really* do with more watermint. It's by far the best thing to treat this sickness."

Her thoughts exactly matched Alderheart's own, but he was still doubtful. "That means going to RiverClan," he responded. "The only other place I know it grows is by the border stream between RiverClan and WindClan. And RiverClan isn't exactly being a friendly group of cats right now."

"I know all that," Leafpool retorted. "But our cats haven't been getting better, and we need watermint if we're to contain the sickness and stop it spreading."

Alderheart knew she was right. And after giving himself a moment to think, he even felt a tingle of excitement at the thought of going to RiverClan.

I could check in and see how they're doing. Maybe I could even convince them to return to the Clans. Then we wouldn't be three anymore.

"I'll go and see Bramblestar," he mewed.

Beside the fresh-kill pile, where Alderheart found him, Bramblestar thought for a long time about the suggestion of going to RiverClan to collect watermint.

"Okay," he agreed eventually. "But take a couple of warriors with you. Mistystar was pretty firm about wanting to be left alone."

"But medicine cats are supposed to be able to cross borders freely," Alderheart pointed out.

"Even so," the Clan leader meowed. "We need you in one piece, Alderheart, not shredded by a RiverClan patrol. You're not going by yourself."

"I'll go."

Alderheart started in surprise at the sound of his sister's voice, and turned to see Sparkpelt standing behind him. She and Twigpaw were just approaching the fresh-kill pile with prey dangling from their jaws.

"Is that okay, Bramblestar?" she added, dropping her vole on the pile.

A warm feeling of anticipation swept through Alderheart as Bramblestar agreed. It would be good to go with his sister on his expedition to RiverClan, especially since that meant Twigpaw would be going with them.

I've been worried about Twigpaw. She looks so sad and anxious all the time. Now I'll be able to see how she's getting along with Sparkpelt, and if she's feeling any better.

"Let's go," Sparkpelt said, dipping her head respectfully to her Clan leader. "Alderheart, you can tell us what it's all about on the way."

* * *

Sparkpelt took the lead as the ThunderClan patrol crossed the border stream and headed through WindClan territory, keeping close to the lakeshore. The rain had stopped; a damp wind still gusted across the lake, fluttering its surface. A heaving mass of cloud still covered the sky, though now and then a few watery rays of sunlight managed to break through.

"How are you?" Alderheart asked Twigpaw as they padded along side by side behind Sparkpelt.

"Fine, thanks," Twigpaw responded.

The curt answer wasn't at all like her, and Alderheart had the definite feeling that there was something she wasn't telling him.

"Are you getting along with Sparkpelt?"

Twigpaw shrugged. "She's okay."

Now Alderheart was sure something was wrong, but before he could question Twigpaw any further, Sparkpelt called out, "WindClan patrol!"

Looking up, Alderheart spotted three WindClan cats streaming down the swell of the moor. As they drew closer he recognized Featherpelt, Hootwhisker, and Larkwing; they veered sideways and picked up their pace to intercept the ThunderClan patrol at the water's edge.

The three ThunderClan cats bunched together. Twigpaw slid out her claws, while Sparkpelt's shoulder fur bristled, as if they were expecting a fight.

"Take it easy," Alderheart murmured. "We're not doing anything wrong."

To his relief, none of the WindClan cats looked hostile as they drew to a halt. "Greetings," Featherpelt meowed, dipping her head politely. "Are you on your way to see Harestar?"

"No, we're going to RiverClan," Alderheart replied, glad that his sister seemed willing to leave the talking to him. "We need to collect some watermint from over there. There's not much left in our border stream."

The three WindClan cats exchanged a rather guilty glance. "Sorry," Featherpelt responded, giving her gray tabby fur a couple of embarrassed swipes with her tongue. "We have belly sickness in WindClan, and I guess we used it all."

"Not to worry," Alderheart assured her. "But we have the same sickness, and we really need watermint."

"One of our border patrols told me there's watermint on the banks of the RiverClan stream, but on our side," Hootwhisker put in.

Alderheart nodded. "That's where we're heading. It should be okay to take some without bothering RiverClan."

"Then can we come with you?" Hootwhisker asked. "We can pick some for our own stores."

"Yes, that should please Kestrelflight," Larkwing added. "Most of our cats are improving, but it can't hurt to be prepared."

Alderheart heard a faint hiss of annoyance from Sparkpelt. He couldn't help wishing that the WindClan cats had used this other supply all along. But he knew there was no point in starting an argument about that now.

"Sure you can come," he mewed. "Are you okay with that, Sparkpelt?"

"I suppose so," Sparkpelt replied. "I suppose six cats will be better than three if we do run into trouble from RiverClan."

"But surely there won't be trouble when we have a medicine cat with us?" Hootwhisker asked. "At least . . ."

His voice trailed off, and all the cats exchanged doubtful glances. *We have no idea how RiverClan will react,* Alderheart thought. Not too long ago, it had been WindClan who had closed their borders, and they had been reluctant to share herbs that grew on their land with any of the other Clans.

Together the two patrols set off toward the RiverClan border, still keeping close to the water's edge. The wind had dropped now, and the lake lay flat and still. There was no sign of a storm, but the sky above still looked bleak and gray. Alderheart's feelings of dread wouldn't be banished, as if he had fox dung clinging to his fur.

As they approached the horseplace, Featherpelt suddenly halted and began to taste the air. "There's a really strong smell of horse," she murmured, looking slightly uneasy. "I wonder if we should take a different way around."

"No, what's the point?" Sparkpelt objected; Alderheart suspected that his sister was reluctant to take suggestions from a WindClan cat. "The horses are always penned in the horseplace. They won't bother us unless we bother them. We'll just sneak past."

Alderheart felt that maybe they should pay more attention to Featherpelt, since WindClan knew more about the horseplace than any cat. But he said nothing, just happy to take the more direct route that would get them to the watermint faster.

But as the cats made their way alongside the horseplace, their ears twitched at an ominous thundering sound.

Something's coming our way! Alderheart thought, feeling the ground tremble under the force of giant paw steps. The creature was hidden for the moment by the barn where Smoky and Coriander lived, but it was drawing closer by the heartbeat.

All the cats had halted, staring toward the barn. Then the charging creature burst into the open. Alderheart gazed at it, transfixed. It was a horse, much smaller than any of the horses he had seen before, but its muscles were powerful, and its huge, hard paws threw up tussocks of grass as it thundered toward the cats.

"A horse kit!" Hootwhisker gasped.

There was a shiny metal mesh between the cats and the horse kit, but it rampaged across the grass straight for them, as if it meant to leap the barrier or break straight through it.

"Scatter!" Sparkpelt squealed.

The group broke up as every cat raced in a different direction. Alderheart headed for the marshes and found himself squelching through belly-deep mud with reeds raking through his pelt. For a few moments he had no idea where the other cats were.

Glancing over his shoulder, Alderheart saw the horse kit come to a snorting halt at the barrier. Tossing its head, it trotted alongside the mesh for a few paw steps, then halted and lowered its head to start cropping the grass.

Alderheart realized that the horse kit probably hadn't meant to frighten them. *Maybe it didn't see us here at all. It was just playing, like our kits.* All the same, he was grateful for the mesh barrier.

After struggling to pull each paw out of the glutinous mud, Alderheart made his way back to the lakeshore. Gradually the other cats joined him. Sparkpelt was even stickier than he was, Larkwing was limping from setting her paw down on a sharp pebble, and Featherpelt had dashed into the lake to stand shivering in the shallows until she realized the danger was over. She waded out, hissing irritably, and showered the other cats with water droplets as she shook herself.

"I'm never going to get my pelt clean!" Sparkpelt exclaimed.

"We'll find some long grass for you to roll in," Twigpaw meowed; she had escaped with no more than a few muddy splashes on her fur.

Sparkpelt let out a snort. "It'll take from now to next new-leaf!"

"Let's get going," Alderheart urged with a sigh. *There had better be watermint, after all this!*

The two patrols continued along the lakeshore, passing the tree-bridge that led to the Gathering island, until they reached the stream that marked the RiverClan border.

"There's the watermint!" Twigpaw squealed in excitement. "Lots of it! I'll get some."

She bounded forward to where thick clumps of watermint were growing on both sides of the stream, purple flowers still visible at the end of the spiky stems.

"Be careful!" Sparkpelt called after her.

Twigpaw plunged in among the plants and began to pick the stems, biting them off carefully toward the bottom. The other cats followed her more slowly; Featherpelt began picking herbs for WindClan, while Hootwhisker and Larkwing kept watch on the RiverClan territory across the stream.

Alderheart was padding up to the nearest clump of watermint when a yowl of alarm came from Twigpaw. Alderheart spun around to see her tottering on the very edge of the stream. She would have fallen in if Sparkpelt hadn't dived forward through the herbs, grabbed her by the scruff, and dragged her back to safety.

"Stupid furball!" Sparkpelt snapped, standing over her apprentice with her tail lashing. "I told you to be careful. And she dropped all her watermint into the stream," she added to Alderheart as he hurried up. Her voice was loud, echoing for fox-lengths, and Alderheart was worried that the noise, along with Twigpaw's yowling, would attract attention from River-Clan across the stream.

"Never mind; there's plenty more," Alderheart pointed out. "Twigpaw, are you okay?"

Twigpaw nodded; she was looking particularly miserable. "I'm sorry," she mewed. "I was only trying to help. The edge of the bank gave way under my paws."

"Well, think what you're doing in the future." Sparkpelt still looked annoyed, though Alderheart guessed she had been afraid that her apprentice would be hurt, or even drowned. "Stay by me from now on. Alderheart, you'd better do the picking."

Alderheart headed for the clumps, but before he could reach the nearest, he heard a swishing sound from RiverClan territory, and looked up to see two RiverClan warriors emerge from the reeds on the far side of the stream.

"What do you think you're doing?" Shimmerpelt, in the lead, halted at the water's edge and glared across at Alderheart and the others, her silver-gray pelt fluffing up. "Let me remind you that our border is *closed*. Now kindly leave the watermint where it is, and get lost, or I'll call up reinforcements."

"Excuse *me*," Sparkpelt retorted, stepping up beside Alderheart. "Do you see any of us on RiverClan territory? If we were to ask permission, it would be from WindClan. Besides, this is medicine-cat business. We have the *right* to take watermint for our sick Clanmates. That's the warrior code!"

Shimmerpelt looked harassed, exchanging an uncertain glance with her Clanmate Havenpelt. "Please don't make trouble," she meowed. "Just go!"

Alderheart wondered whether Mistystar's insistence on closing her borders had left her own warriors agitated and unsure. He slapped his tail across Sparkpelt's muzzle as she drew breath for an angry response.

"We understand the problem," he began, dipping his head respectfully to the RiverClan cats. "Would you allow us to cross so we can explain to Mistystar why we are so close to your territory?"

"We don't *need* permission to be here," Sparkpelt growled softly behind him, but Alderheart ignored her.

"Surely, even though your border's closed," he went on, "you'll agree that it's in every cat's interest for the sickness to be stopped before it spreads too far."

The two RiverClan warriors glanced at each other, then

leaned their heads together for a low-voiced conversation. Alderheart strained to overhear, but he couldn't make out a word.

Finally both cats straightened up again. "Okay," Havenpelt meowed. "*You* can come across, Alderheart, but the warriors must stay behind."

"That's not right!" Sparkpelt protested. "Alderheart, don't go into their camp alone. StarClan knows what they might do!"

Shimmerpelt gave her a cold glance. "RiverClan *respects* medicine cats," she hissed.

"I'm fine with it, Sparkpelt," Alderheart assured her. "I'm not scared of RiverClan. Besides, if Mistystar sees warriors from two Clans walking into her camp, she might think we're getting ready to attack."

Sparkpelt glared at her brother. "Well, if you want to be a mouse-brain . . . Just don't blame me if it all goes wrong."

Alderheart padded forward and looked at the stream. The current ran fast and deep, and just here it was too wide to leap across. He glanced over at the RiverClan cats, and thought he could catch a glint of amusement in their eyes.

"Oh, yes, you don't swim, do you?" Havenpelt purred. "Never mind. Come upstream a little way, and there's an easier place to cross."

Alderheart obeyed, while the two RiverClan cats paced him on the far side. A few fox-lengths farther up there was a place where a large rock jutted out of the water near the middle of the current.

"Are you okay with that?" Shimmerpelt asked, waving her tail at the rock.

"Fine, thanks!" Alderheart responded. *Oh, StarClan, please don't let me fall in!*

Gritting his teeth, he bunched his muscles and pushed off from the bank to land easily on top of the rock. Taking off for the second leap was harder, because the rock was smooth and his paws slipped as he thrust himself forward. For a horrible moment Alderheart thought he would fall short of the bank, but his forepaws landed hard on dry ground. Digging in his claws, he was able to bring his hind legs up and stand to face the RiverClan warriors.

"Lead on," he meowed.

There was a second stream that bordered the RiverClan camp, but this was shallow enough for Alderheart to splash through. As he climbed the bank beyond it, he could see RiverClan cats gathering around, ears pricked in surprise to see a cat from another Clan.

"Stay here," Havenpelt directed. "I'll fetch Mistystar."

Alderheart halted at the top of the bank, uncomfortable under the stares of the RiverClan cats. He was relieved when only a few heartbeats passed before he spotted Mistystar slipping through the cluster of her warriors to stand in front of him.

"Greetings," the RiverClan leader meowed, with a slight dip of her head. "Why are you here, Alderheart? You know our borders are closed."

"Greetings, Mistystar," Alderheart responded politely. He described the sickness in his own camp and WindClan's, and how he and the WindClan cats had come to collect watermint from the border stream. "I promise you, we stayed on the far side of the border," he finished. "We never intended to set paw on your territory, or collect herbs from there."

Mistystar's blue gaze rested on him thoughtfully. "But you came very close to crossing our borders," she mewed at last.

Alderheart felt a stab of fear like a claw tearing at his belly. *Is she going to consider this an act of aggression?* he wondered. *We weren't even planning to trespass! Well, she can think what she likes—I'm not going home without watermint . . . I just hope that doesn't mean we'll have to fight for it.*

"But I understand your needs," Mistystar continued, "and I wish no ill on any cat. Take your watermint, and then go."

"Thank you! We—"

"But next time you think of approaching our border," Mistystar interrupted, "think again. The border is closed—do not forget that."

Yes, I think I've gotten the message by now. Alderheart noticed that Willowshine, one of the RiverClan medicine cats, was among those gathered around Mistystar. She was shifting her paws uncomfortably, and there was an unhappy expression in her bright green eyes. *There's a cat who doesn't agree with her Clan leader.*

Alderheart didn't speak his thoughts aloud. Instead he bowed his head to Mistystar in a show of deepest respect. "You are very generous, Mistystar," he meowed. "ThunderClan thanks you for your graciousness. May StarClan light your path."

Mistystar made no response, and after a moment Alderheart turned to go. But his paws were dragging, and there was a huge weight on his heart. Unsure what was compelling him, he turned back.

"Mistystar, won't you change your mind?" he begged. "Don't you know that ShadowClan has collapsed, and is now part of SkyClan? Suppose it's catching, like a sickness, the way Clans fall apart? Surely it's in every Clan's interest that we're all strong?"

The RiverClan leader drew herself up, her blue-gray fur rippling in the breeze and her blue eyes intent. Alderheart could see that his news had affected her. He held his breath, waiting, hoping, for her to take some action.

Then Mistystar relaxed, her spine settling. "Our borders are closed," she repeated, "while RiverClan rebuilds. I am sorry to hear what happened to ShadowClan, but it is not RiverClan's responsibility." She hesitated, then added, "That is the way things are now."

With a wave of her plumy tail, she dismissed Alderheart.

Struggling to hide his disappointment, Alderheart left the camp. He had always thought of Mistystar as the most reasonable of the Clan leaders, and for a heartbeat he had believed that he had reached her.

The wounds Darktail dealt her Clan have gone too deep. But what will happen to the Clans if the storm in StarClan's prophecy is unleashed on us?

Shimmerpelt and Havenpelt escorted him, one on each

side, until they reached the border stream and the place where he could leap across by the jutting rock.

His Clanmates and the WindClan cats were waiting for him. "Well?" Sparkpelt demanded. "What did Mistystar say?"

Alderheart angled his ears to where the two RiverClan warriors were still watching from the opposite bank. "Mind what you say," he muttered. "We don't want trouble now." More loudly, he added, "She says we can go in peace."

"I should think so," Hootwhisker commented under his breath.

All six cats collected as much watermint as they could carry, making sure that they picked stems that were growing farthest from the stream.

"This might be the only chance we get," Alderheart warned them. "Mistystar told me not to come back."

When they had bundled up the herbs, they set off, back along the lakeshore; Alderheart was aware of Shimmerpelt and Havenpelt still guarding the stream until they were out of sight.

The WindClan patrol said their good-byes at the other side of the horseplace and headed up the moorland slope toward their camp. Alderheart and his Clanmates made their way back to the stone hollow. They padded mostly in silence, and Alderheart tried to feel optimistic.

I might have failed with Mistystar, but at least now we can treat the sickness.

But as soon as Alderheart pushed his way through the

thorn tunnel into the camp, he spotted Jayfeather bounding toward him.

"Where have you been?" the blind cat demanded. "What took you so long? More cats have come down with the sickness—and the worst of them is Squirrelflight!"

CHAPTER 4

"No, no, no! Let's try that exercise again," Sparkpelt meowed. "You should be rearing up on your hind legs, then a double slash with your forepaws. Keep your claws sheathed for now."

That's exactly what I am doing. Twigpaw suppressed a sigh. She had been doing battle training since dawn with Finpaw and Larksong, and she was bored. *I learned all this in my first apprenticeship,* she thought resentfully. *I've known how to do it for moons! Why do I have to go through it all again?*

"Twigpaw!" Sparkpelt's annoyed voice dragged Twigpaw away from these dark thoughts. "When you're *quite* ready . . ."

Trying to work up some enthusiasm for the basic exercise Larksong was teaching Finpaw, Twigpaw reared up on her hind legs and aimed two swift blows at the empty air.

"Hmm . . . not bad," Sparkpelt grunted as Twigpaw landed on all four paws again.

Not bad? It was perfect!

Twigpaw suspected that Sparkpelt's grudging praise was because she was still upset at having been made Twigpaw's mentor. *But we would get along better if she didn't insist on training with*

Larksong and Finpaw the whole time. I wish she would teach me something I don't know!

Twigpaw wondered when Sparkpelt would get past the fact that she had switched Clans more than once. Twigpaw could understand that might have seemed a bit disrespectful of ThunderClan, and of the warrior code, but she felt different now—older and wiser—than when she was a kit, or when she was going through her first apprenticeship with Ivypool. She was certain that her place was as a ThunderClan warrior.

I'm just going to have to prove it to the rest of the Clan.

Twigpaw watched as Finpaw went through the exercise, and listened to Larksong instructing him on how to use his tail for balance, something the young cat had found difficult ever since the accident when he had lost part of it. Twigpaw knew that she could have repeated the instructions word for word, and when she practiced the move, she automatically flicked her tail into the right place.

This is so frustrating! I wonder if Sparkpelt is doing it deliberately, to test my commitment.

"Twig*paw*!" Sparkpelt's voice was harsher still, and Twigpaw had to stop herself from bristling at the emphasis on her apprentice status. "When you've finished staring at that tree like a moonstruck rabbit, maybe you could try the exercise again?"

Twigpaw sighed. It was going to be a long morning.

Back in camp just after sunhigh, Twigpaw went to fetch herself a piece of prey and noticed that there was hardly anything on the fresh-kill pile. She prodded a scrawny mouse and a blackbird that was mostly bones and feathers, but neither of them tempted her. *I'm starving! Where are all the hunting patrols?*

Glancing around and tasting the air, Twigpaw guessed that most of the Clan was gathered here in camp. She knew that there were fewer cats to hunt now that the sickness was so bad. Some of her Clanmates had begun to recover, but they were still too weak and shaky to do more than totter around the camp. At least Squirrelflight had started getting better, though she wasn't strong enough yet to take up her deputy's duties.

What if I went out to hunt and brought back some great prey? Maybe that would convince Sparkpelt I'm ready to be made a warrior. It has to be worth a try!

Twigpaw didn't hang around thinking. When she glanced around again, she saw that the cats who were in sight seemed more concerned with snoozing and recovering their strength than watching what one unimportant apprentice was doing. Sparkpelt and Larksong had both disappeared into the warriors' den, and Twigpaw couldn't see Finpaw at all.

However, Thornclaw was on guard at the entrance of the tunnel, sitting there with ears pricked alertly. Twigpaw didn't want to explain herself to him. It wasn't forbidden for apprentices to go out of camp on their own, but Thornclaw might ask if she had permission from her mentor, and she didn't want to lie to a senior warrior.

Instead Twigpaw headed for the dirtplace tunnel, picked

her way around the dirtplace with her nose wrinkled, then slid quietly into the undergrowth and away from the camp.

She was beginning to relax, thinking she had gotten away with it, when a cheerful voice behind her mewed, "Where are you creeping off to?"

Twigpaw whirled around to see Finpaw standing a tail-length away, his eyes glinting with anticipation. "What are you doing here?" she asked. "Go back to camp, and don't tell any cat that you saw me."

Even while she was speaking, Twigpaw realized that Finpaw wasn't going to listen. The young brown tom scampered around her, his voice squeaking in excitement. "Are you going on an adventure? Can I come?"

Twigpaw sighed. She should have known from the beginning that there would be no getting rid of Finpaw. *Besides,* she thought, *if I bring back prey and look after an apprentice, it'll prove that I'm a real warrior.*

"Okay," she sighed. "Just stop making that racket. You'll scare off all the prey in the forest."

"Is that it?" Finpaw lowered his voice, to Twigpaw's relief. "Are we going hunting? Cool!"

He padded at Twigpaw's side as they headed deeper into the forest, taking care to set his paws down lightly. The forest was cool and shady under a covering of cloud, with here and there a brighter patch where the sun was struggling to break through. Twigpaw kept halting to taste the air, alert for prey and also for cat-scent; she didn't want to risk meeting any of her Clanmates.

Finpaw spotted prey first: a mouse scrabbling around in the debris at the foot of an oak tree. He dropped into the hunter's crouch and crept up on it, but just before he was close enough to pounce, he put one paw down on a dead leaf. The crackling sound alerted the mouse, which darted toward the shelter of the oak roots.

"Mouse dung!" Finpaw exclaimed.

But Twigpaw had been watching, and was ready. With a massive leap she hurled herself on top of the mouse and slapped a forepaw down on it, cutting off its squeak of terror.

"Thank you, StarClan, for this prey," she mewed.

"Hey, great catch!" Finpaw padded up and sniffed the mouse. "Sorry I missed it."

"It's not a problem." Twigpaw touched his ear with her nose. "We make a good team."

The two cats went on hunting. When she had caught another mouse and a shrew, Twigpaw dug a hole and buried her prey, ready for her to collect later. *My idea's working well,* she thought. *Sparkpelt will be really impressed!*

Looking around, she realized that they were close to the WindClan border. "Maybe we should go as far as the stream," she suggested to Finpaw. "We might even be lucky and find more watermint."

Finpaw agreed, but before they had gone much farther, Twigpaw spotted a squirrel climbing down the trunk of an ash tree and set off across an open stretch of ground just ahead. It was taking its time, bobbing along for a few paw steps, then stopping to sit upright with its tail curled upward.

Clearly it was unaware of the two cats.

Twigpaw angled her ears toward the squirrel. "Stay back and stay quiet," she murmured to Finpaw.

Eyes bright, Finpaw nodded enthusiastically.

Twigpaw began to follow the squirrel, creeping forward with her belly brushing the grass. The gap between her and the squirrel grew narrower. But before she could reach her prey, the squirrel sat upright. Twigpaw gritted her teeth with annoyance as she realized the breeze had shifted, carrying her scent toward it.

In the next heartbeat the squirrel pelted for the nearest tree, its tail streaming out behind it. With a yowl of frustration, Twigpaw followed. Her muscles bunched and stretched as she tried to force every last scrap of speed out of her legs.

The squirrel reached the tree and fled up the trunk. Twigpaw was running so fast that she couldn't stop. Her legs carried her on for a few more strides; then suddenly there was nothing under her paws anymore. She let out a screech as she fell into cold water, and the current closed over her head.

For a moment Twigpaw thrashed helplessly, trying to get to her paws as she was bumped along the bottom of the stream. Then her head broke the surface. She couldn't see much for the water in her eyes, but a green blur loomed up beside her, and she reached out with both forepaws.

Her claws caught in the gritty soil of the bank, and with a massive effort Twigpaw hauled herself out of the water and scrabbled her way upward until she could collapse, choking and gasping, on level ground.

For a moment Twigpaw lay there, eyes closed, catching her breath. Then, at a distance, she heard Finpaw calling, "Twigpaw! Twigpaw!"

"I'm okay . . . ," she managed to choke out.

Much closer, another voice meowed, "What are you doing here?"

Twigpaw opened her eyes. At first all she could see were paws: gray paws, standing around her in a half circle. Her gaze traveled upward, and her heart lurched as she recognized a WindClan patrol: Featherpelt with Emberfoot and his apprentice, Smokepaw. All three of them looked hostile, with bristling fur and claws extended.

Oh, StarClan! I've come out on WindClan territory!

"What are you doing here?" Featherpelt repeated.

"I'm sorry," Twigpaw gasped. "I didn't mean to be here."

She staggered to her paws and wanted to shake the water out of her pelt, but she realized in time that if she did that she would shower the WindClan patrol. *And I don't suppose they'd be pleased with me,* she thought, frustrated at having to put up with her wet pelt.

"Your clumsiness cost us prey," Emberfoot hissed. "We were stalking a pigeon, but when you made all that noise falling in, it flew away."

I'll try to fall in quietly next time, Twigpaw thought, but all she dared to say aloud was "Sorry."

"'Sorry' fills no bellies," Featherpelt snapped. "And what are two apprentices doing out here anyway, so far from camp and without your mentors?"

Twigpaw glanced across the stream to see Finpaw standing there, his eyes huge and worried. She wished he had hidden himself in the undergrowth, so that he wouldn't be in trouble too.

At first she wasn't sure how to answer Featherpelt's question. She wasn't sure if she ought to admit that she and Finpaw were hunting, but also she didn't want to suggest that ThunderClan mentors were so careless that apprentices could just wander off without them knowing. *It makes ThunderClan look so bad. . . . It's not the way for me to earn my warrior name.*

"Uh, we . . . we just went out for a bit and got distracted," she stammered at last.

Even while she spoke, she felt a stab of fury at looking like a dumb apprentice in the hope that the WindClan cats would let them go.

But at least her tactic seemed to work. Featherpelt's claws slid back, and her fur smoothed out. Emberfoot and Smokepaw both took a pace back, though they kept a wary gaze on Twigpaw.

"In that case," Featherpelt meowed, "we'll escort you back to the ThunderClan camp. Just to make sure that you don't get distracted again."

"There's no need!" Twigpaw protested, thoroughly alarmed. "We'll go straight back, I promise."

"No, I think your Clan leader needs to know what you've been up to," Featherpelt responded with a dismissive wave of her tail. "Emberfoot, you come with me. Smokepaw, go back to camp and tell Harestar what happened. Meet me back here, and we'll carry on hunting."

The apprentice dashed off through the trees, while Feath-erpelt and Emberfoot padded farther upstream to a place where the stream was narrow enough to leap across. Twigpaw was forced to go with them.

Anger and shame burned through her as she and Finpaw made their way back through the forest, firmly escorted by the two WindClan warriors.

What will Bramblestar say to us? she asked herself. *And Sparkpelt? Oh, great StarClan, could this be any worse?* She was frustrated, too, that she had no chance to pick up the prey she had caught ear-lier. *It'll be crow-food by the time I can go back for it!*

Thornclaw was still on guard when Twigpaw and the oth-ers arrived back at the stone hollow. He leaped to his paws as he saw the WindClan cats. "What are you doing here?" he demanded, sliding out his claws.

Featherpelt dipped her head politely, not reacting to his challenging tone or the hostile stares of the other Thunder-Clan cats who began to gather around. "We would like to speak to your Clan leader, please," she mewed.

Berrynose immediately broke away from the crowd and raced across the camp to the tumbled rocks. Thornclaw waved his tail, allowing the WindClan cats to advance a few paces farther into the camp, while the rest of the Clan waited in a ragged circle around them.

Now that she was standing still, Twigpaw could feel the cold seeping into her wet pelt, and she started to shiver. She hoped none of the other cats thought it was because she was scared. Finpaw brushed his pelt against hers and murmured into her ear, "It'll be okay. You'll see."

Twigpaw wished she could share his boundless optimism.

She felt as if she had been waiting for moons before Bramblestar thrust his way through the cluster of cats and stood in front of her. "What's going on?" he asked the Wind-Clan cats. "Why are you here?"

"We brought these apprentices back," Featherpelt explained, dipping her head respectfully. "This one," she added, angling her ears toward Twigpaw, "fell into the border stream and pulled herself out on our side. I know she didn't mean to trespass, but she cost us a catch."

"It was an accident," Twigpaw defended herself as Bramble-star turned his amber gaze on her.

"I know that," Featherpelt meowed, "but she could have got herself into serious trouble. Some of our warriors might not have been as lenient as Emberfoot and I. Or suppose she had strayed onto RiverClan territory. . . ."

That's mouse-brained, Twigpaw thought, beginning to bristle. *We don't even have a border with RiverClan. And I barely made it onto WindClan territory, so I don't see what all the fuss is about. It's all so unfair!*

However, she had the sense to keep her mouth shut as Bramblestar listened calmly to what the WindClan warrior was telling him. His expression was unreadable, unnerving Twigpaw even more, as he thanked Featherpelt for her courtesy.

"I'll make sure my cats respect the boundaries better," he promised. "And if the next ThunderClan hunting party happens to catch prey close to the border, they'll bring some of it to WindClan to prove our goodwill."

Twigpaw's belly lurched as she listened, and she kept her gaze fixed on her paws. She didn't dare to look up; she could feel the gazes of her Clanmates boring into her for costing them food.

She heard the WindClan cats saying their farewells, then felt Bramblestar's tail flick her shoulder.

"Come to my den, Twigpaw," the Clan leader meowed. "You and I need to talk."

Twigpaw's heart sank right down into her paws. Being scolded by Sparkpelt was one thing; it was ten times worse to be scolded by the Clan leader. Her paws felt like heavy stones as she toiled up the tumbled rocks and followed Bramblestar into his den.

"You may be an apprentice, Twigpaw," he began, sitting down at the edge of his nest. "But you're old enough and experienced enough not to make this kind of mistake. What's going on with you?"

Every word sliced through Twigpaw like a blow from unsheathed claws. She would rather Bramblestar had growled at her instead of speaking in the calm and weary voice that he was using now.

"I'm sorry," she mewed. "It really was an accident."

"But you and Finpaw shouldn't have been out there in the first place," Bramblestar responded. "Come on, Twigpaw, tell me what the problem is. I know you sacrificed a lot to come back to ThunderClan, so you must want to be here. Why are you finding it so hard to settle in?"

Twigpaw sighed, and decided this was the moment to tell the truth. *If the Clan leader will listen to me, things might get a whole lot better.*

"Training is . . . a challenge," she admitted, "because Sparkpelt insists on training me at the same level as Finpaw. I understand," she added in a rush, "and it's perfectly fine. I don't expect special treatment. But—"

"But that is a little strange," Bramblestar interrupted. "You've been an apprentice twice before. It seems like a waste of your time and Sparkpelt's to teach you the basics." His gaze grew thoughtful. "I'll talk to Sparkpelt about it," he promised. "Is there anything else that's bothering you?"

Twigpaw was silent for a moment, but she couldn't go on trying to push her worries aside. "The prophecy!" she blurted out.

Bramblestar's gaze lightened; for a moment he looked almost amused. "What prophecy?" he asked.

"I know Alderheart believes that StarClan wants there to be five Clans," Twigpaw replied. "And with ShadowClan gone and RiverClan having closed its borders, there are only three. I'm worried that terrible things will happen to *ThunderClan* if we don't do something."

Bramblestar was silent for several heartbeats, just looking at her, a bemused expression on his face. "It isn't a warrior's job—much less an apprentice's—to worry about StarClan's messages," he mewed gently. "We have medicine cats to interpret StarClan's meaning for us." His head tilted to one side.

"I remember you hanging around the medicine-cat den with Alderheart when you were a kit," he continued. "Do you feel you might like to be a medicine cat yourself?"

Not another *apprenticeship!* Twigpaw thought. Confidently she shook her head. "When I was a kit, I used to think I might like to be a medicine cat," she replied, "but now I realize I'm much better suited to be a warrior."

Bramblestar nodded. "I appreciate your concern about the prophecy," he told her. "It shows you're a thoughtful and dedicated cat. But ThunderClan can't tell the other Clans what to do. Unfortunately, ShadowClan is its own problem, and only time will tell what will happen there. Meanwhile," he went on, "you must focus on being a good apprentice. That is the best way you can serve your Clan. Do you understand?"

"Oh, yes!" Twigpaw responded. "I really will do my best."

"Good," Bramblestar meowed. "You can go now. Please find Sparkpelt and send her up to me."

Twigpaw ducked her head and left the den. As she scrambled down the tumbled rocks, she felt a mixture of satisfaction and apprehension. *Did I just get my mentor into trouble?*

Early the following morning Larksong appeared at the entrance to the nursery to fetch Finpaw for training. Twigpaw followed her fellow apprentice out into the camp, looking around for her mentor.

"Where's Sparkpelt?" she asked.

"I have no idea," Larksong replied, looking faintly anxious. "She wasn't in the warriors' den when I woke up. Perhaps you'd better look for her. Finpaw and I will wait."

Oh, StarClan! Twigpaw thought, feeling guilty. *Surely Bramble-star can't have sent her away because I complained?*

Twigpaw began to scour the camp, sticking her head into the elders' den, where Graystripe and Millie were still asleep, and into the apprentices' den, where most of the sick cats were curled up. There was no sign of Sparkpelt.

Then, as Twigpaw was approaching the medicine-cat den, she heard her mentor's voice raised in a loud and annoyed meow. "I haven't got *time* for this! I have an apprentice to train."

Twigpaw's ears twitched at Jayfeather's growl, though she couldn't make out the words. She brushed past the bramble screen and saw Sparkpelt sitting at the side of the den, licking up some leaves that looked like watermint.

"Twigpaw," she rasped as she looked up to see her apprentice, "I have this StarClan-cursed sickness. You'll have to train with Larksong today."

"And for the next few days," Jayfeather added. "Now eat the rest of those leaves and get yourself over to the apprentices' den."

With an irritated twitch of her whiskers, Sparkpelt obeyed. Her belly heaved, but to Twigpaw's relief the healing herbs stayed down.

"I'm really sorry," Twigpaw mewed. "I'll come and see you later."

"Thanks," Sparkpelt growled. Her eyes were glazed and she looked exhausted; she seemed a different cat from the energetic Sparkpelt Twigpaw knew. "Twigpaw," she added as Twigpaw turned to go, "I'll give you some more challenging tasks when I recover. But for now, you'll have to learn what you can with Larksong and Finpaw."

"I'll do my best," Twigpaw promised.

She retreated from the den, dashed across the camp, and joined Larksong and Finpaw, who were waiting beside the entrance to the thorn tunnel.

When she gave them the news, Larksong glanced wistfully at the medicine cats' den, as if he wanted to see Sparkpelt himself. Then he gave his pelt a shake. "Come on," he meowed. "Hunting practice this morning."

Twigpaw prepared to be bored as she followed Larksong and Finpaw into the forest. She tried hard to be patient while Larksong got Finpaw to practice the hunter's crouch, even though she could see that Finpaw had forgotten all about what he should do with his tail.

Finally she had to speak. "Finpaw, if you keep letting your tail bob up and down, you'll alert any prey you're trying to stalk."

"Oops. Okay, thanks, Twigpaw." Finpaw tucked his tail in.

"Yes, thank you so much." Larksong's voice was heavily sarcastic. "I'm sure I'd never have noticed his tail. I couldn't possibly have been waiting until I was sure he'd gotten his paws in the right position." Then he relaxed a little and gave Twigpaw a friendly shove. "Come over here a moment." Glancing over his shoulder, he added, "Finpaw, practice by yourself for a bit. Pretend that dead leaf over there is a mouse."

"What do you want?" Twigpaw asked, as she and Larksong withdrew a few tail-lengths from where Finpaw was busy creeping up on the leaf.

"It's not helping Finpaw to train with you," Larksong told her. "You're much more advanced, and it's not fair to him. He's so enthusiastic, and he'll try to do the things you can do. If he fails, he might get despondent, and that will affect his confidence."

Do you even know your apprentice? Twigpaw thought. *That cat has enough confidence to fill up the stone hollow, and then some!*

"I get that," she meowed to Larksong. "So what do you want me to do?"

"You might as well go back to camp for now," Larksong decided. "See if the elders need anything, or if you can help the medicine cats."

Twigpaw dipped her head. "Okay." As she padded off toward the camp, she heard Finpaw's voice behind her, raised in a triumphant yowl. "Hey, Larksong, I killed the leaf!"

Back in camp, Twigpaw took fresh-kill to Graystripe and Millie, then looked in on the medicine cats. Sparkpelt had gone to join the other sick cats in the apprentices' den; White-wing was still curled up in her nest, though by now Plumkit was getting better and had gone back to her mother in the nursery.

"Hi, do you need me for anything?" she asked the medicine cats.

It was Alderheart who replied. "I don't think so, right now, thanks. But I'll call you if we do."

Disappointed, Twigpaw retreated into the camp again. Her paws itched to be doing something, but she didn't dare go off by herself to hunt, not after what had happened the day before.

Glancing around, she spotted Lilyheart stretched out on a rock at the side of the stone hollow, and padded over to join her. Lilyheart looked up at her, blinking affectionately.

"Hi, Twigpaw. No training today?"

"No, Sparkpelt is sick," Twigpaw replied, not wanting to go into all the problems about training with Finpaw.

"Then you can come and talk to me." Lilyheart gestured with her tail for Twigpaw to join her on the rock.

Twigpaw felt soothed by her welcome. When she had first come to ThunderClan as a tiny kit, Lilyheart had taken her into the nursery and cared for her as her own mother had never had a chance to. Twigpaw still felt a strong bond between them.

At least one cat is happy to see me, she thought, but a pang of grief pierced through her at the memory of when Lilyheart's mate, Snowbush, had died in a rockslide. *I wasn't even in ThunderClan to comfort her when that happened.*

"How are you today?" she asked, remembering that Lilyheart had been one of the first cats to fall ill.

"Better, but it's a slow job," her foster mother replied. "I just long to get out into the forest to have a good run and stretch my muscles. But when I get up, I can barely totter over to the fresh-kill pile!"

"Would you like some fresh-kill now?"

Lilyheart shook her head. "I'm fine, thanks." Giving Twig-paw a more penetrating look, she added, "But I can see that you're not. Something's bothering you, isn't it?"

Twigpaw hesitated, but her foster mother's loving gaze encouraged her to speak. "I feel a little restless here in ThunderClan," she confessed. "I don't want to leave—far from it—but I'm not sure yet what my place is. I know I'm being stupid, but . . ." She paused again, needing to make sure her voice would be steady. "I guess I expected my Clanmates to be more excited to have me back."

Lilyheart stretched out her neck to rasp her tongue over Twigpaw's ear. "You're not being stupid at all," she mewed gently. "But, you know, it's because we all loved you so much that we were so upset when you left. Now *I'm* happy, because I feel like I have all my kits back with me."

Twigpaw nuzzled Lilyheart's shoulder. "It's Violetshine, too," she continued. "Things are so strained between us now, and I hate it."

"She'll always be your sister," Lilyheart reminded her.

"Yes, but I wish I had *kin* here in ThunderClan, too," Twig-paw meowed. "They would understand me, or at least make things less difficult."

Lilyheart reached her tail around to touch Twigpaw's shoul-der. "The Clan will trust you again," she promised. "Maybe you need to prove to *yourself* that you belong here, instead of proving it to other cats."

Twigpaw bowed her head and touched noses with Lilyheart,

grateful for her foster mother's wisdom and feeling much better about herself. "Thank you," she purred.

Just then a triumphant voice rang out from the entrance to the thorn tunnel. "Twigpaw! Look!"

Twigpaw turned to see Finpaw bounding across the camp, a vole dangling from his jaws. Larksong followed more slowly.

"Look!" Finpaw repeated, dropping his vole on the fresh-kill pile. "I caught it all by myself!"

"That's great!" With a dip of her head toward Lilyheart, Twigpaw raced over to join her friend and inspect his prey. It was a very small vole, but Finpaw looked as proud and excited as if he had brought back the fattest squirrel in the forest.

"Larksong," he asked his mentor, "please can I share it with Twigpaw?"

Larksong looked almost as delighted as his apprentice. "Of course you can."

Eyes shining, Finpaw picked the vole up off the fresh-kill pile and settled down with Twigpaw to eat. As she bit into the warm prey, Twigpaw felt a moment of happiness. But she still wondered what she could do to prove herself a loyal Thunder-Clan cat.

CHAPTER 5

♣

"Sandynose, I want you to lead a border patrol," Leafstar meowed. "And you can take a look at the old ShadowClan camp on the way. Violetshine, you can go with him."

Pleased to be chosen, Violetshine stepped up beside her Clanmate, while Leafstar fixed Tree with a serious gaze. "Tree, it's been half a moon, and Frecklewish tells me you don't seem too interested in learning the ways of a medicine cat," she continued. "So I think you'd better join this patrol, too. Let's see how the life of a warrior suits you."

The muscular yellow tom was sitting at the edge of the group, watching the clouds drift by. He didn't respond when his Clan leader addressed him.

"Tree," Leafstar repeated. "Are you with us?"

Tree gave a sudden start. "Uh . . . sorry, Leafstar, what did you say?"

"I told you to join this patrol," Leafstar replied, flicking her tail toward Sandynose and Violetshine.

Tree looked uncertain. "But that sounds like a warrior task," he protested, "and I'm not a warrior."

Violetshine studied Leafstar anxiously, afraid that the

Clan leader would lose patience with Tree. He had been living with SkyClan for more than a moon now, and he still hadn't decided where he fit into the Clan, or even whether he wanted to stay.

"Even if you don't think of yourself as a warrior," Leafstar responded, her eyes and her voice calm, "you must contribute if you're going to stay here. That rule applies to *all* cats."

Her final words held a challenge, or even a taunt, making Violetshine uneasy for a completely different reason. *Maybe Tree will just say, "No thanks," and then leave. I really don't want that to happen.* She couldn't imagine not seeing Tree anymore. But if he became a loner again, how could he fit into her life?

"Well . . . okay." Tree was still looking unsure. "But won't I slow down the patrol if I haven't been on one before?"

"Every cat has to start somewhere," Leafstar told him briskly. "Your instincts will probably serve you well. And you'll be with Violetshine. It'll be a good way for you to see what the warrior life is all about."

"Yes, I'll help," Violetshine mewed eagerly. *Then he might be convinced to stay for a little while. . . .*

The sun, barely visible through a layer of cloud, was skimming the tops of the trees when Sandynose led his patrol out through the fern tunnel. By the time they reached the border, the previous day's scent markings had started to fade.

Tree had already irritated Sandynose by wandering off, then stopping to yawn and groom himself. Violetshine heard Sandynose muttering to himself, "StarClan knows why Leafstar puts up with this cat!"

Violetshine had to admit that Tree's behavior was annoying. *He'll cost himself a place in the Clan, if he's not careful.* Hoping to help him act more like a warrior, she showed Tree how to renew the markers, aware all the time of Sandynose keeping a watchful eye on them. She felt a little wary of the stocky brown tom: he had been Twigpaw's mentor, and spent a lot of time grumbling about her defection to ThunderClan. Not only that, but he was Finpaw's father. Violetshine knew how much he missed the energetic young tom since he had made the decision to go with Twigpaw.

And maybe Sandynose thinks it was my fault somehow, because Twigpaw's my sister, Violetshine thought. *But I miss Twigpaw too.*

She tried not to dwell on how it felt to be abandoned by kin, but as she brushed her pelt against Tree's, she felt a hollow ache in her chest.

If even my littermate doesn't belong with me, then why would Tree?

Violetshine left Tree to set a scent marker on a boulder while she sniffed around the entrance to a dark hole in a nearby bank, picking up only the stale scent of rabbit.

"Oh, for StarClan's sake!"

Sandynose's exclamation made Violetshine turn back, to see that instead of setting the marker, Tree had climbed on top of the boulder and was stretched out in a shaft of sunlight that broke through the clouds.

"Tree, get down off there!" Sandynose continued. "Honestly, the smallest kit in the Clan has more sense!"

Unoffended, Tree slid down from the boulder. "Keep your fur on," he meowed. "What's the rush? We've got all day."

"There are other duties—" Violetshine began, only to be interrupted by a growl from Sandynose.

"I give up! Tree, you can come with us or not, but I'm not standing around waiting for you to rearrange your whiskers. Violetshine, set the marker, and then we'll go and have a look at the old ShadowClan camp."

He swung around, hardly giving Violetshine time to obey, then stalked off between the pine trees. Violetshine hastily set the marker and bounded after him; to her surprise, she heard Tree padding after them.

Just as she caught up to Sandynose, the brown tom halted suddenly and lifted his head, beginning to taste the air.

"What is it?" Violetshine asked, keeping her voice low in case Sandynose had detected an attack. "Is it rogues?"

Sandynose tasted the air again. "I'm not sure," he replied. "But there are definitely cats up ahead. They're inside the border here, and that means they're trespassing."

Violetshine drew in the air for herself. They were not far away from the ShadowClan camp, and a stiff breeze was blowing from that direction, carrying the scent toward them.

"Don't you think those scents are familiar?" she asked Sandynose.

Sandynose shook his head. "Not to me. If they are, there's probably nothing to worry about—but there has to be a reason why cats are crossing borders and snooping around the old ShadowClan camp." He drew back his lips in the beginning of a snarl. "And that's unlikely to be anything good, right?"

Violetshine pricked her ears like she was trying to pinpoint prey. Her muscles tensed as she braced herself for trouble. "We ought to go and check it out," she whispered.

Sandynose gave a curt nod. "Follow me."

As he set off, flattening himself to the ground and setting his paws down as lightly as if he was creeping up on a mouse, Violetshine turned to Tree.

"You'd better stay back," she told him. "We don't know what we're getting into here."

"Certainly not!" Tree hissed. "I'm not going to run and leave you to fight by yourselves."

There was no time to argue. Violetshine headed after Sandynose, thankful for the thick covering of pine needles that silenced her paw steps, and the breeze still carrying their scent away from the camp and the intruders. Tree padded alongside her.

When they reached the rocky slope that led up to the ShadowClan camp, Sandynose raised his tail to halt the others. "From now on, absolute silence," he whispered, with a hard look at Tree. "And Violetshine, if there is trouble, I want you to run back to camp and fetch help. You're the fastest," he added, as Violetshine opened her jaws to protest.

"Okay, Sandynose."

Together the three cats crept up the slope until they reached the top and could look down into the shallow dip that had been the ShadowClan camp. The scent of cats was even stronger here, and Violetshine felt more than ever that she ought to recognize it.

As they watched, a golden-furred she-cat appeared at the

far side of the hollow, a mouse dangling from her jaws. She bounded down into the camp and disappeared into the bramble thicket that had once been the nursery.

"Sleekwhisker!" Violetshine breathed out. "She was a ShadowClan cat, but she joined Darktail." She suppressed a shudder as she remembered how viciously Sleekwhisker had supported the rogue leader. "She helped kill Needletail."

"Not a cat we want around, then," Sandynose responded. "Let's go and deal with her."

He led the way, paw step by careful paw step, down into the hollow and across to the bramble thicket. A narrow tunnel led inside; Sandynose plunged into it and Violetshine followed, with Tree bringing up the rear.

"Watch our backs," Violetshine instructed him. "There might be more of them."

Before she finished speaking, she heard a yowl of alarm from up ahead. Pressing forward, she emerged into the old nursery and halted in amazement at what she saw. Sleekwhisker was there, and so was Yarrowleaf, another former ShadowClan cat who had been part of Darktail's Kin, stretched out in a nest of moss. Her rounded belly showed that she was close to having kits.

Sandynose stood over them. His claws were out and his tail lashing, but he was obviously reluctant to attack a cat so near to kitting. Sleekwhisker crouched between him and Yarrowleaf, her fur bristling and her lips drawn back as she hissed defiance.

"Violetpaw!" Yarrowleaf exclaimed, her yellow eyes wide

and frightened. "What's happening? Where is ShadowClan?"

"Are these both ShadowClan cats?" Sandynose asked Violetshine.

"Yes. This is Yarrowleaf."

Uneasiness stirred in Violetshine's belly. Sleekwhisker and Yarrowleaf were two of the cats who had been closest to Darktail. *What do they want here?* she asked herself.

Sandynose still didn't sheathe his claws. "That's all well and good," he meowed, "but they've still crossed our borders without permission."

"But you're not going to attack a pregnant queen, are you?" Tree asked; his eyes were warm with sympathy for Yarrowleaf, who looked so scared and confused.

Sandynose hesitated for a moment, then relaxed with a sigh. "No, I can't do that. But don't expect me to welcome them. Not if they're the ShadowClan warriors who betrayed Rowanclaw."

"Not only that," Violetshine told him, "but they were both really loyal to Darktail when he made them part of his Kin. They helped *drown* cats." She shivered, remembering how Sleekwhisker had flung herself at Needletail, trying to force her underwater. *Needletail was one of the first friends I ever had.*

"We've left Darktail," Sleekwhisker told them. "We realized what a mistake we'd made, and we came back looking for ShadowClan, to come home again. Where *is* ShadowClan?"

"The ShadowClan cats have a different camp now," Sandynose said shortly. "And you aren't part of their Clan anymore."

"Oh, please let us stay," Yarrowleaf begged. "We just want

to be ShadowClan cats again."

"You were fine letting your Clanmates die when Darktail was in charge," Violetshine accused Yarrowleaf. "Is it because you're expecting kits that now, all of a sudden, you see the value in a Clan?"

Yarrowleaf cringed away from her. "It's not like that," she protested. "Sleekwhisker and I have been living with the remains of Darktail's group, but it bothered us more and more, the way that none of the cats seem to care about one another."

"That's right," Sleekwhisker growled, her muscles still tensed to spring as she glared up at Sandynose. "Now that Darktail is gone, they don't even have the idea of Kin anymore. It's every cat for themselves."

"Spikefur died." Yarrowleaf's voice was shaking. "He was sick. We tried to help him, but the other cats wouldn't forage for herbs, or . . ." She gave way altogether, and buried her nose in her forepaws, her whole body shaking.

"No cat would help treat him, or fetch him fresh-kill," Sleekwhisker went on. "I did my best, but I couldn't look after him and Yarrowleaf as well. So he died," she finished bleakly.

"I took Nettle as a mate," Yarrowleaf began again, clearly making a massive effort to control herself. "These are his kits, but I was so scared about the idea of raising my kits among the rogues. I kept remembering what it was like when I was a kit, here in the nursery, safe and surrounded by cats who cared about me. I want that for *my* kits. I want ShadowClan."

For a moment none of the SkyClan cats responded, gazing warily at one another. Violetshine didn't know how to find the words, to break the news to Yarrowleaf that what she wanted didn't exist anymore. She noticed, too, that Tree looked deeply disturbed, as if he had begun to realize how serious the loss of ShadowClan was.

The silence seemed to stretch out for moons, until Sleek-whisker sat up, flattening her bristling fur, a look of concern in her eyes. "Violetpaw, what did he mean"—she glanced at Sandynose—"when he said Rowan*claw*? He meant Rowanstar, surely?"

"I'm Violetshine now," she replied. She glanced at Sandy-nose, but his gaze was fixed on his paws; she was obviously not going to get any help from him in explaining. "SkyClan has returned to the lake," Violetshine went on, "and Shadow-Clan . . . Rowanstar decided he couldn't go on leading a Clan that hardly existed anymore. So now he's Rowanclaw again, and what's left of ShadowClan has joined SkyClan."

Sleekwhisker and Yarrowleaf exchanged a stunned glance. "But—but how can ShadowClan not *exist* anymore?" Yar-rowleaf stammered.

Violetshine couldn't think of any way to answer that.

"You both need to think long and hard about what you want to do now," Sandynose meowed sternly. "Leafstar, the leader of SkyClan, is in charge, and I'm not sure what she'll say about allowing you into the Clan. If it was ShadowClan you wanted . . . perhaps you should think again."

Yarrowleaf and Sleekwhisker were silent for a moment, looking deeply troubled. "Then we want to join SkyClan," Yarrowleaf declared at last.

"Yes, we've been through a horrible time since we left," Sleekwhisker mewed. "We had no idea that things would turn out like this. We're not here to cause trouble."

Her voice was so fervent that Violetshine was almost convinced, yet she found it hard to forget what Sleekwhisker had done when she was one of Darktail's Kin.

"Any Clan is a Clan," Sleekwhisker continued. "That's the only kind of life we want."

"That's right," Yarrowleaf agreed. "I'm so sorry for turning my back on ShadowClan. I know now this is where I need to be."

Violetshine was doubtful about whether they ought to trust either of these cats. *I can't believe that Yarrowleaf is having a rogue's kits. Should we really be bringing half rogues into Clan territory?*

At the same time, she couldn't deny that the ShadowClan cats looked sincere when they said all they wanted to do was get back to normal.

I wonder if anything will ever be normal again, for ShadowClan cats.

"I suppose we can start by bringing them to Leafstar," Violetshine suggested to Sandynose. As the brown tom nodded a curt agreement, she realized that she had no idea what the SkyClan leader would say.

Sandynose led the way into the SkyClan camp, with Violetshine and Tree bringing up the rear behind the two ShadowClan she-cats. Yarrowleaf was quickly exhausted; Violetshine was impressed by her resolve to keep going, when the weight of her kits must be dragging at her.

As soon as she emerged from the fern tunnel, Yarrowleaf halted, her legs shaking as she gazed around. Violetshine could see she was finding it hard to accept how things had changed, and that she was making her way into a totally strange camp and strange Clan.

At the far side of the camp, in a quiet corner near the nursery, Rowanclaw and Tawnypelt were sharing tongues, not looking like leaders or senior warriors at all. Yarrowleaf stared at them for a moment, then let her head droop.

"This is terrible . . . ," she hissed to herself. "I feel so responsible. . . ."

As she spoke, Tawnypelt lifted her head and spotted the two ShadowClan cats. Instantly fury flooded her green eyes and she sprang to her paws. "I thought I smelled a traitor!" she snarled.

Before any cat could react, Tawnypelt raced across the camp and came to a halt in front of Yarrowleaf. Her claws were out, with one paw raised to strike. For a heartbeat she froze, as if she had just realized that Yarrowleaf was expecting kits. Then she lowered her paw, but her gaze still glittered angrily. "This is all your fault!" she spat. "You and the other deserters. It's because of you that ShadowClan fell!"

The other ShadowClan cats in the camp also rose to their paws. Snowbird and Scorchfur bounded across to Yarrowleaf and stood beside her, supporting her. Violetshine remembered that she was their kit. Juniperclaw padded up and touched noses with his littermates, Sleekwhisker and Strikestone. More of the lost Clan gathered around and stood in shocked silence, waiting for what would happen.

"Things were so bad with the rogues," Yarrowleaf began hastily, as if she was desperate to explain. "Spikefur, who was my mentor, is dead, and I realized that I wanted to come home to ShadowClan to have my kits."

"But this isn't ShadowClan anymore." Leafstar's voice joined the debate. "It's SkyClan."

Every cat turned to see Leafstar standing at the entrance of her den in the hollow cedar tree. Calm and unhurried, she jumped down and padded over to the group of cats surrounding the newcomers.

Before she reached them, Tawnypelt broke away and raced across to confront her. "Don't let them in!" she meowed. "They're traitors who attacked and killed their own Clanmates. They're unforgiveable! They—"

Leafstar raised a paw to silence Tawnypelt. As she joined the group, Yarrowleaf thrust her way through the cats who surrounded her and stood trembling in front of the SkyClan leader.

"Please take us in," she begged. "We've nowhere else to go, and we have kin here."

"You should have thought of that before you betrayed your Clanmates," Tawnypelt growled.

"No—stop." Violetshine hadn't noticed Rowanclaw approaching, but now he stood beside his mate and curled his tail across her shoulders. "Whatever Yarrowleaf and Sleekwhisker have done in the past, I forgive them. It will do no good for Clans to hold grudges. That's a sure way to drag every cat into trouble again. We should—"

Rowanclaw suddenly broke off and gave his chest fur a couple of embarrassed licks. He had obviously just realized that he was making a speech like a Clan leader. With a guilty look at Leafstar, he added, "Of course, this is SkyClan now. It's your decision about whether these cats are welcome or not."

Leafstar stepped forward and gazed at the two newcomers with narrowed eyes. "Give me one reason why I should trust you," she meowed, "after everything that's happened."

Violetshine could hear several cats murmuring agreement, while beside Yarrowleaf, Snowbird and Scorchfur exchanged anxious looks.

"We're ready to dedicate ourselves to SkyClan," Sleekwhisker assured Leafstar, her eyes wide and pleading. "We'll do whatever we need to prove ourselves."

Leafstar seemed unimpressed. "It seems you were willing to dedicate yourselves to *ShadowClan*, not to SkyClan," she mewed with a sniff. "And I'm not even sure I believe that, if what I understand about you is true. You *did* leave ShadowClan to join Darktail's group?"

The two she-cats nodded, looking wretched.

"Are you aware," Leafstar went on, her tone suddenly as icy as a wind in leaf-bare, "that before Darktail came to the lake, he wormed his way into SkyClan, posing as our friend? And that then he and his rogues attacked us in the dead of night and drove us out of the gorge—out of our home?"

Sleekwhisker and Yarrowleaf exchanged horrified glances. This was the first they had heard of SkyClan's story.

"We were left homeless," Leafstar went on inexorably, "wandering for moon after moon, searching for the other Clans. It's only recently that we arrived here at the lake and were given this territory. Have you any idea how many cats died because of Darktail's treachery?"

The two cats shook their head. "No," Sleekwhisker responded.

"Too many," Leafstar meowed grimly. "And Darktail is responsible for the deaths of many of your ShadowClan Clanmates, too. I'm not sure I could ever trust a cat who chose to leave a Clan to follow Darktail. Why in the name of StarClan would you do that?"

"I was young and stupid!" Yarrowleaf wailed. "I blamed Rowanstar for things that weren't his fault. Now I know my life would have been better if I'd been loyal to my Clan."

"I thought our leader was weak," Sleekwhisker added simply as Leafstar's cold gaze turned to her.

Her words brought a gasp of outrage from Tawnypelt and some of the others, but Rowanclaw looked unsurprised, dipping his head in acceptance.

For a few heartbeats, silence fell. Violetshine felt herself holding her breath as she waited for Leafstar's decision. *I don't know whether I want them to go or stay.*

Leafstar's steady gaze rested on the two cats as if she was trying to read their thoughts. Then she lowered her eyes. "I'm sorry," she mewed. "But this is a difficult time for the Clans, and I can't welcome into my Clan any cat I don't completely trust. Knowing you followed Darktail—knowing what you did while you were with him—I can never trust you completely. You can never be part of SkyClan."

Yowls of protest came from many of the assembled cats. Snowbird and Scorchfur drew closer to Yarrowleaf as if to protect her, while Juniperclaw's fur bushed up and he looked ready to attack any cat who came near his sister.

"I'm sorry," Leafstar meowed decisively. "But I want the two of you off SkyClan territory right away. If you're so keen on joining a Clan, perhaps you should talk to ThunderClan or WindClan . . . but I cannot have you here."

Even before she had finished speaking, Yarrowleaf let out an anguished yowl. "But this is my home! These are my kin!" More quietly she added, "I could never be a ThunderClan or WindClan cat."

"You will never be a SkyClan cat, either," Leafstar responded calmly. "Sandynose, Macgyver, escort them to the border."

The two warriors she had named stepped to the side of the two ShadowClan cats. Sandynose jerked his head toward the fern tunnel, while Macgyver gave Sleekwhisker a shove. She responded with a furious hiss but didn't try to resist.

For a moment Violetshine was afraid that the former ShadowClan cats would attack. Scorchfur in particular was growling with rage, his tail lashing. But he did nothing as his daughter and Sleekwhisker were led away.

"What about my kits?" Yarrowleaf was wailing as she vanished into the tunnel with Sandynose hard on her paws. "I have nowhere to go. . . ."

Violetshine could feel tension in the air as the sounds died away, like the ominous sensation before a thunderstorm.

"How could you?" Snowbird turned on Leafstar, her eyes full of grief. "That was *my* daughter—the daughter I thought was dead! And you've driven her out to have her kits in the forest."

Juniperclaw faced Leafstar at Snowbird's side. "There are cats in SkyClan *right now* who followed Darktail," he pointed out, his whiskers quivering with fury. "I'm one of them. Will you drive us out too, one day? Don't you believe that a cat can change?"

"Obviously she doesn't," Scorchfur sneered. "I wanted to believe that this combination of Clans would work, but this has just made it clear that Leafstar has no business making decisions for ShadowClan cats. She didn't grow up with us. She doesn't understand our bonds!"

More than ever, Violetshine was afraid that the argument would grow into a full-scale fight. She glanced around for Hawkwing, knowing that her father would help, but there was no sign of him; clearly the SkyClan deputy wasn't in camp.

Then, to Violetshine's amazement, Tawnypelt turned on her Clanmates, standing at Leafstar's side.

"Be quiet, all of you!" she snarled at them. "Like it or not, Leafstar is our leader now. She was chosen by StarClan. Do you want to go against StarClan?"

"Leafstar was chosen by StarClan to lead *SkyClan*," Juniperclaw muttered. "Not us."

Tawnypelt merely glared at him, and after a moment

Juniperclaw turned his head away.

"Leafstar made the right decision," Tawnypelt went on. "Those cats are *traitors*. If any of the rest of you want to be traitors, the way out of camp is right there."

Violetshine half expected that some of the cats would leave. Snowbird took a hesitant step or two toward the tunnel, but Scorchfur shook his head, laying his tail comfortingly on her shoulder. Gradually, the tension subsided.

"Well, why are you standing around here?" Leafstar asked, fighting to take back control. Violetshine thought she sounded shaken, perhaps more by Tawnypelt's unexpected defense than by the hostility of the other cats. "There's work to be done."

Gradually the group broke up, most of them heading for their dens. Frecklewish called to her apprentice, Fidgetpaw, and led him out of camp to collect herbs. Rowanclaw gathered a patrol and left camp to hunt.

Violetshine stood still, gazing at the fern tunnel where Sleekwhisker and Yarrowleaf had vanished, not sure what she should do. *Did I mess up by bringing them here?* she asked herself. *What will happen to them now?*

Then she felt a tail stroke gently along her flank, and turned to see Tree. He stood close to her, nuzzling her shoulder. "Are you okay?" he asked.

"I'm not sure *how* I feel," Violetshine murmured. "I don't really trust Yarrowleaf and Sleekwhisker. It was so terrible when Darktail was in control of ShadowClan, and it was Sleekwhisker who helped him kill Needletail."

Tree rasped his tongue over her ear. "I know she meant a lot to you."

"She was my best friend—my only friend. Sleekwhisker and Darktail tried to drown her in the lake, while Roach and Raven held me back so I couldn't help her." Violetshine shivered. "I still dream about it."

"You never told me that before," Tree mewed. "It must have been terrible. I can see I'll have to stay and keep an eye on you."

Oh, yes! Violetshine thought, warmed by his promise. "Tree," she asked after a moment, "did you . . . did you see any ghost cats walking with Yarrowleaf and Sleekwhisker?"

"Yes," Tree replied. "I saw a dark brown tom with a tuft of fur on his head."

"That must be Spikefur. They said he had died."

"I sense they tried to help him when he was alive," Tree went on. "I think they might be good cats. . . ."

Violetshine didn't know whether to be relieved by that, or horrified. She wanted to think that Yarrowleaf and Sleekwhisker were good cats, but if that was true, then Leafstar had just driven them out undeservedly, while their kin watched. They would struggle to survive with no Clan, no cat to help them.

I can't imagine this ending well. . . . Oh, StarClan, is there any way you can look after two Clanless cats?

CHAPTER 6

♣

Alderheart toiled up the moorland slopes toward the Moonpool. The half-moon appeared fitfully through gaps in the cloud, and there was a tang of frost in the air. Leaf-fall was clearly upon them, and the hungry days of leaf-bare were not far off.

Leafpool and Jayfeather were walking ahead of him, while Puddleshine and Frecklewish, with her apprentice, Fidgetpaw, brought up the rear. So far there was no sign of Kestrelflight from WindClan, or the RiverClan medicine cats, Mothwing and Willowshine.

I don't think the RiverClan cats will come, Alderheart thought. *Not when Mistystar is still keeping the borders closed.*

"So how is Twigpaw adjusting?" Leafpool asked Alderheart, dropping back to pad alongside him. "I saw you talking to her earlier, and I thought she looked sad."

"I know." Alderheart felt a pang of pain when he thought about the young cat who had been his friend ever since he'd found her as a kit in the tunnel under the Thunderpath. "I think she's just having trouble fitting back into ThunderClan."

Leafpool's ears twitched in surprise. "I hope she's not thinking of leaving again."

"I don't think so." Alderheart shook his head. "She knows she belongs with us, but she's missing her kin, and she's frustrated at having to be an apprentice again. But I haven't spent as much time with her as I would have liked," he added. "I've been worrying about the prophecy, and what it means now that we've lost ShadowClan and RiverClan has shut itself off."

Jayfeather, just ahead, let out a snort. "Aren't we all!"

"Well, perhaps we'll get some guidance when we meet with StarClan at the Moonpool," Leafpool meowed.

"We'd better," Jayfeather snapped.

The night grew colder as the cats approached the Moonpool, and by the time they clambered up the final rocky slope beside the stream, a brisk wind had arisen, flattening their fur to their sides. Turning to look back the way they had come, Alderheart spotted the small figure of a cat bounding across the moor.

"There's Kestrelflight!" he exclaimed.

"Thank StarClan," Leafpool mewed. "I was beginning to think there must be trouble in WindClan, too. I can't bear the thought that we might be down to two Clans."

"Have you seen any sign of Mothwing and Willowshine?" Jayfeather asked Kestrelflight as he scrambled up the rocks and stood panting at the top.

The WindClan medicine cat shook his head. "Not a whisker."

"Then I suppose they're not coming," Frecklewish murmured. "After all, the RiverClan borders are still closed."

"Maybe we ought to wait a little while," Puddleshine

suggested. "Just in case they show up."

Jayfeather let out an irritated sigh, but none of the other cats objected. Moment after moment slid past, but the moorland was empty.

"They're not coming," Leafpool meowed at last. "We'd better get started."

Along with his fellow medicine cats, Alderheart pushed his way through the line of bushes that surrounded the Moonpool and followed the spiral path down to the water's edge. A shiver ran through him as his paws slipped into the paw prints made by other cats so long ago. His worries seemed to fade as he listened to the sound of the water falling into the pool, and watched the shimmer of moon and starlight on its surface.

When every cat had settled around the edge of the pool, Leafpool rose to her paws. "We have an outbreak of belly sickness and vomiting in ThunderClan," she announced. "Our sick cats are recovering, thank StarClan, but many of our cats are sick."

"We have it in WindClan, too." Kestrelflight sounded eager to share information. "Several of our cats—six now—have the sickness. We and ThunderClan have used all the watermint from our border stream and the border with RiverClan."

"Have you got it in Shad—in SkyClan?" Alderheart asked the other medicine cats.

"No," Frecklewish replied. "Not yet, at least."

"Then let's try to keep it that way," Leafpool meowed. "I'll warn our border patrols to stay away from yours, and you should do the same. But enough of this," she went on briskly.

"Kestrelflight, stay in touch with us over the sickness. Now it's time to think about the prophecy."

"'The dark sky must not herald a storm,'" Alderheart murmured, remembering how hard he had struggled to understand the meaning. It was all too obvious now. "We have darkened the sky by going from five Clans to three," he went on, "at least until RiverClan decides to join us again—if they ever do."

"Have any of you had another message from StarClan?" Leafpool asked. "Any sign of what we should do next?"

The other medicine cats shook their heads.

"The spirit cats that Tree helped us see told us we must find the missing ShadowClan cats," Alderheart mewed.

"And I'd like nothing better," Puddleshine told him. "But we have no idea where they went, so how can we send out a patrol to find them?"

Leafpool blinked thoughtfully. "The loss of ShadowClan concerns me deeply," she murmured. "I do believe that River-Clan will one day return, but without ShadowClan how can we ever be five Clans? Puddleshine, do you think there's any hope of your Clan reviving?"

Puddleshine looked down and studied his paws. "No," he meowed reluctantly. "All our efforts now are to unite around Leafstar. The ShadowClan I knew is gone."

A heavy silence fell. Alderheart could feel disaster looming, like a storm cloud about to unleash its fury on the Clans.

It was Kestrelflight who spoke next. "Maybe StarClan will have some wisdom for us tonight."

Leafpool nodded. "Let's hope so. It is time to speak with them."

Along with the other medicine cats, Alderheart stretched out his neck and touched his nose to the surface of the Moon-pool. At once a deep chill flowed through him, so that he felt like a cat made of ice. Darkness was all around him; he opened his eyes and found himself sitting in dappled shade underneath a tree, with the murmuring sounds of greenleaf all around him.

"Hi there," a voice behind him said.

Alderheart whipped around to see Needletail standing behind him, a friendly glimmer in her green eyes and starlight dazzling in her fur.

"Needletail!" he gasped, springing to his paws. Relief and joy flooded over him at the sight of the cat who had been his friend ever since she had joined his quest to find SkyClan. "You made it to StarClan!"

Needletail dipped her head. "Yes. Once we had delivered our message, we were able to move on to join StarClan."

"And are you okay?" Alderheart asked.

"Oh, yes. It's great here." Needletail padded forward to touch noses with him. "But I still worry about Twigpaw and Violetshine. You will keep an eye on them, won't you?"

"You know that Violetshine is in SkyClan now, and she has her father and her kin to look after her," Alderheart responded. "But I'll certainly take care of Twigpaw. You can trust me."

Needletail let out a purr. "Let me down, and I'll come over

to ThunderClan and claw your ears off!"

Alderheart suppressed a small *mrrow* of laughter, then sobered, remembering the message of the spirit cats. "Needletail, I need to ask you something important. Do you know where the missing ShadowClan cats are?"

Needletail did not reply; her amusement vanishing, she only fixed Alderheart with her intense green gaze. "The shadows are approaching," she meowed at last, "and must not be dispelled."

Before Alderheart could ask Needletail what she meant, her starry form began to fade. Darkness swept over him again, and he blinked his eyes open to find himself once more beside the Moonpool. His fellow medicine cats were stirring around him.

As they rose and shook out their fur, Alderheart could not free himself from the sense of frustration that filled him from ears to tail-tip. *There were no answers in that vision,* he thought, deeply disappointed. *I'm even more confused than I was to start with!* From their confused looks, none of the other cats seemed to have learned anything, either. His head bowed with dejection, Alderheart prepared to set out on the long journey home.

But before any cat could start to climb the spiral path, Puddleshine suddenly exclaimed, "Dawnpelt came to me!"

At once the other cats gathered around him.

"What did she say?" Jayfeather demanded. "What did you see?"

Puddleshine closed his eyes, as if he was trying to cling to the vision before it faded from his memory.

"She didn't seem in pain from her death," he began, sounding relieved. "And she's in StarClan now."

"But what did she *say*?" Jayfeather lashed his tail impatiently.

"She told me that the shadows are approaching, and must not be dispelled," Puddleshine replied. He and Frecklewish exchanged a concerned glance, as if the words meant something to them that they didn't mean to the other medicine cats.

Alderheart's dejection vanished like ice under the strong sun of greenleaf. "I saw Needletail!" he mewed excitedly. "She told me exactly the same."

"And I saw Lioneye." Kestrelflight's eyes were filled with awe as he spoke. "She gave me the same message, too. They came to every Clan!"

"The shadows are approaching . . ." Frecklewish's voice was thoughtful. "Maybe that means the missing ShadowClan cats are on their way back to us!"

"And 'they must not be dispelled,'" Kestrelflight added. "Perhaps that means we should be open to the returning cats, and listen to what they have to say."

Puddleshine glanced around the group of medicine cats, his eyes worried. "This gives me hope," he mewed. "Perhaps ShadowClan isn't gone forever. But we'll have to convince Leafstar. . . ."

"We must take the message back to our Clanmates," Leafpool declared. "The meeting is over. And may StarClan light our paths, now and always."

"This is the best news we've had from StarClan in a long time," Kestrelflight declared as he and the other cats climbed the spiral path.

The others murmured their agreement. Alderheart could sense excitement and optimism in the air, as if every cat was eager to return to their Clan and pass on the message.

But as he thrust his way through the bushes and paused beside Leafpool before leaping down the rocks, Alderheart could see that his Clanmate looked troubled. The other cats, even Jayfeather, had gone on ahead, so Alderheart hung back to speak to her alone. "What's the matter?" he asked. "This is what we've been hoping for, isn't it?"

"I'm just not sure . . . ," Leafpool murmured. "Fine, Shadow-Clan cats might be coming back, but which cats are they? Not all of them were good—many of them joined with Darktail, and fought for him against their Clanmates."

"But not all of them," Alderheart pointed out. "And some were just scared, and didn't know what else to do."

Leafpool let out a worried sigh. "There's SkyClan, too. They have just returned to us. What effect will this have on them? Leafstar has been very patient with ShadowClan so far. But it's asking a lot of her, creating one Clan out of two, and then maybe splitting up again when these other cats arrive."

Alderheart considered what his fellow medicine cat had said. He could understand her worries, and he didn't know Leafstar well enough to guess how she would react.

"We don't know that's what StarClan's words mean," Alderheart cautioned Leafpool. "We don't even know for sure that any ShadowClan cats will return. Perhaps 'shadows' means something else."

"True," Leafpool admitted, gazing up at the sky as if she could read an answer there. "But I still feel uneasy."

Alderheart couldn't think of anything to say that would reassure her. The other medicine cats were already heading out across the moor; Alderheart bunched his muscles to leap down the rocks and follow them. Then his ears twitched as he caught the sound of movement in the bushes. He froze.

"Did you hear that?" he asked Leafpool.

"No—what?"

Alderheart parted his jaws to taste the air, but all he could pick up were the scents of the other medicine cats. He shrugged. "I must have been imagining it. Let's go."

Chapter 7

That was close!

Hidden deep within the bushes that surrounded the Moonpool, Twigpaw stood shivering. She had watched the other medicine cats leave, and had almost jumped out of her fur when she thought Alderheart had detected her presence. It took a long time before her heart stopped pounding.

Twigpaw knew that she shouldn't have come. But when she had heard Alderheart and Jayfeather talking about the prophecy, she had just had the feeling that if she followed them, she could learn something, or do something to help.

From her hiding place among the bushes, Twigpaw had heard nothing of what went on when the medicine cats were gathered at the Moonpool. She couldn't bring herself to go closer—the Moonpool was *only* for medicine cats. Her ears twitched with irritation at herself as she huddled in the bushes while the medicine cats were at the Moonpool—she should have thought of that. But she had been close enough to catch scraps of the conversation between Leafpool and Alderheart as they passed by on their way home.

Leafpool says that she's worried. . . .

Twigpaw stayed still, crouching close to the ground and not even twitching a whisker until she was sure the medicine cats were gone. She had a lot to think about. She knew Alderheart was convinced there should be five Clans, and how worried he was now that there were only three.

Twigpaw wondered what would happen to ThunderClan if ShadowClan was truly gone, and if RiverClan never came back. She knew that Sparkpelt thought the remaining Clans would be stronger, but Twigpaw wasn't so sure. StarClan had warned of a storm.

Sure now that she wouldn't be discovered, Twigpaw slid out into the open, shaking leaves and debris from her pelt. She was about to launch herself down the rocky slope, when a sudden thought struck her.

Suppose I go to the Moonpool? Maybe I can help figure out how to drive back the storm.

Twigpaw knew that she wasn't a medicine cat, and that she had no right to be down there. But if she could somehow get some information, she could reassure Leafpool, and prove her own allegiance to ThunderClan once and for all.

I'll do it!

Twigpaw took a swift glance over the slope and across the moor to make sure that the medicine cats were gone. Only Alderheart, Leafpool, and Jayfeather were still in sight, and they were a long way off, their figures tiny in the distance.

Taking a deep breath, Twigpaw slid through the bushes and stood at the top of the spiral path.

At first she was transfixed, gazing at the beauty in front

of her. Except for the pounding of her heart, she felt as if she had been turned to stone and would never move a paw again. She stood gazing down, drinking in the glimmer of the moon, reflected on the surface of the water. The stream that flowed down the rock face into the pool looked like liquid starlight.

I don't care if I'm punished for this! It's worth it, just to see. . . .

Slowly, torn between fear and wonder, Twigpaw began to descend the path, fitting her paws into the depressions made by countless cats before her. At last she reached the water's edge, and crouched beside it with her nose a mouse-length from the surface.

At first everything was dark and quiet, the only sound the falling water and a soft breeze gently caressing the surface of the pool. Above her head, the stars shone brightly in the deepening dark of the night sky.

Twigpaw bent her head farther and touched her nose to the water. This was how the medicine cats were swept into their visions of StarClan. But for Twigpaw, nothing happened. She raised her head again, twitching water droplets from her whiskers and feeling remarkably silly.

Well, what did you think would happen, you stupid furball?

Feeling that she shouldn't have come, Twigpaw began to retreat from the water's edge when a change in the silver light on the surface caught her eye. It had become an ominous scarlet, as if the water were running with blood. She jumped with shock as a loud boom of thunder echoed and echoed around the hollow of the Moonpool.

With a gasp of fear, Twigpaw looked up to see that flame lit the sky from horizon to horizon. At first she flattened herself to the ground, terrified that the warriors of StarClan were coming to punish her.

Then she realized that an image was taking shape. Fire was roaring through the ThunderClan camp—or at least Twigpaw thought it was the ThunderClan camp. There were so many downed trees and piles of smoldering debris that it was hard to be sure.

This can't be real! Twigpaw thought frantically. *I just left the camp, and it was fine.*

"Why is this happening?" she asked aloud, hoping that StarClan would answer her.

But the answer that came was not reassuring at all.

The image of an old, grizzled cat with a broad face formed amid the flames in the sky. Scarlet fire was reflected in her eyes. Her voice rolled out like thunder as she growled, "You don't belong here!"

Remembering the stories Alderheart had told her when she was a kit, Twigpaw thought she recognized Yellowfang, the former ShadowClan medicine cat who had come to live with ThunderClan, back in the old forest. But she was too terrified to ask the spirit cat's name or question her again.

Instead Twigpaw leaped back from the water's edge and raced up the spiral path. Plunging through the bushes, oblivious of the twigs that scraped her sides and snagged in her pelt, she half fell, half scrambled down the rocky slope and fled across the moor.

But when Twigpaw had to stop for breath and looked

around her, she noticed a glow on the horizon that showed her where the sun was about to rise. A chill struck through her paws as if she was walking on ice.

How can that be? I was only at the Moonpool for a few heartbeats.

Twigpaw went on more slowly, trying to stop her legs from trembling. The whole experience had shaken her to the depths.

What did that vision of the ruined camp mean? And what did Yellowfang mean when she said I didn't belong there? Did she mean I didn't belong at the Moonpool? Or . . . did she mean I shouldn't be in ThunderClan?

Horror almost overwhelmed Twigpaw as she considered it might be her own presence in ThunderClan that would bring about their destruction. *Is it because my kin are in SkyClan, so I belong there? Or do I not belong in ThunderClan because I abandoned it before?* That might have been why Yellowfang showed her the vision of the camp destroyed.

Is it possible that the ThunderClan cats who didn't want me back were right? Maybe I really don't belong there. . . .

Determinedly Twigpaw shook off the thought. She wouldn't believe it. She had needed some time to figure it out, but now she knew that ThunderClan was her true home.

I'm sure I belong in ThunderClan. I just have to convince the others, too.

And she knew she had to do it right away, while the terrifying vision was still fresh in her mind.

Picking up the pace again, Twigpaw raced back to camp, barely pausing to take a breath. She was relieved to see it looking just as she'd left it, not like the terrible ruined camp of her vision. As soon as she emerged from the thorn tunnel, she spotted Bramblestar and Alderheart, standing just outside the medicine-cat den, deep in conversation. Hoping neither cat would see her, she crept close enough to overhear. "So what do you suggest we do?" Bramblestar was asking.

"I suppose we must wait and see," Alderheart replied. "But it worries me that there's no right answer about ShadowClan. I don't want to see the Clan disappear, but if they manage to revive it, it will really test SkyClan's patience."

"It will all become clear soon," Bramblestar responded, resting his tail-tip reassuringly on Alderheart's shoulder. "StarClan clearly has a plan. You need to focus on your duties here. Several of our cats are still sick."

Alderheart murmured agreement. "I think Leafpool may be coming down with it. She vomited on our way back from the Moonpool."

Bramblestar sighed. "There you are, then. ThunderClan needs your skills."

Though Alderheart nodded warily, Twigpaw thought he still looked worried. *I hate seeing him like this.*

Trembling shook Twigpaw's limbs as she remembered her terrifying vision at the Moonpool. *Alderheart's wrong that there's no right answer about ShadowClan. They* must *be revived, or the storm will destroy us.*

She couldn't tell Bramblestar and Alderheart what she'd seen at the Moonpool. The Moonpool was a place *only* for medicine cats. She couldn't let them know she'd trespassed there, not when some cats didn't even think she belonged in ThunderClan.

Twigpaw almost despaired. She knew she was only a ThunderClan apprentice. She had no idea how she could affect what happened in ShadowClan.

Then a thought struck her. *Maybe I should reach out to my sister. She might be a SkyClan warrior these days, but she used to be in Shadow-Clan. They're the same Clan now; she's Clanmates with all the ShadowClan cats again. And she won't tell anyone I went to the Moonpool.* But a fresh chill of fear coursed through her as she considered the idea. *What if Violetshine turns me away?*

CHAPTER 8

♣

"You have to do something."

This wasn't the first time Violetshine had heard those words from her Clan leader. A quarter moon had passed since Leafstar had turned Sleekwhisker and Yarrowleaf away from SkyClan, and Tree still hadn't decided what his place in the Clan should be. The Clan leader was losing patience; she had asked Violetshine to bring Tree to her den, and now her tail-tip twitched to and fro as she confronted the yellow tom.

"If you don't want to be a medicine cat, you must train to be a warrior. You can't just sleep in the sun all day."

Like we've had much sun lately, Violetshine thought as she listened to the argument. But she could see Leafstar's point. No Clan cat had the right to sit around and do nothing.

"But it's not right for me to be a medicine cat *or* a warrior," Tree objected. "Why do I have to fit into a specific position?"

"Because that's how Clans work," Leafstar retorted, her voice tense and her neck fur beginning to bristle. "If you don't want to be part of the Clan—"

"No," Tree interrupted. "I *do* want to stay here. I just haven't found my place. . . ."

"Then it's time you did," Leafstar snapped, "and stop all this dithering around. We're not going to keep you here if you don't contribute."

A pang of fear shook Violetshine like a gust of icy wind. *She mustn't send Tree away. . . .*

"Tree, why don't you come hunting with me?" she suggested desperately. "While you try to figure it all out, you might as well learn some warrior skills, right?"

Tree blinked, hesitating, then reluctantly mewed, "Okay."

"Well, thank StarClan for that!" Leafstar exclaimed, still looking irritated. "And thank you, Violetshine. Maybe if Tree tries the warrior way of hunting, he'll get to like it."

And maybe hedgehogs fly, Violetshine thought. She knew that she had to find a place for Tree, but she couldn't imagine what that would be.

As Violetshine led the way across the camp to the fern tunnel, she spotted the group of former ShadowClan cats, all of them glaring after Leafstar as she returned to her den. Scorchfur muttered something to Snowbird with a hostile lash of his tail.

Violetshine suppressed a sigh, reflecting how much tension there had been in the Clan since Leafstar had turned Yarrowleaf and Sleekwhisker away. Juniperclaw, Scorchfur, and Snowbird had been all but ignoring orders from the leader and deputy, or being as slow and uncooperative as they could. Every one of them had been criticizing Leafstar, loudly and openly where the whole Clan could hear them. Only rebukes from Rowanclaw and Tawnypelt had kept them from outright defiance; they were listening to Rowanclaw as if he were their leader still.

I'm not sure how I would feel if Leafstar had turned my kin away, Violetshine thought. But she wasn't sure either if she trusted Yarrowleaf and Sleekwhisker. *Perhaps Leafstar is right, and this is a time for caution. But then, Tree wondered if they might be good cats . . . .*

"Let me show you the hunter's crouch," Violetshine mewed when she and Tree were out in the forest. "It's like this. Keep your paws well tucked in, and your tail close to your side so you don't alert the prey."

"Like this?" Tree asked.

Staring at him, Violetshine had to let out a loud *mrrow* of laughter. Tree had taken up an almost perfect hunter's crouch, except that he was lying on his back, with his paws in the air.

"What do you expect to catch like that?" she asked. "Low-flying blackbirds?"

Tree rolled over and sprang to his paws. "Well, it's a bit different from how I usually hunt," he remarked.

"It's how we do things out here in the wild." Violetshine was glad that Leafstar couldn't see Tree messing around. "Now try it the right way up."

Tree crouched down, impressing Violetshine this time with how quickly he had mastered the position.

"That's very good," she told him. "Now creep forward, setting your paws down as lightly as you can. Remember that a mouse will feel the vibrations of your paws on the ground long before it hears you coming."

Tree pressed his belly to the ground and began to creep

with long, slow movements of his legs. Watching his muscles rippling underneath his pelt, Violetshine realized that he would be a formidable hunter and fighter if he could be bothered to learn.

Tree went on creeping until he came to the top of a steep bank. Instead of stopping, he launched himself downward and rolled head over paws until he landed with a crunch in a heap of dead leaves.

"I think your mouse just escaped," Violetshine meowed drily, peering down at him from the top of the bank.

Tree sat up with a leaf stuck to the top of his head. "You never told me to stop." His voice was reproachful, but his eyes were sparkling with mischief.

Violetshine skidded down the bank to join him. "You daft furball!" she exclaimed, butting his shoulder with her head. "Honestly, how did you ever manage to feed yourself when you were a loner?"

"Ah, I had a special move for that," Tree explained. "I turned myself into a bush."

Violetshine rolled her eyes.

"No, really. Shall I show you?"

"Go on, then," Violetshine responded with a sigh.

"Okay. You start by crouching down like this," Tree instructed her, tucking his paws underneath him in something like the hunter's crouch. "That's right," he mewed as Violetshine copied him. "Now think bush!"

Violetshine stared at him. "Do what?"

"Think bush. Like your legs are branches and your claws

are twigs, and you have leaves opening up all over your pelt. You've got to keep really still, and then your prey will come to you."

While Tree was still speaking, incredibly, a mouse went skittering past. The yellow tom lazily stretched out one paw and slammed it down on top of the prey. "Like that," he finished.

Violetshine snorted with laughter. *It feels so good to have fun, when everything in camp is so tense.* "Tree, no cat but you could hunt like that!"

"It works," Tree mewed smugly. "Do you want to share?"

"No, we're a hunting patrol," Violetshine responded. "The Clan must be fed first. We'll bury your mouse and then—"

She broke off as Tree stretched out a paw to silence her. He pointed with his tail, and Violetshine spotted movement in the undergrowth. A flash of black fur showed her Juniperclaw, slinking through the bushes in the direction of the old ShadowClan camp.

"What's going on?" murmured Tree. "Why is he out here alone?"

"Maybe he just wants some herbs or something from his old camp," Violetshine suggested. *But in that case, why does he look so furtive?*

"I think we should follow him," Tree mewed.

Violetshine nodded, and quickly scraped some earth over Tree's mouse so they could collect it later. Then, side by side, the two cats slipped through the undergrowth, following Juniperclaw's scent trail.

They caught sight of him again as he climbed the rocky slope up to the ShadowClan camp and disappeared into the brambles at the top. Tree and Violetshine crept up in his paw steps until they could look down into the hollow of the camp.

Down at the bottom of the hollow, where the fresh-kill pile used to be, Yarrowleaf lay stretched out, grooming herself, while Sleekwhisker, beside her, rose to her paws to welcome her brother Juniperclaw.

Violetshine let out a cry of surprise. Alerted, all three cats turned to face her and Tree, as they paced down the slope to join them. Violetshine forced herself not to flinch under the hostile glares from Juniperclaw and Sleekwhisker. Yarrowleaf simply looked terrified.

"Oh, no!" she yowled, while Sleekwhisker asked, "How did you find us?"

"A more important question is, What are you doing here?" Violetshine retorted. "This is SkyClan territory, and Leafstar ordered you to leave."

Sleekwhisker stretched out her neck and hissed at Violetshine. "You don't understand. This is our *home!*"

"Oh, really?" Violetshine refused to be intimidated; she could feel her back fur beginning to bristle. "You think I don't understand what it was like to grow up in ShadowClan?"

"You didn't grow up as a *real* ShadowClan cat," Sleekwhisker sneered, narrowing her eyes. "You proved that when you ran off to SkyClan!"

Fury throbbed through Violetshine. She bunched her muscles, ready to spring forward and confront Sleekwhisker, only to find Tree's tail held across her path as a barrier.

"Sleekwhisker, Yarrowleaf," Tree meowed, "give me one good reason why we shouldn't tell Leafstar you're here right now."

Violetshine gave him a disbelieving stare. *We have to tell Leafstar!* Before she could speak the words aloud, Tree gave her a tiny shake of his head, as if he was telling her to let him continue.

"I can't be wandering the wilderness when I'm about to have kits," Yarrowleaf mewed sorrowfully. "And I desperately wanted to return to ShadowClan. I've changed—I want to come home."

"That's true," Sleekwhisker agreed. "Violetshine, I'm sorry. I'm just so desperate to stay. Will you help us?"

"Please," Juniperclaw added. "Violetshine, you grew up with all of us. You must remember how close we were."

I don't remember that at all, Violetshine thought, but she wasn't going to say it out loud. *You were never my friends.*

"You must understand it's not okay to throw them out," Juniperclaw continued. "Especially when they're sorry."

For a moment Violetshine hesitated. She could understand how the intruders felt, particularly Yarrowleaf, who was so close to kitting. "I'm sorry too," she responded at last. "Yes, we grew up together," she added, lifting her head proudly, "but I'm a SkyClan cat now. And Leafstar must know what's happening on her territory."

Yarrowleaf let out a terrified wail.

"Wait," Tree put in. "Maybe we can work out a solution

that will make every cat happy."

Violetshine glared at him. "Have you got bees in your brain?"

"Yarrowleaf is clearly in distress," Tree murmured to her. "Maybe Leafstar would let her hang around long enough to have her kits."

"Oh, thank you!" Yarrowleaf had heard Tree's low-voiced suggestion. "All I want is for my kits to be born in Shadow-Clan."

"That doesn't look likely," Tree meowed, candid as ever. "But we'll see what we can do. Violetshine, shall we go and talk to Leafstar now?"

Violetshine sighed. *Tree is such fun, and I like him so much, but there are times I could cheerfully rip his pelt off!* "Yes, Tree," she responded. "We'll go now."

Most of the SkyClan cats seemed to be in camp when Violetshine led Yarrowleaf and Sleekwhisker through the fern tunnel. Yowls of outrage came from them as they gathered around to stare at the intruders. Violetshine spotted Scorchfur and Snowbird exchanging glances of shock and fear that their kit had been discovered.

"I'm going to tell Leafstar," Plumwillow meowed, breaking away from the crowd and bounding toward the cedar tree.

When Leafstar shouldered her way through the cluster of cats, her amber eyes were sparking with fury. Her tail lashed, and her fur was bushed up so that she looked twice her size.

Puddleshine and Frecklewish followed her, and to

Violetshine's surprise they looked almost relieved. *That's odd,* she thought. *Something is going on with them.*

Hawkwing appeared, too, and stood at his leader's shoulder; his expression was unreadable as he gazed at the two intruders.

"Well?" Leafstar demanded in a voice as icy as the coldest winds of leaf-bare.

"We found these two cats in the old ShadowClan camp," Tree explained. "They want to stay."

"And I've already told them they can't," Leafstar retorted. Whirling around, her glance raked across her Clan. "How many of you are involved in this?"

"I am," Juniperclaw admitted, stepping forward from where he stood behind Tree.

"So are we," Snowbird added, with a glance at her mate, Scorchfur.

"And me." Whorlpaw, Juniperclaw's apprentice, came to stand beside his mentor. His legs were trembling, and Juniperclaw rested his tail on the young tom's shoulder.

"I knew about it," Strikestone confessed reluctantly.

"All of you went against my orders?" Leafstar snarled. "How can I trust you now? How can we be one united Clan when you only obey me when you agree?"

Violetshine could see the Clan leader's anger reflected in Juniperclaw's eyes. "With respect, Leafstar," he began, "we only went against your wishes because you ignored all the Shadow-Clan cats when you sent Yarrowleaf and Sleekwhisker away."

For a heart-stopping moment Violetshine thought that

Leafstar would throw herself on the black tom in a whirlwind of screeching fury. Then she saw the Clan leader battling to hold on to calm.

"First, that's not true," she meowed. "Rowanclaw and Tawnypelt didn't trust them either. And second, I don't need your agreement. I am Clan *leader*. StarClan chose me to make decisions for this Clan. Or does ShadowClan not believe in StarClan?"

Juniperclaw and Scorchfur exchanged a glance; then each of them opened their jaws as if to yowl defiance at Leafstar.

Tree stepped forward quickly and spoke before they could get a word out. "Listen, surely there's a way to solve this. Like it or not, you're all one Clan now. You have to live together." His glance traveled around the former ShadowClan cats. "Do you want to be in SkyClan?" he asked. "Or would you rather form your own Clan again?"

"It doesn't actually *work* like that," Leafstar muttered.

"We want to be here," Rowanclaw responded swiftly, thrusting himself farther forward with Tawnypelt by his side. "That was my last decision as leader of ShadowClan—and it holds."

"That's right," Tawnypelt agreed, glaring around as if she dared any of her Clanmates to contradict her.

There was murmuring among the ShadowClan cats, with tail-twitching and doubtful glances at Leafstar, but finally they settled down.

"Yes, we want to be here," Scorchfur declared, speaking for all of them.

Looking at them, Violetshine couldn't help wondering, *Do you, really? Or do you just not have any other choice?*

"Leafstar, I'm sorry," Rowanclaw began, stepping up to face the Clan leader and dipping his head respectfully. "I say that on behalf of all my Clanmates."

"Yes, we're sorry," the others muttered. Juniperclaw's fur still bristled angrily, and Scorchfur dropped his eyes rather than meet Leafstar's gaze, but they joined in with the others' meows.

Snowbird took a pace forward that brought her to Rowanclaw's side. "Leafstar, I promise to be loyal to you in future," she meowed. "Nothing like this will happen again."

One by one, the others came up and made the same pledge of loyalty. Leafstar didn't look appeased, but in the end she nodded curtly. "Very well. Make sure you act on the words you've spoken today."

"Leafstar, we still have to decide what to do about Yarrowleaf and Sleekwhisker," Tree reminded the Clan leader with a respectful dip of his head. "If you'll allow me, I'd like to offer you an idea."

Leafstar regarded him warily. "Go on," she mewed eventually.

"It *does* seem sensible to allow Yarrowleaf to stay here," Tree began. "At least until her kits are born."

Violetshine cringed inwardly as Tree spoke, but Leafstar did not react at all, but merely waited for Tree to go on.

"Other cats who are here now *did* follow Darktail," the yellow tom reminded her. "But they've changed. They're loyal to you. The time it will take Yarrowleaf to have her kits and wean them will be a chance to test Yarrowleaf and Sleekwhisker—a time for them both to prove their loyalty to SkyClan. When the kits are weaned, they can be invited to join the Clan, or sent on their way with no hard feelings."

Leafstar flexed her claws, looking torn; Violetshine could see that she would really have preferred to send the two intruders on their way right now. Then she relaxed a little, as if she could see the wisdom of Tree's words.

While she still hesitated, Frecklewish stepped forward to Leafstar's side. "Remember what Puddleshine and I told you," she meowed.

Leafstar faced her medicine cat; unspoken words seemed to flow between them. "I remember," Leafstar murmured after a moment.

"Oh, *please*," Yarrowleaf begged, as if she sensed a softening in the Clan leader's attitude. "I'll do anything you ask to prove my loyalty. I just want to be part of a Clan again!"

"So do I," Sleekwhisker added. "I promise we won't let you down."

Leafstar heaved a deep sigh. "Very well. But remember this, Tree," she went on, swinging around to face the yellow tom. "They're your responsibility. If they put a paw out of line, guess whose ears I'll be clawing off."

Violetshine gasped, then saw that there was a glimmer of amusement in Leafstar's amber eyes.

"Then claw away, Leafstar," Tree mewed easily. "But I'm sure it won't be necessary."

"Of course, that's assuming that you're staying with the Clan," Leafstar added.

"I'd very much like to," Tree responded with a glance at Violetshine. "I just need to find my place here."

Leafstar nodded thoughtfully. "Perhaps we just need to get creative . . . ," she murmured.

With that, the meeting began to break up. Snowbird led Yarrowleaf across the camp to make a nest in the nursery. Frecklewish followed them.

"You'd better go in with the apprentices," Hawkwing told Sleekwhisker curtly. "You're not an official SkyClan warrior yet."

Violetshine thought she caught a flicker of anger in Sleek-whisker's eyes, but the yellow she-cat bowed her head meekly as she replied, "Of course, Hawkwing."

"I'll show you where," Whorlpaw offered, and led her away.

Violetshine watched, troubled, as they padded toward the apprentices' den. Hawkwing had taken no part in the debate, and she hadn't paid much attention to him while it was going on. Now she could see that her father wasn't happy about the decision—and he wasn't the only one. Even Tawnypelt looked anxious, speaking to Rowanclaw in hushed tones, their heads close together.

What is happening to my Clan? Violetshine wondered. *I thought Leafstar—with Tree's help—had brought all the cats together. But now look at us. Will we ever be one Clan?*

CHAPTER 9

Alderheart padded along the lakeshore, enjoying the shimmer of the full moon on the surface of the water. For once the cloud cover had dwindled, leaving an almost clear sky for the night of the Gathering.

"How are you feeling?" he asked Twigpaw, who was walking at his side.

Twigpaw looked up at him. "Much better, thank you," she replied. "As soon as Sparkpelt got better from the sickness, she stopped training me with Finpaw. We're learning *advanced* skills now. It's really exciting!"

"That's great!" Warm approval flowed through Alderheart's pelt at the thought that his friend was making progress at last. But when he glanced at Twigpaw again, he became aware that her gaze still rested on him, and now there was concern in her eyes.

"Is there any more news about the prophecy?" she asked.

Alderheart shook his head. "No, the last I heard is that ShadowClan is still combined with SkyClan, and RiverClan's borders are still closed."

"Isn't any cat worried about that anymore?" Twigpaw's

expression darkened. "Doesn't StarClan want there to be five Clans?"

"I believe they do," Alderheart responded with a sigh. "But there's nothing we can do without more guidance. We just have to wait and see."

For a couple of heartbeats he thought that Twigpaw was about to say something else, but before he could ask her if anything was the matter, she gave him a swift nod and bounded forward to join her mentor.

As Alderheart crossed the tree-bridge and pushed his way through the bushes into the center of the island, he looked around in the hope that RiverClan had returned at last. But there was no sign of Mistystar or any of her Clan.

Taking his place with the other medicine cats, Alderheart could see that no cat was surprised that RiverClan hadn't come, but the mood was somber as Bramblestar, Leafstar, and Harestar leaped up into the branches of the Great Oak.

"Only *three* now!" some cat whispered close behind Alderheart.

"I thought things would get better with the rogues gone," Whitetail, a WindClan elder, mewed despondently. "But now I wonder."

"StarClan will be angry!" another cat murmured.

Alderheart spotted several cats looking up at the sky to see if clouds would cover the moon, but nothing blocked the silver light. At least StarClan was prepared to let the Gathering continue. He shivered a little: the sky was clear now, but the weather had been ominous for a moon—was the storm

StarClan had warned of coming?

"Cats of all Clans!" Bramblestar yowled, stepping forward on his branch so that his muscular tabby figure was visible to all the cats below. "Welcome to the Gathering. Who will speak first?"

"I will," Leafstar responded, from where she stood on a branch just above Bramblestar. "SkyClan is settling into our new camp, and the prey is running well in our territory," she continued. "A few days ago, two former ShadowClan cats, Yarrowleaf and Sleekwhisker, surprised us by returning—"

She broke off as mingled yowls of welcome and protest rose from the clearing as she spoke the names. Clearly many of the cats remembered that the newcomers had been loyal to Dark-tail.

Alderheart gazed, stunned, at his fellow medicine cats, remembering what Needletail had told him when he visited StarClan at the half moon meeting. *Shadows approaching . . . Are these the shadows Needletail was referring to?*

Leafstar held up her tail for silence, and gradually the tumult in the clearing died down. "After some discussion," she continued, "I have decided to allow Sleekwhisker and Yarrowleaf to stay with SkyClan—at their request—since Yarrowleaf is very close to kitting. But they will be on proba-tion until the kits are born and weaned."

Another outcry erupted in the clearing. Though Alder-heart could see that some of the cats approved of Leafstar's decision, most of them did not.

"Traitors!" some cat screeched.

"They followed Darktail!

"Drive them out!"

"No ShadowClan cat could ever be trusted!" Breezepelt of WindClan yowled.

He's hardly the cat to talk about trustworthiness! Alderheart thought. He was glad to see that many cats, including some of his own Clan, turned to glare at Breezepelt.

Bramblestar was one of them. "That's not true," he declared. "ShadowClan was one of the original five Clans, and a noble Clan. Just because it no longer exists doesn't mean that its cats shouldn't be respected."

Breezepelt glared defiantly back, but no cat was paying attention to him now, as the meeting continued.

"Leafstar," Bramblestar continued, gazing up at the Sky-Clan leader, "could these cats be the 'approaching shadows' mentioned in the medicine cats' vision?"

Seeming flustered by the question, Leafstar gave her chest fur a couple of quick licks before replying, "I suppose they could."

"The medicine cats had a vision from StarClan," Bramble-star announced to the cats gathered in the clearing. "They were told that shadows were approaching and must not be dispelled. These ShadowClan cats must be the approaching shadows!"

Murmurs of surprise came from the cats around the Great Oak, their former hostility fading. Some of them broke up into smaller clusters, speaking excitedly together.

"Yes . . ." Leafstar looked a little uncomfortable.

"Puddleshine did make me aware of that, but I'm not sure *these* are the shadows. In any case," she went on quickly, forestalling an objection from Bramblestar, "they will stay with SkyClan until Yarrowleaf's kits are weaned."

Alderheart wasn't really listening as Leafstar gave the rest of her news and Harestar stood up to speak. He spotted Sleekwhisker among the SkyClan warriors, seeing that she was watching the leaders intently.

Leafstar clearly trusts her if she let her come to the Gathering . . . but should she? Should Yarrowleaf?

Guilt pricked Alderheart's pelt, because he had assumed that the "approaching shadows" would be a clearer sign that ShadowClan might revive. *Such as Tigerheart coming home . . .* He wasn't sure that the return of two cats who had followed Darktail was a signal that ShadowClan would rise again.

And that means the storm could be moving closer. . . .

Chapter 10

❦

Twigpaw bounded across the camp toward the medicine-cat den, impatient to speak to Alderheart. A few fox-lengths away she made herself slow down. *The sick cats won't want an apprentice charging in on them,* she told herself.

She brushed past the bramble screen at the entrance to the den and found Alderheart at the back, where the herbs were stored. She padded toward him, careful not to disturb Leafpool and Whitewing, who were curled up in their nests.

"Hi, Alderheart," Twigpaw mewed. "I have a little time before I have to hunt with Sparkpelt. Is there anything I can do to help you?"

"There certainly is," Alderheart replied with a welcoming twitch of his whiskers. "I'm just sorting herbs for the sick cats in the apprentices' den. You can take them over there for me if you like."

"Sure," Twigpaw responded.

Although she was happy to help, that wasn't the only reason Twigpaw was visiting Alderheart. A couple of sunrises had passed since the Gathering, and this was her first opportunity to ask him about the prophecy. The sight of only three leaders at the Gathering had felt so *wrong*, so strange and frightening.

Shall I tell Alderheart what I saw at the Moonpool? she asked herself. A sick feeling gathered in her belly as she wondered what Alderheart's reaction would be. *He's a medicine cat. I'm afraid he'd be very angry.*

"I know you're worried that StarClan wants us to have five Clans," she began at last. "But it looks like ShadowClan isn't coming back."

Alderheart looked up from portioning out stems of watermint. "We don't know that," he responded. "After all, Sleekwhisker and Yarrowleaf have returned, even if they might not be the shadows the vision spoke of. Besides, StarClan sent us that vision, and so far we're following their advice. Perhaps we need to look for more signs."

We could do that until the storm strikes us, Twigpaw thought. "Maybe we should be doing more," she suggested. "Maybe talk to the ShadowClan cats about rebuilding."

Alderheart shook his head. "That won't work. They would just think that bossy ThunderClan was interfering again! Besides, ShadowClan doesn't have a strong leader. Rowanclaw won't change his mind, and no other cat has come forward to replace him. Without a strong leader, no Clan can survive." Sighing, he added, "There's nothing else we can do now except wait and see."

When she left the medicine-cat den with the leaf wraps of herbs, Twigpaw felt frustrated. Even though her apprenticeship was going well now, she couldn't shake off the feeling that she should be doing something really important to show her commitment to ThunderClan. She knew she ought to be going out to hunt with Sparkpelt, but she felt too tense; she was sure that she could never concentrate on finding and stalking prey.

I know I'll get caught, and Sparkpelt will have me on tick duty for a moon, but I really need to sneak off and find Violetshine. It's been more than a moon since I left, and the SkyClan warriors left the Gathering before I had a chance to speak with her. She can't still be angry with me, can she?

As Twigpaw delivered the herbs to the apprentices' den, her mind was racing ahead of her through the forest. She looked forward to talking to Violetshine about ShadowClan.

After all, she was raised as a ShadowClan cat. It has to mean something to her.

Twigpaw hoped too that together she and her sister might be able to convince one of the other ShadowClan cats to be leader. *Surely one of them could manage?*

Twigpaw waited at the SkyClan border, shivering in the cold, damp-laden breeze, until she scented an approaching patrol. As they emerged into the open around a bramble thicket, she recognized Sagenose and Harrybrook.

"Hi!" she called out, stepping right up to the border.

The two cats swerved and bounded up to her, both of them gazing at her warily.

"What do *you* want?" Harrybrook asked.

"I need to talk to Violetshine," Twigpaw responded. "Will

you go and fetch her for me? Please," she added, as the two SkyClan warriors exchanged a doubtful glance. "It's really important."

"I suppose so," Sagenose meowed after a moment's pause. "But don't even think about setting a paw over the border. You're not a SkyClan cat anymore."

The two cats swung around and disappeared into the undergrowth. Twigpaw sat down to wait, her ears pricked and her pelt tingling with apprehension. If a ThunderClan patrol came this way while she waited, she would be in terrible trouble, with nothing to show for it.

As Twigpaw waited, her nervousness mounted, until she felt as if she had a whole swarm of bees nesting in her belly. Every rustle in the undergrowth was an approaching patrol of her Clanmates; every scent wafted on the breeze threatened discovery.

Twigpaw felt she could hardly bear the rising tension for another heartbeat when ferns on the far side of the border parted and Violetshine came into view, her whiskers quivering and her eyes watchful. "Okay, I'm here," she mewed as she padded up to her sister. "What's this all about?"

Twigpaw's tail drooped. *I missed Violetshine! Isn't she pleased to see me?* But there was no affectionate greeting for her from her sister.

"I'm worried about the prophecy," Twigpaw explained, ignoring her hurt. "There have to be five Clans, and how can there be, when there's no ShadowClan anymore? We have to do something!"

To Twigpaw's dismay, her sister's yellow eyes were cold. "What do *you* care about the future of ShadowClan?" she asked. "Besides, I'm a SkyClan cat now. ShadowClan has nothing to do with me either."

"But you were brought up there!" Twigpaw protested.

"Yes, and it was no fun, believe me," Violetshine retorted. "I had to watch Darktail take over and cats die. Going back there is the last thing I want."

"But—" Twigpaw tried to interrupt.

Violetshine ignored her. "Besides, I can see how vulnerable it was under Rowanstar's leadership," she went on, "so perhaps it's not so bad that it fell apart. Rowanstar's weakness gave Darktail the opportunity to take over. And things are going well now, with SkyClan and ShadowClan combined. It's taking some getting used to, but—"

"Going well?" Twigpaw interrupted. "Really? Couldn't you feel the tension at the Gathering? The SkyClan cats were supporting Leafstar, but the ShadowClan cats were furious when she was talking about Yarrowleaf and Sleekwhisker." Twigpaw reached out a paw to her sister. "Please, Violetshine, tell me the truth. Was it really as simple as Leafstar made it sound?"

Violetshine relaxed with a sigh, though she swept the surrounding forest with a glance before she replied. "No, you're right, it wasn't." Seeming relieved to be telling some cat, she went on, "It was really awkward. Leafstar turned them away at first, and then some of the ShadowClan cats—their kin—snuck them into their old camp. Tree and I found them there, and we had to tell Leafstar."

Twigpaw blinked in astonishment. "I don't suppose she was pleased."

"She was furious! She wanted to drive them out all over again. It was Tree who convinced her to let them stay."

Twigpaw felt even more astonished to hear that. "Wow—he must be a good talker!"

"He is," Violetshine admitted. "A bit like you. Except he follows through."

Twigpaw gasped, stung by her sister's words. "Look," she meowed, "I'm sorry about leaving SkyClan, but I just didn't *belong* there, as much as I wanted to." When there was no response from Violetshine, she asked, "Haven't you ever felt that way?"

"More times than I would have liked," Violetshine sighed.

Twigpaw was encouraged to feel that her sister was warming to her a little. "All right," she began, "so hear me out about the prophecy. StarClan wants there to be five Clans. And I have to tell you something I've told no cat before. . . ." Twigpaw hesitated, swallowing nervously. She had no idea how Violetshine would react, and after she had spoken there could be no going back. "At the medicine cats' half-moon meeting, I went to the Moonpool."

Violetshine's eyes stretched wide with shock. "*You* went? What did the medicine cats think about that?"

"They never knew," Twigpaw explained. "I hid in the bushes until they left. But after that, I saw a vision . . . a dreadful vision of fire and a ruined camp. StarClan showed it to me!

And now I'm afraid terrible things will happen unless we can find a fifth Clan."

Before Violetshine could reply, the ferns near the border parted, and a muscular yellow tom stepped into the open. Twigpaw recognized Tree. He padded up to the border, sat down beside Violetshine, and lifted one hind leg to scratch his ear.

"You Clan cats are so *afraid* of StarClan," he meowed, not bothering with a greeting. "If StarClan wants you to do stuff, why can't they be clearer about it?"

"Any medicine cat would ask the same question," Violetshine commented wryly.

Twigpaw turned to Tree. "What are you doing here?" she demanded.

"Oh, I was bored," Tree replied. "I just thought I would follow Violetshine. I've been missing you, too."

Twigpaw could see a glimmer of amusement in Tree's eyes, but she couldn't see what the joke was. *I never could see why some cats think Tree's so funny.*

Violetshine batted Tree over the head with her tail. "You should stop following me!" Twigpaw sensed she didn't mean that seriously. "What do you think about all this?" she added.

Tree shrugged. "I never thought I'd be saying this, but Twigpaw is making a lot of sense. StarClan *does* seem to want there to be five Clans, and for all five Clans to work together. And there *is* tension in the SkyClan camp. Sooner or later it's going to break out into fighting. Perhaps it would be better if the ShadowClan cats split off again."

"But how can we make that happen?" Violetshine asked.

"We should at least *talk* to the ShadowClan cats," Tree replied. "Surely one of them could make a decent leader."

For a few moments Violetshine was silent, clearly deep in thought. "Perhaps we could talk to Tawnypelt," she suggested at last. "She was Rowanstar's deputy after Tigerheart left, and she truly cared about her Clan. Once I saw her with Rowanclaw at ShadowClan's old camp, and she seemed so regretful about all they had lost. Maybe she would be willing to try reviving the Clan."

"Okay," Twigpaw mewed, feeling a tingle of hope in her pads. *Is this plan of mine actually working?* "Let's go and talk to Tawnypelt."

CHAPTER 11

♣

"We can't do that!" Violetshine objected. She couldn't believe that her sister would ignore the way things were done in the Clans. "We have to talk to Leafstar first."

"But this is ShadowClan's affair," Twigpaw pointed out.

"Have you got bees in your brain?" Violetshine demanded. "ShadowClan is part of SkyClan now, and Leafstar is the leader for every cat. And *I'm* a SkyClan cat," she added, narrowing her eyes. "I'm not going to mutiny by convincing ShadowClan to rebuild without warning my leader."

"I suppose so. . . ." Twigpaw sounded hesitant. "The thing is, I don't think Leafstar is exactly a fan of mine since I left to rejoin ThunderClan."

Violetshine flicked her ears in annoyance. *This isn't all about you!* Aloud she mewed, "Don't worry. I'll do all the talking. We'll get Hawkwing to be there, too. That will make it easier."

She turned and headed back to the SkyClan camp, with Twigpaw following her and Tree bringing up the rear. It felt weird to Violetshine to be padding along these paths with her sister, who had been her Clanmate not so long ago, and now was an interloper. *If Twigpaw wasn't with me and Tree, any*

SkyClan cat would be right to attack her.

Grassheart was on guard duty at the camp entrance. "What's *she* doing here?" she asked with a glare at Twigpaw.

"She needs to talk to Leafstar," Violetshine replied. "We all do."

"She doesn't want to come back again, does she?" Grassheart called after them as they padded farther into the camp.

Though she was irritated, Violetshine wasn't surprised her Clanmates would react that way when they saw Twigpaw again. *The sooner we get this over with, the better.*

She was relieved to see Hawkwing talking to Sparrowpelt in the center of the camp, and bounded over to join him. "I need to talk to you," she declared.

Sparrowpelt gave her a friendly nod. "I'll get that hunting patrol together," he meowed to Hawkwing, whipping around and vanishing into the warriors' den.

"So what—" Hawkwing began, and broke off. "Hey, Twigpaw!" He pressed his nose into his daughter's shoulder. "It's good to see you."

Twigpaw looked encouraged to see her father, leaning into him with a happy purr. But she straightened up nervously a moment later as Leafstar appeared through the lichen screen at the entrance to her den.

"What's this?" she asked, leaping down from the roots of the cedar tree and stalking across the camp to Violetshine and the others. "Twigpaw, why are you here?"

Violetshine felt she should be the one to reply. "We need to talk to you and Hawkwing," she mewed. "Please, Leafstar, will you hear us out?"

Leafstar hesitated for a moment, then nodded. "Very well."

"We're worried about the prophecy," Violetshine began. "The way that StarClan says there have to be five Clans, and now there are only three. We think we might have found a way to help."

The Clan leader's gaze was fixed on Violetshine, who felt a wave of relief that Leafstar was clearly taking her seriously. But there was a skeptical look in her amber eyes. *I mustn't put a paw wrong if I want to convince her,* Violetshine thought.

"Go on," Leafstar meowed.

Violetshine swallowed. "We want to ask Tawnypelt if she would be leader and rebuild ShadowClan."

Leafstar's expression changed; her amber eyes smoldered with anger. "Rebuild *ShadowClan*?" she hissed.

Violetshine glanced at her father for support; her heart began to pound harder when she saw that he too looked annoyed, his ears laid back and his claws sliding out.

Maybe I'm making a mistake, Violetshine thought. *I knew I should never have listened to Twigpaw! I only went along with this because I care about her!*

"Leafstar, what do you think?" Tree asked in his usual straightforward manner.

"Enough!" Leafstar swung around on him. "How can you ask that question? I'm angry. Of course I'm angry. All SkyClan has ever wanted is a safe place to live and hunt, surrounded by the other Clans. We suffered terribly to find that, and lost so many of our cats."

"But you're here now," Tree pointed out.

"Yes, we're here now." Leafstar dug her claws into the ground. "When we finally reached the lake, we were told we had to ask another Clan for territory. Then we agreed to share with ShadowClan, and we did our best to satisfy ShadowClan, even when Rowanstar was unreasonable. *Then* I was told that ShadowClan was disbanding, and I had to take their remaining cats into my Clan. *Now*—"

Violetshine tried to interrupt, but Leafstar swept on in a storm of indignation.

"*Now* I've worked really hard to blend every cat into one Clan—and you and Twigpaw want to split ShadowClan off again! Twigpaw, what are you even doing here? You're a ThunderClan apprentice!"

"Leafstar, it's because—" Violetshine began.

"I don't want to hear it. Every hair on my pelt is out of patience with you!"

Leafstar whipped around to go back to her own den, but Tree stepped in front of her, blocking her with his tail. Violetshine cringed, waiting for Leafstar to rake a paw over his ear.

"Leafstar, wait," Tree meowed. "Please listen. This isn't about what Violetshine and Twigpaw want—it's about StarClan. When StarClan is happy, all the Clans are happy, right? Couldn't we save ourselves a lot of trouble by just doing what StarClan wants?"

Leafstar stared at him as if she was wondering where this

cat had sprung from, daring to question her decisions. *At least she didn't strike him,* Violetshine thought.

At that moment, to Violetshine's relief, Hawkwing stepped to his leader's side. "I know you're frustrated, Leafstar," he declared. "I'm frustrated too. We seem to have arrived at the lake at a very difficult time for the other Clans. But . . . perhaps Violetshine and Twigpaw—and Tree—have a point. If StarClan has willed it, then we should at least make an effort to have five Clans. Maybe we *are* missing something. Maybe there is a capable leader left in ShadowClan, who just needs convincing."

Violetshine waited, hardly daring to breathe, while Leafstar stood in silence for what seemed like endless heartbeats. Finally the Clan leader let out a long sigh.

"Fine," she mewed. "You can talk to the ShadowClan cats." With a twitch of her ears toward Violetshine, she added, "Do you intend to leave, too, if ShadowClan splits off again?"

For a moment Violetshine gaped at her, stunned that her Clan leader could ask such a question. "No!" she exclaimed. "I'm a *SkyClan* cat, through and through. I would *never* be disloyal. Besides," she added, "I could never leave Hawkwing."

Leafstar seemed satisfied by her reply, though Violetshine was aware of Twigpaw, standing beside her, shifting her paws uncomfortably. *And no wonder!* Violetshine thought. *She had no problem leaving.*

"But hear this," Leafstar went on. "If ShadowClan decides to leave, I'm *never* taking any more cats into SkyClan. It's disruptive, and it's robbing my Clan of time we could be spending strengthening ourselves. This is it!"

"I understand," Violetshine responded.

Leafstar retreated to her den. Together with Twigpaw and Tree, Violetshine padded around the camp until they found Tawnypelt with Rowanclaw, sharing tongues in the shelter of a rock beside the stream.

"Tawnypelt, we need to talk to you," Violetshine began.

Tawnypelt looked up at them, narrowing her eyes when she spotted Twigpaw. "I saw you talking to Leafstar," she meowed. "You're not expecting to come back again, are you?"

Twigpaw shook her head emphatically. "No! I'm just visiting."

Tawnypelt gave a grunt of approval. "So what is all this about?"

Violetshine sat beside the two ShadowClan warriors and wrapped her tail neatly around her paws. Twigpaw crouched down beside her, while Tree draped himself over the rock, seemingly lazy, though his eyes were alert as he looked down at the others.

Gathering her courage, Violetshine took a deep breath. "We're all worried about the prophecy," she meowed. "StarClan wants five Clans, and things will only get worse until ShadowClan comes back. So, Tawnypelt, we wanted to ask you if you would consider leading a revived ShadowClan."

Tawnypelt exchanged a shocked glance with Rowanclaw. "Why me?" she asked. "You've got a Clan leader right here. Why don't you ask him?"

"Oh, no," Rowanclaw interrupted, shaking his head. "I

don't want to lead ShadowClan again. I've made that very clear. Besides . . ." He hesitated and then went on, "I've been dreaming about Tigerheart, and I haven't given up hoping that one day my son will come back—especially since the medicine cats had the message about returning shadows."

Tawnypelt gazed at him, her green eyes suddenly softened. "I hope that's true," she whispered.

"I'll support Tawnypelt if she wants to do it," Rowanclaw went on. "She was deputy, after all, after Tigerheart left."

"That's great!" Violetshine mewed, though she had the feeling that Rowanclaw wasn't that enthusiastic. "So, Tawnypelt, what—"

"Of course, we would need approval from StarClan," Rowanclaw interrupted. "In fact, Violetshine, why are you and Twigpaw the ones bringing this up? Where are the medicine cats?"

You stupid furball! Violetshine scolded herself. If she had thought for a heartbeat, she would have realized that she should have spoken to a medicine cat first: probably to Puddleshine, who had been ShadowClan's medicine cat. *I was thrown off balance by Twigpaw's showing up, and then Leafstar's being so angry. . . .*

She was about to suggest going to find Puddleshine when she heard approaching paw steps, and turned her head to see Sleekwhisker and Yarrowleaf, now very heavy with her kits.

"We overheard," Sleekwhisker mewed. "We'd love to see ShadowClan rise again!"

"Yes," Yarrowleaf agreed, her yellow eyes shining with hope. "Imagine if my kits could be born into a revived ShadowClan!"

Every cat's gaze went to Tawnypelt, who still looked undecided. "I'll think about it," she meowed, "provided that Puddleshine—"

She broke off at a loud gasp from Yarrowleaf.

"What's wrong?" Tree asked.

"The kits aren't going to wait for ShadowClan," Yarrowleaf explained, her breathing fast and shallow. "I think they're coming now!"

CHAPTER 12

♣

The sun was going down, shining fitfully through gaps in the cloud and casting dark shadows across the stone hollow. Alderheart brushed past the bramble screen into the camp, and stood taking deep breaths. The air was warm and clammy, and all day the clouds had been so low they almost touched the tops of the trees.

Alderheart gave silent thanks to StarClan that Leafpool was recovering from the sickness, though she was still too shaky to return to her duties. Whitewing had also taken a turn for the better, and could be treated in the apprentices' den with the other sick cats. Squirrelflight was responding well to his treatment and getting stronger every day.

However, for all his efforts, sickness was still rampaging through the camp. Molewhisker and Hollytuft had joined the sick cats in the apprentices' den, and worst of all, that morning Jayfeather had started vomiting.

He has to be the worst patient ever, since the Clans came to the lake, Alderheart thought with a sigh. He felt that every hair on his pelt was drooping with exhaustion.

As Alderheart stood outside his den, a thin, chilly breeze

started up, rattling the leaves of the trees at the top of the cliff. In the distance he spotted a crack of lightning, followed almost at once by a boom of thunder that echoed around the stone walls of the hollow.

Alderheart stiffened, his fur prickling with apprehension. *Great StarClan, that sounded close!*

The breeze strengthened and became a powerful wind that scoured through the camp, flattening the ferns and throwing up dust from the earth floor. Fat drops of rain began to fall. Overhead, lightning cracked again, and thunder rolled out even closer than before.

"Take shelter!" Alderheart yowled to the other cats who were out in the camp, staring up at the sky with bristling pelts.

Seeing them dive for their dens, he whipped around and went back into his own den, wondering what he needed to do for all the sick cats. After the Great Storm, the Clan had worked out how to deal with another flood, but Alderheart wasn't sure whether this would be a big enough storm to start evacuating the camp.

Slipping back into the den, Alderheart saw Leafpool sitting up in her nest, alarm in her eyes as she listened to the chaos outside. Jayfeather was resting with his nose on his paws, apparently asleep.

Thank StarClan for that! Alderheart thought.

"Do you think we ought to start moving the cats into the tunnels?" he asked Leafpool.

She hesitated for a moment, then shook her head. "Bramble-star will give the order if he thinks the storm is bad enough," she replied. "Meanwhile, all we can do is wait and see." She flinched at another growl of thunder that sounded as if a gigantic cat was crouched at the top of the cliff. "Maybe we'd better move Briarlight, though," she added. "She'll be harder to move if the weather gets any worse."

"I'll see to it," Alderheart mewed.

He pushed past the bramble screen once more and stared up at the sky. Rain swept across the camp, driven by the wind, and as Alderheart gazed upward, he flinched at another crackling claw of lightning.

Is this the storm? he wondered. *The storm that the dark sky must not herald?*

A weight of apprehension gathered in Alderheart's belly. He couldn't help thinking that maybe Leafstar's gesture of letting Sleekwhisker and Yarrowleaf stay in SkyClan was not enough. *Perhaps we should have done more to revive ShadowClan, like Twigpaw said—and perhaps we should have tried harder to bring River-Clan back among us.*

Bracing himself for the cold and wet, Alderheart dashed out into the storm and headed for the warriors' den. The rain had turned the dusty earth of the camp into mud that splashed up into his belly fur as he pelted across the open space. Sticking his head through a gap in the brambles that lined the walls of the den, Alderheart saw his Clanmates curled up in their nests, buried as deeply as possible in moss and bracken to avoid the chilly drops of rain that penetrated the roof.

"Wake up," he meowed. "I need two of you to come and help me move Briarlight."

"I will," Sorrelstripe volunteered immediately.

Ambermoon rose to her paws and shook off the scraps of bedding that clung to her pelt. "And me."

Together the two she-cats brushed past Alderheart and raced across the camp to the nursery. Alderheart followed.

At the entrance to the nursery Twigpaw was crouching, peering out at the sky. "Are you as worried about this as I am?" she asked, as Alderheart slipped into shelter and stood shivering.

"Maybe," Alderheart responded, his voice a bit sharper than he had intended.

It was less than a half-moon since Twigpaw had come back from sneaking off to SkyClan camp, excited at the idea the two of them had come up with, to persuade Tawnypelt to become the leader of a rebuilt ShadowClan. Sparkpelt and Bramblestar had both been furious with Twigpaw.

It sounded like Tawnypelt and some of the other former ShadowClan cats were intrigued by the idea. But it wasn't a *ThunderClan* apprentice's job to challenge the leadership of other Clans.

I understand she's concerned, Alderheart thought. *But even I have to admit she really overstepped. ShadowClan is none of our business.*

He was a bit hurt, too, that Twigpaw hadn't taken his advice, or seen fit to talk over her idea with him before heading off to SkyClan. *I'm a medicine cat, and I would have told her that no cat can install a new leader without StarClan's approval.*

"Did you hear anything about ShadowClan at last night's half-moon meeting?" Twigpaw asked.

The question did nothing to make Alderheart feel friendlier toward her. The meeting at the Moonpool was medicine-cat business, and it was up to them how much they revealed. But in this case, there was nothing much to say.

"Puddleshine reported that he was busy looking after Yarrowleaf and her two kits," he replied. "But he can't support the idea of reviving ShadowClan without a sign from StarClan. And none of us received a sign last night."

Twigpaw was visibly disappointed, crouching lower with her head drooping. Alderheart instantly felt sorry that he had been cool toward her. But just then Ambermoon and Sorrelstripe approached from the depths of the nursery, carrying Briarlight between them, and he decided that he had better concentrate on what he had to do.

"Take her up to the tunnel where the Clan camped in the Great Storm," he directed. "I'll follow in a few heartbeats and check on her."

"Don't worry about me," Briarlight meowed stoutly. "I *love* getting my fur wet!"

Alderheart noticed, as the two warriors carried her past him, that Sorrelstripe was staggering a little, and her eyes were fixed and glassy. *Oh, not another one!* was his first thought. Then he decided that the dark brown she-cat was probably just tired. *StarClan knows, life's been tough enough lately.*

When Briarlight and her escorts had disappeared into the rain, Alderheart headed toward the medicine-cat den. But before he had gone more than a few paw steps, a yowl of alarm from behind made him turn back.

He was in time to see the wind lift a whole section of the nursery roof and send it flapping away into the storm. More yowls came from the cats inside, and shrill wails of terror from the kits.

Alderheart splashed back through the puddles and dived into the nursery. Rain was pouring through the gap in the roof, soaking the side of the nursery where Briarlight had been sleeping.

We moved her just in time! Alderheart thought. *Thank StarClan!*

Cinderheart and Blossomfall had shrunk away from the gap to the far side of the nursery, each drawing her kits close to the curve of her body to shelter them from the cold and wet. Ivypool, Daisy, and Twigpaw were dragging over what bedding they could save from the rain.

"Alderheart, what shall we do?" Blossomfall asked. "We can't stay here—what if the rest of the roof gives way?"

For a heartbeat Alderheart struggled with panic. *Where can they possibly shelter?* "The elders' den is closest," he meowed at last. "Graystripe and Millie will be delighted to have kits to look after."

Stemkit immediately bounced to his paws. "Will Graystripe tell us stories?" he asked.

"Yes!" his sister Eaglekit squealed. "I want to hear about Firestar and the old forest."

"Certainly not. You need to sleep," their mother, Blossomheart, scolded. "And so does Graystripe."

In the midst of the chaos, Alderheart stifled a small *mrrow* of amusement. *I don't think any of them will get much sleep tonight.*

When he had sent his Clanmates on their way—the she-cats carrying Cinderheart's younger litter, while Blossomfall's kits pattered alongside—Alderheart raced back to the medicine-cat den. The wind was stronger still, almost enough to carry him off his paws. It had blown rain into the den past the brambles; Leafpool and Jayfeather—who was awake now, Alderheart noticed with a sinking heart—were both crouching in their nests, cold and wet and miserable.

"Where have you been?" Jayfeather rasped, rising to his paws and arching his back. "Get me out of here before I'm washed away in the flood! And I need more watermint."

Alderheart sighed. Jayfeather was a brilliant medicine cat, but when *he* was ill, taking care of him was worse than facing down a whole den of badgers.

"No cat is going to get washed away," Alderheart assured him. "The ground is muddy, but there's no flooding. But I *am* worried about the prophecy," he admitted. "'The dark sky must not herald a storm.'"

Jayfeather looked briefly disconcerted. "You said yourself, there's no flooding," he reminded Alderheart after a moment. "Perhaps this is just a little rain. When StarClan wants to make a point, they're not what you could call subtle."

Unconvinced, Alderheart let out a sigh. "As for the watermint," he told Jayfeather, "it's stored safely in the rock, where it will keep dry. You'll just have to wait for a while. And Leafpool," he added, turning to the other medicine cat, "don't let him bully you into fetching it. You need to rest."

"Yes, O great one," Leafpool murmured, a glimmer of

amusement in her amber eyes.

"Some medicine cat you are," Jayfeather grumbled, wrapping his tail over his nose. "You should have a bit of what you need on you at all times."

And where do I put it? Alderheart asked himself. *In my ears?*

After heading out of the den, he left the camp and climbed the slope to the tunnel openings where the Clan had sheltered during the Great Storm. Alderheart hadn't been born then, but he had heard the stories of what had happened, especially from the old tabby Purdy.

A pang of grief shook Alderheart. *Great StarClan, I miss Purdy!*

He found Ambermoon and Sorrelstripe with Briarlight near the mouth of the biggest tunnel. Somewhere they had managed to find some dry bracken to make a nest.

"Is every cat okay?" he asked.

"We're fine," Ambermoon replied cheerfully. "Don't worry about us."

"It's good to get out of camp for a while," Briarlight added.

Alderheart gave Sorrelstripe a close look, but though she was quiet she didn't seem ill, and he couldn't scent sickness on her.

"I'll come and tell you when it's safe to return," he meowed, and left them with a wave of his tail.

By this time it was almost dark. Alderheart had to watch where he was putting his paws as he made his way back down the slope. The grass was slippery from the rain, and more than once he almost lost his balance, digging in his claws to stop himself rolling down head over paws.

Before he had gone many fox-lengths, he jumped as he heard the loudest crack yet, and stood frozen while the hillside around him was bathed in a brilliant frosty light.

That's the closest so far, he thought.

From where he was standing, way above the camp, he could see into the far distance. An orange glow lit up the sky in the direction of SkyClan territory.

Fire!

Alderheart tried to work out exactly where it was. Dread filled him like rain filling an upturned leaf as he realized that flames could be devouring the SkyClan camp.

Forgetting to be careful, Alderheart launched himself down the slope. He slipped and skidded on mud and wet grass, desperate to reach the camp. Once, his paws shot out from under him, and he rolled over and over until he slammed into a jutting rock, the breath driven out of him. He picked himself up, then pelted on until he bounded through the thorn tunnel and into the camp.

"Bramblestar!" he yowled. "Bramblestar!"

Bramblestar appeared on the Highledge, his pelt soaked and plastered to his sides, as if he had just been making the rounds of the camp. "What is it, Alderheart?" he called.

"Fire!" Alderheart replied, gesturing with his tail. "Over there, near SkyClan!"

Bramblestar leaped down the tumbled rocks. By now the fire had risen so high in the sky that the orange glow was visible from the stone hollow. The Clan leader took one look, then dived into the warriors' den, reappearing a moment later with Stormcloud and Leafshade.

"Go and find out what's happening," Bramblestar ordered. "Don't get too close—just find out if it's near a camp, and if any other Clan needs our help."

"We're on it," Leafshade meowed.

The two cats bounded past Alderheart, who heard Stormcloud mutter, "This is just like old times!"

Alderheart remembered that Stormcloud had been a kittypet who had sheltered with ThunderClan during the Great Storm, and had decided to stay and train as a warrior. *It must be tough for him, remembering what the last flood was like. Purdy told me his brother died.*

Alderheart watched the two warriors go, then turned toward the medicine cats' den. *There might be nothing I can do about the storm, but I can at least find Jayfeather his watermint, and maybe that will shut him up for a while.*

By moonhigh, the rain had almost stopped, and the clouds had cleared enough for a faint silver light to filter down into the camp. Alderheart's fear receded, and he began to feel more confident.

Perhaps Jayfeather was right. Perhaps it was just a little rain.

Cats were out in the open, beginning to clear away the debris. Brackenfur was busy patching the nursery roof, with Twigpaw and Finpaw fetching bramble and ivy tendrils to help him. Already the gaping hole had almost vanished.

Things will be back to normal before we know it, Alderheart thought. *At least, I hope they will.*

He was about to head out of camp to tell Ambermoon and Sorrelstripe to bring Briarlight back, when he saw Stormcloud and Leafshade thrusting their way through the thorn tunnel. Alderheart was relieved to see them both returning unhurt, and took a pace forward to greet them.

Then he halted in surprise. Two cats Alderheart had never seen before followed his Clanmates into the camp. In the lead was a little tom with fuzzy ginger tabby fur, bouncing energetically around the warriors' paws so that they almost tripped over him. Behind him, limping a little, was a she-cat with long, silky gray fur and amber eyes.

Wow, she's a pretty cat! Alderheart thought.

She was holding something in her jaws; at first Alderheart thought it was a mouse, but then he realized it was just a scrap of fur. *Why is she carrying that?* he wondered.

While Alderheart hesitated, Bramblestar had appeared from his den, and he halted beside him with a disapproving glare. More of the Clan were padding over too, gathering around to stare curiously at the newcomers.

"What's this?" Bramblestar demanded. "Strange cats?"

"They're kittypets," Leafshade explained. "We ran into them when we were on our way to investigate the fire. They say it's in the Twolegplace over there, and they were running away from it."

"My name's Fuzzball!" the small, lively tom announced, bouncing confidently up to Bramblestar. "And my friend is called Velvet. She got burned, so we came to you to ask for help."

"How do you know about the Clans?" Alderheart asked.

"Oh, I kind of knew where you were," Fuzzball replied. "And I knew if anyone could help us, it would be warrior cats! I've heard how you fight, and stalk prey, and talk to the stars, and how you're the bravest cats ever! I know how—"

"You'll have to excuse Fuzzball," Velvet mewed, dropping the piece of fur she was carrying. "There's nothing between his ears except for dreams of Clan cats, so he's very excited to be here."

"That's all very flattering," Bramblestar meowed, giving the little tom a harassed glance. "But the Clans don't take in kittypets. It's for your own good," he added, as Fuzzball's whiskers drooped dejectedly. "It's a different life here in the forest, and kittypets aren't prepared for the dangers. You'll have to leave."

Alderheart couldn't bear to see the disappointment in the kittypets' eyes, particularly Velvet's. "Look at them," he told Bramblestar. "The she-cat is wounded. They're covered with soot, and obviously exhausted. They must have traveled a long way to ask for our help. At least let me treat Velvet's wound before we send them back to their Twolegs!"

When Bramblestar still seemed undecided, Stormcloud stepped forward. "You took in kittypets during the Great Storm," he reminded his Clan leader. "I know, because I was one of them. And that didn't turn out too badly, did it?"

Bramblestar sighed. "I thought you might say that. . . ."

"Please," Velvet begged him. "My burn is hurting a lot. A huge bolt of fire came from the sky, right outside my housefolk's den. It hit a tree, and the tree fell onto the den, so that caught fire too. And so did all the dens around it. Fuzzball and I only just managed to get out, and I grabbed what was left of my favorite toy." She reached out one paw and gave the scrap of fur an affectionate pat. "I suppose you wild cats think that's silly, but it gives me comfort."

Alderheart was aware that Leafshade and some of the other cats who had clustered around were suppressing amusement, but he didn't think it at all funny that the beautiful she-cat had needed something from her old home to help her face the dangers of the forest. "It's not silly at all," he defended her.

"We'd go home if we could," Velvet went on with a grateful glance at Alderheart, "but there were horrible wailing noises, and a huge monster showed up with its lights flashing. Our housefolk fled; we don't even know where they are."

"It would be cruel to turn them away," Alderheart pointed out to Bramblestar. "They've got nowhere else to go, and they're tired and wet from their journey."

Bramblestar clearly wasn't happy about letting in the two kittypets, but eventually he nodded. "I suppose you can stay until the fire is out and your Twolegs come back," he meowed with a snort. "But not a heartbeat longer."

Fuzzball let out a long, excited screech and began jumping up and down. "Thank you! Thank you!"

"Thank you," Velvet mewed more quietly, her amber gaze warm. "I promise you, we won't be any trouble."

"See that you're not," Bramblestar grunted. "And stay out from under every cat's paws." With that he stepped back and gathered his warriors around him with a wave of his tail, beginning to give them instructions about checking out the camp after the storm.

"Come with me," Alderheart directed the two kittypets. "My name is Alderheart, and I'm a medicine cat. You can stay in my den while—"

"What's a medicine cat?" Fuzzball interrupted, gazing up into Alderheart's face.

"I heal cats who are hurt or sick," Alderheart explained, leading the way to his den, "and I'll heal Velvet's burn and check you over if—"

"Oh, I'm fine," Fuzzball assured him. Alderheart wondered if he would ever be allowed to finish what he was saying. "I'd like to help. What can I do?"

Alderheart thought that the best way of shutting him up would be to give him a job to do. *But what could a kittypet do to help Clan cats?* Then he halted, blinking. *I've just had a great idea!*

"Come with me," he told Fuzzball. "I've got the *perfect* job for you."

"Great!" Fuzzball squeaked. "I'm going to be a Clan cat!"

On the way back to his den, Alderheart spotted Twigpaw carrying a bundle of wet bedding out of the nursery. He beckoned her over with his tail.

"Twigpaw, is the nursery okay now?" he asked.

Twigpaw nodded vigorously. "Brackenfur's really good at repairs," she mewed.

"We won't disturb the kits until tomorrow," Alderheart continued. "But when you've dumped that bedding, will you go up to the tunnel and tell Ambermoon and Sorrelstripe that they can bring Briarlight back? I'll come and see her when she's settled in the nursery again."

"Sure thing!" Twigpaw responded, spinning around and bounding toward the thorn tunnel.

"Thanks!" Alderheart called after her.

He padded on, with Velvet and Fuzzball still following, gazing around at the camp with wide and wondering eyes. As he reached his den, Birchfall limped on three legs, holding up one of his forepaws. Cherryfall was just behind him.

"Alderheart, I trod on a thorn in all this mess," Birchfall announced. "And I can't get it out. Can you help?"

"And I slipped in the mud and wrenched my shoulder," Cherryfall added.

"Okay, I'll deal with you in a minute," Alderheart responded. "Wait out here, and I'll be back when I've seen to these kittypets."

Leading the way past the bramble screen, Alderheart saw that Leafpool was curled up asleep in her nest, while Jayfeather was sitting up, irritably scratching at his ear with one hind paw. To Alderheart's relief he saw that there was enough dry bedding stored by the back wall of the den to make nests for the two kittypets.

"This is Leafpool," he told them, pointing with his tail, "and this is Jayfeather. They're both medicine cats, but right now they're here because they're sick with bellyache."

"Greetings," Velvet mewed with a polite dip of her head, while Fuzzball squeaked, "Hi!" with another excited bounce.

Jayfeather merely glared at the pair of them, not returning

their greeting. "My nest is full of thorns," he snapped at Alderheart.

"Then I've got just the thing for you," Alderheart responded. "This is Fuzzball." He urged the little tom forward with a sweep of his tail, and Fuzzball seemed to be trembling with eagerness to help. "Fuzzball will be looking after all your needs from now on," he continued. "Thorns in your nest? Need your bedding fluffed? Ask Fuzzball. Need water? Ask Fuzzball!"

"I don't believe this!" Jayfeather growled. "What are you meowing about?"

Before Alderheart could reply, Fuzzball hurled himself at Jayfeather and crouched down beside him, beginning to part the fern fronds and clumps of moss as he searched for thorns.

"Are you blind?" he asked Jayfeather, staring at his eyes. "What's it like being blind? How did it happen?"

Jayfeather opened his jaws: not to reply, Alderheart guessed, but to deliver a stinging rebuke. But Fuzzball chattered on obliviously. "Was it in a fight with a badger? Or a dog? Did the dog *die?* Is your belly hurting? How bad? Would you like me to rub it?"

Turning his head, Jayfeather glared at Alderheart, almost as if he could see him. "When I get better, I'm going to kill you," he grumbled.

Alderheart backed away, whiskers twitching with amusement, and saw the same amusement glimmering in Velvet's eyes. "We'll make a nest for you," he told her, "and then you can get some sleep."

Velvet put down the scrap of fur she had brought with her into the den. "Later," she mewed. "I wouldn't be able to relax, knowing how busy you are. You have a lot of cats to take care of, and I'd like to help you."

Alderheart gave her a doubtful look; he didn't think she would know enough to help a Clan medicine cat.

"I lived as a stray for a while," Velvet continued, clearly understanding his hesitation. "I had to take care of myself, and I learned a thing or two about herbs and healing. If you don't mind, I'd rather help you tend the sick cats and make myself useful."

Surprised, Alderheart blinked in gratitude at her offer. "Okay," he mewed. "Let me treat your wound first, and then you can help, as long as you don't move around too much."

"Okay," Velvet agreed.

Alderheart headed for the back of the den to the herb store in the cleft rock. He skirted Jayfeather's nest, where Fuzzball was telling him all about the fire.

"The flames were so high—higher than our housefolk's nest! The sparks flew right up into the sky...."

Jayfeather had his eyes closed and his tail over his nose, as if he was pretending none of this was happening.

Alderheart returned to Velvet with a fat black root in his jaws. "This is burdock root," he told her. "You can chew it up, if you like, but don't swallow it. I'll use it to make a poultice for your burn."

Velvet sniffed the root, then licked the end of it. "Ooh, bitter!"

"I can do it if you'd rather," Alderheart offered.

"No, I'll do it. I'd like to learn new things while I'm here."

Alderheart watched Velvet chewing a bite of the root, then asked her, "So you haven't always been a kittypet?"

"No," Velvet replied, spitting out the pulp. "My first house-folk went away and left me behind, so I was a stray for a couple of seasons, but then the weather got cold, so I found some new housefolk."

"How did you do that?" Alderheart asked as he began to pat the burdock-root pulp onto Velvet's burned leg.

Velvet let out a small *mrrow* of laughter. "I sat outside their den and meowed, and when they came out, I looked sad." She raised her head with her eyes stretched wide and a pathetic expression on her face. "It worked."

I'm sure it did. Alderheart couldn't imagine Twolegs being able to resist such a pretty cat. *Talking to her is really nice,* he thought. *But I'd better get back to work.*

"Keep still," he mewed, "and I'll fetch some cobweb to bind the poultice in place."

"It feels better already," Velvet told him, with a long sigh of relief. "You must be a great medicine cat."

Alderheart heard a snort from the direction of Jayfeather's nest, but he took no notice.

Once Velvet's leg was firmly bound up, Alderheart headed outside to see to the cats who were waiting for him. Velvet followed him.

"Can you take out a thorn?" Alderheart asked her.

"Oh, yes, no problem," Velvet replied. "If you don't mind?"

she mewed, with a questioning glance at Birchfall.

Birchfall looked surprised, but for answer he sat down and stretched out the injured paw. "I'd put up with a badger if it could get rid of this wretched thing," he meowed.

After making sure Velvet knew what she was doing, Alderheart was turning to Cherryfall when Sorrelstripe came padding over from the nursery.

"Is Briarlight okay?" Alderheart asked her.

"Yes, she's settled in again," the brown she-cat replied. "But I have to tell you . . . I vomited while we were up in the tunnel. And my belly aches really badly."

Oh, no, not another one, Alderheart thought. Aloud he mewed, "You need watermint, and—"

He broke off as the skies opened again and without any warning rain began falling in torrents, a renewed storm even fiercer than the one before. Alderheart's pelt was soaked in heartbeats.

"Quick, into the den!" he yowled, turning to the other cats. "Squeeze inside and—"

An enormous *crack* interrupted him, and another claw of lightning crashed down, impossibly bright and leaving Alderheart half blinded and stumbling through the puddles. As his vision cleared, he saw orange light flaring into the sky.

Fire had struck again, but this time it was much closer. The ominous glow was lighting up the sky over the territories of WindClan and RiverClan.

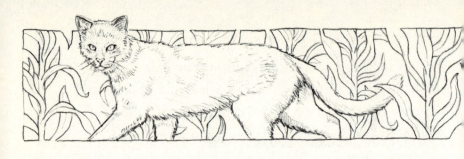

CHAPTER 13

Twigpaw stuck her head out of the nursery and gazed out into the storm. She could make out Alderheart at the opposite side of the camp, yowling louder than the thunder that echoed and echoed around the stone hollow.

"Bramblestar! Bramblestar!"

The Clan leader was already racing down the tumbled rocks.

"Fire!" Alderheart yowled again, dashing to meet his Clan leader in the center of the camp. "It's not the one I saw at first, in Velvet's Twolegplace. This is on the other side of the lake. WindClan or RiverClan might need our help."

Twigpaw shuddered, sure that this was the storm StarClan had warned them about. Memories of her vision at the Moonpool haunted her. *Has lightning struck another Clan's camp?*

Velvet, the long-haired kittypet, appeared from the medicine-cat den and joined Alderheart and Bramblestar, mewing in shock. As the thunder died away, Twigpaw could hear what they were saying.

"If Alderheart's treated your wounds, perhaps you should head back toward the Twolegplace," Bramblestar mewed curtly. "If Clan cats are hurt, we may need the space in the medicine cats' den."

"No, they can't," Alderheart objected. "Velvet knows about healing, and if the fire's as out of control as it looks, then some of the RiverClan cats might be injured. Leafpool and Jayfeather are still sick, so we're going to need all the help we can get."

"I suppose you're right," Bramblestar agreed reluctantly. "And there's no time to stand around arguing. We have to go *now!*"

Twigpaw raced out into the storm, ignoring the mud that splashed up around her, and skidded to a halt beside her Clan leader. "I want to go!" she gasped.

"And me!" another voice piped up behind her.

Glancing over her shoulder, Twigpaw saw that Finpaw had followed her. She gave him an approving flick with her tail, admiring the young tom's courage.

Bramblestar dived into the warriors' den and emerged a moment later with Sparkpelt and Larksong. Ambermoon and Rosepetal appeared hard on their paws.

"We'll come too," Rosepetal announced.

Bramblestar took the lead as the cats left the camp and plunged into the forest, heading for the lake. The darkness under the trees was so thick that Twigpaw could hardly make out the tail of Ambermoon, who was just in front of her. The heavy rain had made the ground spongy; Twigpaw struggled to run, but her paws were clogged with mud. As she forced her aching legs to carry her, she pictured the terrible vision she had seen at the Moonpool, smoldering trees and undergrowth as fire roared through a camp, devouring everything in its path.

I thought I was seeing the ThunderClan camp at the Moonpool . . . but maybe I was wrong. Twigpaw's relief that the destruction was happening to a different camp was mixed with guilt and anxiety for whichever Clan was facing the fire.

Is my vision really happening now? Will we be too late?

Once the patrol broke out of the trees to reach the lakeshore, the going became easier. The rain had lessened, too; now it was no more than a fine drizzle, with gaps in the clouds where fitful moonlight showed through. For a heartbeat Twigpaw felt relieved, then realized that the heavy rain might have helped to put the fire out. There was nothing to stop it now.

Clear of the trees, Twigpaw could see the orange glow of fire at the other side of the lake, not far from the water's edge. *It's not WindClan—it's RiverClan! And it looks like it's in their camp!*

Pelting along the lakeshore, Twigpaw spotted three WindClan cats sweeping down from the top of the moor. As they drew closer, she recognized Gorsetail and Nightcloud with her apprentice, Brindlepaw.

"You're heading for the fire?" Gorsetail panted as the WindClan cats joined the ThunderClan patrol. "We'll come with you. It looks bad!"

The combined patrols raced along the shore past the horse-place. As they reached the end of the tree-bridge they could hear noise ahead of them: the roaring of flames and terrified cats yowling for help or screeching in pain. Twigpaw's belly tightened with compassion, and she tried to force her legs to run even faster.

At the border stream the cats came to a halt. Ahead of her Twigpaw could see a barrier of fire; a fallen tree was blazing, along with undergrowth and dried reeds that grew along the water's edge. Beyond the barrier more flames leaped into the sky; the whole of the RiverClan camp was alight.

For a few heartbeats Twigpaw stood frozen, stunned to see her vision taking place for real in front of her. *This is what StarClan was warning me about!* At first, she felt renewed relief that it wasn't ThunderClan's camp being destroyed. But her relief was swamped by the horror of seeing what the fire was doing to RiverClan.

These are Clan cats! We have to help them!

In the midst of the flames she could see the dark shapes of fleeing cats. Some of them had leaped into the lake and were swimming to safety. But Twigpaw could see injured cats and an elder huddled together beside the water, unable to swim to safety. Twigpaw spotted Mistystar with them; clearly the Clan leader was refusing to leave the weakest of her Clan.

The fire was creeping across the ground to the spot where they were standing; soon they would have to swim or be devoured by the flames.

"Somehow we have to get to those cats," Alderheart declared.

"Will they want us to?" Gorsetail murmured anxiously. "Will they be angry with us for interfering? RiverClan's borders are closed!"

Oh, sure, flea-brain! Twigpaw thought, anger clawing through her. *Maybe they don't want to be rescued. So what are you here for?*

"We *must* help," Bramblestar asserted, glaring at the Wind-Clan warrior. "I can't imagine a Clan leader refusing help to save their Clan."

"But how?" Ambermoon asked. "None of us are strong swimmers, and without swimming there's no way to get past that burning tree."

"Then we'll have to make a way," Alderheart meowed. Glancing around, he spotted a log lying in the mud on their side of the stream. "We could push that into the water," he suggested. "Then the cats will be able to cross."

"Good thinking." Bramblestar nodded approvingly.

"It's pretty big," Ambermoon mewed doubtfully. "Will we be able to move it?"

"We will if we all put our strength together," Bramblestar responded, quickly beckoning the cats to take their places on the side of the log farthest from the stream. "Now—*push!*" he yowled.

Twigpaw thrust at the log with her shoulders but felt her paws slipping out from under her as the log refused to budge.

It's too heavy! she thought despairingly.

"Push! Harder!" Bramblestar yowled again.

Just when Twigpaw was ready to give up, she felt the log shift slightly. "Yes!" she screeched.

Every cat started pushing even more strongly, encouraged as the log moved faster and faster until it reached the stream. Alderheart, Nightcloud, and Larksong pushed at one end to maneuver it into the right place; then every cat gave one final thrust to drive it across the current. Panting and shaking with the effort, Twigpaw saw that it was just long enough to reach the opposite bank.

Thank StarClan! she thought.

Meanwhile Finpaw had leaped up onto the nearer end of the log and was jumping up and down, waving his stump of a tail. "Here! Over here!" he yowled to the stranded RiverClan cats.

Mosspelt, the RiverClan elder, spotted him, and a heartbeat later all the stranded cats were streaming across the open ground to the log. One by one they staggered across it, struggling not to lose their balance on the muddy surface, and leaped down to the safety of the other side.

"Thank you!" Mosspelt gasped as she stumbled onto the bank. "I thought we'd burn for sure."

Mistystar, crossing last of all, dipped her head to Bramblestar. "You have the thanks of all RiverClan," she mewed.

Twigpaw looked at the shivering cluster of cats and wondered what they would do now. It was no use escaping from the fire, only to die later from cold and exposure. More RiverClan cats came to join them, dragging themselves out of the lake, but Twigpaw noticed that there were still cats missing.

Where are the others? she wondered. *Oh, StarClan, don't let them be dead!*

Mistystar and Bramblestar were talking together, with Nightcloud from WindClan; Mistystar was clearly agitated, flexing her claws in and out. Twigpaw drew closer to hear what they were saying.

"I won't leave any cats behind," Mistystar was meowing. "Some of them are still missing."

"But no more are coming," Bramblestar pointed out patiently.

"I saw some cats escaping the other way," Podlight put in.

"And the cats here need your care," Bramblestar continued. "Some of them will die if they don't find shelter. You can bring them back with us to our camp for now."

"I'm sure Harestar would take in some cats, too," Nightcloud added.

Mistystar hesitated, then let out a long sigh. "You're right. We can't stay here."

"Then let's get going," Bramblestar meowed. "We can work out the details later."

The RiverClan leader began to gather her cats together, but before they could move off, Twigpaw heard a desperate yowl coming from the other side of the stream. Whipping around, she spotted a RiverClan apprentice tottering toward the bank. Twigpaw gasped at the sight of her pelt; it seemed to be burned away down one side, exposing the flesh underneath.

She was trying to reach the log and cross the stream, but by now the fire had reached the far end of it, and flames were leaping up in her face.

"Help me!" the young cat yowled. "I can't get on!"

"Softpaw!" The shriek of horror came from a RiverClan

cat behind Twigpaw; she didn't stop to see who it was. "Soft-paw, no!"

Twigpaw was closest to the log. Before any other cat could respond, she darted across it and leaped over the licking flames at the far end. Her paws landed on hot ash, and she drew in a painful, hissing breath.

The young apprentice Softpaw was crouching on the ground in front of her, with ears flattened and her eyes screwed shut.

"It's okay," Twigpaw reassured her. "I'll get you out."

Gently she grabbed the young cat by the scruff and carried her up to the blazing end of the log. Swinging her backward to build up momentum, she tossed her high above the flames.

Softpaw let out a squeal of alarm. She landed on the log, and for a moment her paws skidded on the slick surface. Twigpaw cringed, expecting with every heartbeat that she would fall into the stream.

But at last Softpaw managed to dig her claws in and regain her balance. She scurried across the log; Shimmerpelt and Mistystar met her on the other side and covered her ears with licks.

Twigpaw spotted Alderheart standing at the far end of the log. "Twigpaw, get back over here *now*!" he yowled.

"I'm coming!" Twigpaw called back.

Bracing herself, she took a few paces back from the bank, then raced up to the log and hurled herself into the air with a powerful thrust of her hind paws. She felt the heat of the flames as she leaped over them. For a heartbeat she thought she had beaten the fire, but as she came down to land she felt an explosion of heat scorching along one of her back legs.

Twigpaw let out a screech of agony. She thumped down onto the log, flailed briefly with her paws, and felt herself slipping sideways. A moment later the icy water of the stream surged around her and her head went under. As she sank, she heard Alderheart yowling, "No!"

Twigpaw struggled blindly underwater, losing all sense of direction. Then her head broke the surface. Gasping for air, she thrashed with her paws and tried to propel herself to the bank. The current was much stronger here than at the border stream with WindClan, and the water deeper. The bank seemed to be racing past her at a tremendous rate.

I'll be swept into the lake, and then I'll never get back!

She caught a glimpse of Alderheart pelting along the bank to keep pace with her, and heard Mistystar's voice. "Alderheart, you can't swim! If you jump in, we'll have to rescue both of you."

Twigpaw was growing tired, and her waterlogged pelt was weighing her down. It was harder and harder to keep on struggling. Then, as she was sinking again, she saw Shimmerpelt and Mallownose diving into the water, with a smaller cat following them.

Finpaw? Oh, no!

Shimmerpelt and Mallownose grabbed Twigpaw, one on each side, and held her up as they pulled her toward the bank. Finpaw swam in front of her, encouraging her; Twigpaw couldn't believe how confident he was in the water. "You'll be fine, Twigpaw. We won't let you drown."

Alderheart was waiting as they reached the far side of the stream, and reached down to sink his teeth into Twigpaw's scruff and help haul her to safety.

"Are you okay?" he demanded.

Twigpaw nodded feebly, tried to speak, and coughed up a mouthful of water. "Thank you," she gasped when she could breathe again. "Finpaw, I never knew you could swim like that."

Finpaw shrugged. "I was born by a lake," he responded. "Don't all cats swim?"

Mistystar let out a faint *mrrow* of amusement. "Maybe you should be a RiverClan cat," she told Finpaw.

"Paws off!" Alderheart retorted. "He's ours!"

Bramblestar padded up, looking down at Finpaw and Twigpaw with an approving glow in his amber eyes. "Finpaw is full of surprises," he murmured. "And as for you, Twigpaw, that was very brave."

"It was," Mistystar agreed, bending down to touch Twigpaw's head with her nose. "Thank you, from the bottom of my heart."

Twigpaw struggled to her paws, pride warming her from ears to tail-tip. But then, gazing past Mistystar, she saw the fire still burning in the RiverClan camp.

What does StarClan have in store for us next? she wondered anxiously. *Our troubles aren't over, not by a long shot. But how much worse can everything get?*

CHAPTER 14

❧

Frosty lightning flashed over the forest for a heartbeat, leaving Violetshine blinking as the dim, leafy daylight surged back. She winced as thunder crashed overhead and rolled on through the trees until she felt as if her head would burst with the sound.

"Fox dung!" Sandynose, who was leading the hunting patrol, let out a furious exclamation as the sound died away. "I nearly had that blackbird, until the lightning scared it off."

Macgyver winced from the noise and dropped the mouse he had just caught. "Maybe we should call it a day," he suggested.

Before he had finished speaking, Violetshine could feel a chilly wind rising. Branches above her began to creak, and dead leaves whirled in the air. All three cats exchanged alarmed glances.

"I think you're right," Sandynose meowed. "Let's take what we've caught so far and head back to camp. This is going to be a powerful storm!"

Violetshine gazed upward to where dark clouds were massing, covering the setting sun and casting an eerie twilight over the forest. She shivered as the first icy drops of rain splashed onto her fur.

The words of the prophecy crept unbidden into her mind: *The dark sky must not herald a storm.*

The ominous prediction reminded her of how she had talked to Puddleshine and Tawnypelt over the last quarter moon. She knew that Puddleshine wasn't sure that Shadow-Clan should rise again, or that StarClan would support Tawnypelt as leader.

But what if that's a mistake? Violetshine wondered, shivering more deeply at the thought. *Is this the storm we've been warned about? Are we too late to stop it?*

Macgyver picked up his mouse again while Violetshine fetched the squirrel she had left among the roots of an oak tree, and Sandynose retrieved another mouse and a thrush. Carrying their prey, the three cats set off at a fast trot toward the SkyClan camp. The rain grew heavier with every paw step they took, until the sound grew to a steady pattering on the canopy. The trees shielded the cats from the worst of the deluge, though Violetshine flinched at the lash of icy rain whenever wind thrust the branches apart.

As she followed Sandynose, Violetshine spotted the gleam of a golden pelt among the trees several fox-lengths away. It vanished almost at once; Violetshine paused for a moment, her whiskers twitching in puzzlement as she gazed after it.

Was that Sleekwhisker? she asked herself. *Where does she think she's going, all by herself?*

It wasn't wrong for warriors to hunt alone, or just to go

for a walk, but it was odd for any cat to be heading away from camp when the storm was getting worse with every heartbeat.

Then Violetshine shrugged. *Maybe it wasn't Sleekwhisker. And even if it was, it's none of my business what she does. I might say something to Leafstar, though, once the storm is over.*

"Hey, Violetshine!" Sandynose called back to her. "Are you coming, or do you want to get soaked all the way through?"

Violetshine raced to catch up with her Clanmates. As they drew closer to the camp, she could feel anxiety prickling through her pelt, as though she were trying to push her way through a thicket of brambles. She knew it wasn't because of the odd sighting of Sleekwhisker, but she couldn't think of any other reason.

What's the matter with me? she asked herself.

Then, as she approached the fern barrier that surrounded the camp, Violetshine suddenly began to understand. *Tree! I hope he's okay!*

She thrust her way into the camp, her pelt soaked as she brushed against the walls of the tunnel. Emerging into the open again, Violetshine felt a sudden rush of relief as she spotted the muscular yellow tom crouching in the shelter of a boulder, with Sparrowpelt and Blossomheart close beside him.

Around them the life of the Clan seemed to be carrying on as usual, with cats gathered around the fresh-kill pile and Hawkwing calling another patrol together, ready to go out. The rain had eased, but wind still buffeted the cats' fur.

Violetshine bounded across to Tree, pausing only to drop her squirrel onto the fresh-kill pile. "Are you okay?" she asked.

Tree stretched his jaws in a yawn. "Fine," he replied at last. "We're all fine."

"If this StarClan-cursed storm doesn't get any worse," Sparrowpelt muttered.

As if his words were a signal, a fiercer gust of wind hit the camp. It swept leaves, twigs, and debris into the air; Violetshine blinked at the sting of grit blowing into her eyes. Around the camp, the pine trees swayed and dipped with the force of the blast. Flowerpaw, the smallest of the apprentices, was knocked off her paws and lay on her back, waving her legs and tail in the air, until her mentor, Scorchfur, bounded over to her and hauled her upright again.

A frightened squeal came from the nursery. Puddleshine, who had just emerged from the medicine cats' den, broke into a sudden dash across the camp to check on the three she-cats and their kits.

"Take cover!" Leafstar yowled, emerging from the mouth of her den. "No cat must leave camp!"

Her words were almost lost in the howl of the wind and the buffeting of pine branches. An even stronger gust pushed Violetshine under the boulder next to Tree, and was followed by a horrific *crack* from somewhere overhead.

Craning her neck out of shelter, Violetshine saw the top of one of the pine trees tear loose, whirl in the air for a heartbeat as if it were a twig, then come barreling down into the camp.

"StarClan, no!" she shrieked as the tree landed with a deafening thump on top of the apprentices' den, shattering the bramble walls. A cloud of dust billowed into the air. For a couple of heartbeats the sight of the devastation was blotted out.

Thrusting down panic, Violetshine hurled herself across the camp toward the ruined den, with Tree, Sparrowpelt, and Blossomheart hard on her paws. With Hawkwing in the lead, more of her Clanmates converged on the den, too, yowling the names of the apprentices. "Flowerpaw! Whorlpaw! Snakepaw! Reedpaw! Dewpaw!"

Meanwhile Leafstar bounded into the center of the camp and let out a piercing caterwaul, rising above the noise of the wind. "Apprentices! Report to me!"

Violetshine glanced around to see the young cats scurrying up to their Clan leader, Flowerpaw still shaking dust out of her pelt. Breathlessly she counted, until she realized that all the apprentices were safely in the open. She saw Leafstar's shoulders sag with relief.

"Thank StarClan!" she exclaimed. "Right, every cat take cover. Apprentices, you'll have to go in with the warriors for now."

"Yes!" Whorlpaw's eyes stretched wide. "We'll be great warriors, we promise!"

They won't be so pleased when they have to rebuild their den, Violetshine thought.

She was heading for the warriors' den, thrusting hard against the force of the wind, when Strikestone exclaimed, "Wait!"

Violetshine turned to see him staring out across the camp in the direction of the lake.

"I can smell smoke!" he announced. "And there's a red glow in the sky!"

Violetshine parted her jaws to taste the air, and picked up an acrid tang flowing over her scent glands. Following Strikestone's gaze, she spotted the dull red glow, and thought she could see wisps of smoke rising for a heartbeat before the wind whipped them away.

"Lightning must have struck and started a fire," Hawkwing meowed. "Could it be in one of the other Clans?"

Panic stabbed through Violetshine at her father's words. She remembered the vision her sister had told her about, of fire raging through a camp. *Could ThunderClan be in danger?* she asked herself. *Oh no—Twigpaw!*

"This isn't the time to find out," Leafstar replied to her deputy. "The storm is too dangerous! We must take cover and ride it out, and then when it's over we can start to fix the apprentices' den, and send out patrols to check on the other Clans."

Several of the SkyClan cats had already retreated to their dens, and the rest hurried to obey their leader's command. But the former ShadowClan warriors stayed where they were, shifting their paws uneasily. *Sleekwhisker isn't with them,* Violetshine noticed.

"Get inside!" Leafstar yowled. "Have you got bees in your brain?"

Tawnypelt stepped up to her with a respectful dip of her head. "Maybe it's different for SkyClan," she began, "since you're not used to having other Clans around. But we can't let another Clan suffer, if they might need our help."

Violetshine thought that there was a leader-like glint in the tortoiseshell's green eyes. *We're right,* she thought. *Tawnypelt would make a strong leader for ShadowClan.*

Leafstar glared at her. "Are you implying that SkyClan cares less for other Clans than ShadowClan does?" she spat furiously. "Because that isn't true. We care about all the Clans, but my first responsibility is to *SkyClan*—and in case you forgot, you're a SkyClan cat now, Tawnypelt. And I just ordered you to go inside!"

For an uncomfortable moment that Violetshine thought was stretching out for seasons, Tawnypelt stayed still. The storm had begun to fade. Wind still ruffled their fur, yet the rain was easing off. The last icy drops lashed their faces, though the sky remained an ominous gray.

The storm could start again at any moment, Violetshine thought.

"I'm sorry, Leafstar, but I can't," Tawnypelt mewed in response to her Clan leader. "I'm going to find out where the fire is, and see if another Clan needs help."

"I'll go too," Juniperclaw added, stepping up beside Tawny-pelt.

Rowanclaw joined them. "And me."

Violetshine felt dreadfully torn. She wanted to obey her Clan leader, but she couldn't help thinking that Tawnypelt was right. And she couldn't stifle her terrible anxiety about her sister.

She glanced at Hawkwing, who was standing beside her. "Twigpaw," she whispered.

Her father nodded. "Leafstar, I mean no disrespect," he began, "but I have a daughter in another Clan. I really need to find the fire and check out if Twigpaw is okay."

"I'd like to go too," Violetshine meowed.

Leafstar gazed at them, understanding and irritation warring in her eyes. Violetshine could see concern there, too. "You're making the choice to take a huge risk," she pointed out.

"I know," Hawkwing replied. "But we will be careful."

Leafstar hesitated for a heartbeat more, then let out a long sigh as she nodded reluctantly. "Very well. Hawkwing, you're in charge," she declared, with a stern look at Tawnypelt.

Violetshine padded just behind her father and Tawnypelt as the patrol headed out into the forest. By now night had fallen; only a few fitful gleams of moonlight struggled through the trees to guide their paws.

Tawnypelt was casting awkward glances at the SkyClan deputy.

"I didn't mean to undermine Leafstar," she mewed at last. "I just needed to check on the other Clans."

Hawkwing was looking straight ahead, not meeting Tawnypelt's gaze. "You must decide who is leader," he told her. "Leafstar or you. Because right now, it doesn't feel like we're one Clan. It feels like we're two Clans sharing the same camp. And that isn't fair to SkyClan."

Tawnypelt looked taken aback at Hawkwing's brusque tone. Slackening her pace, she dropped back to walk beside Rowanclaw; Violetshine shot her a sympathetic glance as she passed her to take the lead beside her father.

I know Tawnypelt is trying to do the right thing, she thought. *She said that if StarClan approved, she would take over as leader of ShadowClan.*

But Violetshine also knew that Puddleshine was still waiting for a sign from StarClan. And no sign had come at the last half-moon meeting.

Tawnypelt is in a really awkward position.

Violetshine wasn't sure whether ShadowClan should rise again. The storm was telling every cat that StarClan wasn't happy with the way things were, but even if the wind and rain continued for seasons, the cats would be no closer to understanding what StarClan wanted from ShadowClan or its former warriors.

Why can't StarClan just say what they want, in a straightforward way—like Tree?

Hawkwing broke into Violetshine's thoughts. "How are you coping with life as a warrior?" he asked her. "I know you must be missing Twigpaw."

Violetshine nodded. "Being a warrior is great," she replied. "But I wish Twigpaw had stayed with us. I was so happy when I thought we would be warriors together, in the same Clan."

"I miss her too," Hawkwing agreed. "But I think it was the right decision for her. She'll be happy in ThunderClan."

"I hope so," Violetshine murmured. "I hope she'll be okay."

"Me too," Hawkwing meowed fervently. Glancing at Violetshine with warmth in his eyes, he added, "You're really finding your place in the Clan, aren't you?"

"I think so," Violetshine responded. "It's great to—"

"And I think you're finding your place with a certain other cat, too."

Hot embarrassment flooded over Violetshine. "I don't know what you mean," she mumbled, all the while sure that she *did* know what her father meant.

"I've seen you and Tree spending time together," Hawkwing continued, amusement in his voice. "I'm glad you've found each other. Tree is a bit weird, but I think he has a good heart. He would probably make a good father."

Violetshine felt even more embarrassed and confused, though at the same time she was pleased that her father approved of Tree. *But I don't want to talk about having* kits *with him! It's way too soon for that!*

She sought desperately for some way to change the subject, but before she could decide what to say, Hawkwing halted and pointed with his tail. "Look!" he exclaimed. "We can see the fire now. It's coming from RiverClan territory. Come on!" he urged, glancing back at the ShadowClan cats who followed him.

Hawkwing picked up the pace until the patrol was racing through the forest. Ahead of her Violetshine could see leaping flames, and as they drew closer, she could hear the crackling of fire and the screeches of panic-stricken cats.

"Faster!" Hawkwing yowled.

The sounds were dying away by the time the patrol broke out of the trees near the halfbridge and pelted across the little Thunderpath. Ahead, Violetshine saw a smoldering glow in the direction of the RiverClan camp, with clouds of smoke surging around it. A small group of cats was huddled together at the edge of the lake.

So few! Violetshine thought, fear gripping her with icy claws. *Are we too late?*

She halted, panting, on the lakeshore as the RiverClan deputy, Reedwhisker, staggered forward and dipped his head to Hawkwing.

"What happened?" Hawkwing asked. "Where's Mistystar?"

"Lightning struck a tree," Reedwhisker answered. His eyes were wild and his fur was bristling. "It caught fire and fell on our camp. And I don't know where Mistystar is."

Willowshine limped forward to stand at Reedwhisker's shoulder. "I think she and some of the others escaped the other way, toward WindClan," she replied. "Oh, StarClan, I hope so!"

"What can we do to help?" Hawkwing asked.

Reedwhisker and Willowshine exchanged a glance; both cats looked overwhelmed.

"We need shelter," Reedwhisker responded at last.

"And help with healing," Willowshine added. "The fire destroyed our store of herbs. Mothwing was badly hurt trying to save them."

Glancing past her, Violetshine spotted the golden-pelted medicine cat lying stretched out on the ground, and her belly clenched with compassion. Mothwing was so limp and still that she almost looked like she was dead.

She's so brave! She could have gotten herself killed, trying to save the herbs for her Clan.

While Hawkwing and the ShadowClan cats began to discuss what was best to do, Violetshine gazed along the shoreline. By now the fire was dying down, leaving blackened debris at the water's edge. Beyond the stream that marked the border, she caught sight of small, dark figures moving to and fro, half hidden by the swirling smoke.

"Look!" she called out.

Reedwhisker spun around and let out a cry of pure relief. "Our Clanmates!"

Seeming suddenly energized, he headed along the water's edge, hardly seeming to notice the scraps of smoldering bark and twigs. The other RiverClan cats streamed after him, while Hawkwing followed more cautiously with his patrol.

As they drew closer, Violetshine recognized Mistystar among the group on the far side of the stream, along with the rest of her Clan. Most were on their paws, though a few were lying on the ground, clearly injured.

But at least they're safe, Violetshine thought.

She saw too that more cats were gathered around; she spotted Bramblestar, Ambermoon, Larksong, and other warriors from ThunderClan and WindClan. And a slender, gray figure who was achingly familiar. *There's Twigpaw!* she realized with a sudden lifting of her heart.

"Typical ThunderClan," Juniperclaw muttered from just behind her. "Always sticking their whiskers in."

Violetshine ignored him. Bounding forward, she reached the edge of the border stream and called out to her sister. "Twigpaw! You're okay!"

Twigpaw stumbled up to the water's edge; her pelt was soaked and plastered to her body, she was limping on three legs, and she looked exhausted.

"What happened to you?" Violetshine asked, full of anxiety for her sister.

"Twigpaw is a hero," Alderheart replied, padding up to the bank of the stream. "She saved Softpaw."

"Really? Oh, well done!" Violetshine exclaimed. She could see the small, dark gray RiverClan apprentice crouching beside the stream. She looked battered, but out of danger, and she was gazing at Twigpaw with eyes full of gratitude.

Beside Violetshine, Hawkwing let out a purr of praise. "Twigpaw, I'm so proud of you," he meowed.

Twigpaw's legs were shaking, and she ducked her head to give her chest fur a couple of embarrassed licks, but her eyes were shining. "I just did what any cat would have done," she murmured.

Meanwhile, Bramblestar stepped forward and dipped his head to the cats who had just arrived. "We're discussing what to do next," he explained. "ThunderClan and WindClan are going to divide up the RiverClan cats to take shelter in our camps."

"But that's mouse-brained!" Tawnypelt exclaimed.

Even though Violetshine knew that Tawnypelt was Bramblestar's sister, she was still shocked that any warrior would address a Clan leader like that.

"If RiverClan needs a place to stay," Tawnypelt went on,

"they should stay in ShadowClan's old camp. It's empty, and it's closer. They—"

She broke off suddenly with a sideways glance at Hawkwing, who returned her look with whiskers twitching, as if he was saying, *That wasn't your offer to make.*

But after a moment's pause, Hawkwing gave a brief nod. "That seems sensible," he meowed. "You could stay there until you can get your own camp back in order—if Leafstar agrees."

Mistystar blinked at him gratefully. "Thank you," she responded. "RiverClan will not forget this day."

As the RiverClan leader began to gather her cats together, Violetshine felt a purr welling up from deep inside her chest. She finally felt hope that RiverClan's long estrangement from the other Clans was over.

Violetshine's belly churned with nervousness as she followed Hawkwing into the SkyClan camp. The RiverClan cats crowded in behind her.

Leafstar is already losing patience. What is she going to think about this?

The center of the camp was empty when Violetshine and the others arrived, but the sound of the new arrivals brought heads popping out of the warriors' den to see what was going on. Soon cats were emerging into the open, staring at the hu crowd.

"Great StarClan!" Sparrowpelt exclaimed. "How going to find space for all these cats?"

No cat answered him; instead a murmur of ant

broke out as Leafstar appeared from her den, leaped over the cedar roots, and bounded up to meet Hawkwing and Mistystar beside the stream.

"Greetings, Leafstar," Mistystar mewed, bowing her head with deepest respect.

"Greetings," Leafstar responded with an irritable flick of her tail. To Hawkwing she added, "What's all this about?"

Violetshine thought her leader looked startled, and not at all pleased as she surveyed the RiverClan cats. She wondered what would happen if Leafstar decided to refuse them shelter and ordered her Clan to drive them out of SkyClan territory.

She wouldn't do that . . . would she?

Hawkwing explained how the fire had led his patrol to the RiverClan camp. "I thought it would be a good idea if the RiverClan cats stayed in the old ShadowClan camp," he continued. Violetshine noticed that he didn't say it had been Tawnypelt's idea. "Only temporarily, of course. I hope you don't mind that I offered."

"Of course not," Leafstar responded. "After all the help the other Clans have given us, it's the least we can do."

For all the friendliness in Leafstar's words, Violetshine thought she could detect an edge in the Clan leader's voice. However, all Leafstar did was to beckon Juniperclaw, Bellaleaf, and Plumwillow.

"Escort the RiverClan cats to the old ShadowClan camp," she ordered. "And see that they have everything that they need."

"My Clan and I thank you, Leafstar." Mistystar bowed her

head again. "We are in your debt. And you can be sure that we won't trespass on your generosity for long."

Leafstar acknowledged Mistystar's words with a nod. Her voice sounded a little warmer as she added, "It's good to see you again."

The SkyClan leader remained standing in the center of the camp while the RiverClan cats filed out through the fern tunnel, accompanied by their escort. When they were gone, Leafstar flicked her ears to summon Tawnypelt to her side. Violetshine could feel the tension between the two cats, as if another, even worse storm were about to break.

"Leafstar, I'm sorry," Tawnypelt began. "I meant no disrespect when—"

"Enough!" Leafstar interrupted in a cool, crisp voice. "Tawnypelt, you and the other former ShadowClan cats must decide which you want to be: ShadowClan or SkyClan. If you want to be ShadowClan, you must get off SkyClan territory. If you want to be SkyClan, you must never question my judgment again."

Tawnypelt's tail drooped. "Of course, Leafstar," she responded with a dip of her head.

A murmur rose among the listening crowd of cats. None of them sounded happy, and the former ShadowClan warriors were exchanging disturbed glances.

Violetshine's gaze sought out Puddleshine. The medicine cat looked deeply troubled—just as troubled as she felt.

I don't think this is the end of it, Violetshine thought. *What is going to happen to ShadowClan?*

CHAPTER 15

❧

Thin clouds dotted the sky, too few to cover the full moon that shone out above the lake. The night air was cool and fresh as Twigpaw padded along the lakeshore with her Clan. Almost a half-moon had passed since the fire that had devastated the RiverClan camp, and the injury to her hind paw was completely healed.

Bramblestar was leading his Clan, with Squirrelflight by his side. Leafpool and Alderheart were with them too, though Jayfeather was still lying sick in the medicine cats' den. But he was the only cat still suffering from the bellyache, and Twigpaw hoped that better times were ahead.

Her paws tingled with anticipation as she and her Clanmates crossed the border stream and headed along the water's edge through WindClan territory.

Maybe RiverClan will be there! If they are, it will be the first time for moons that they've been to a Gathering.

It gave her a good feeling to think that RiverClan had opened its borders again, though Twigpaw still wondered what StarClan thought of what was happening around the lake. ShadowClan's fate wasn't resolved yet; Twigpaw had managed a quick chat with Violetshine when they were patrolling their shared border, and her sister had told her that there were still tensions between the SkyClan warriors and those who had belonged to ShadowClan.

We survived the storm, Twigpaw thought. *But what's next?*

When Bramblestar led his Clan through the bushes into the clearing at the center of the island, the other Clans were already there. Twigpaw looked up into the Great Oak to see Mistystar perched on a branch as well as Harestar and Leafstar. Reedwhisker was sitting on the oak roots with the other deputies.

Twigpaw was happy to see the RiverClan cats back in their proper place, but she spotted several cats from the other Clans muttering together and casting hostile looks at the RiverClan cats, who were clustered together at the far side of the clearing. She could tell that not every cat shared her feelings.

"I thought every cat would be glad to see RiverClan back," she whispered to Finpaw, who was sitting beside her in the shelter of an elder bush.

Finpaw shrugged. He was about to reply, but Sparkpelt cut off whatever he meant to say.

"RiverClan should never have left in the first place," she snapped, her green eyes wide. "Now they think they can just stroll back and have everything like it was? That's not happening!"

Twigpaw blinked in alarm at her mentor. She didn't want to get into an argument, so she was relieved when Bramblestar, who had leaped up into the Great Oak, stepped forward to start the meeting.

"Greetings, cats of all Clans," he began. "I'd like to welcome Mistystar and RiverClan among us again. They've been missed."

There was some muttering at the ThunderClan leader's words, as if not every cat agreed, but Bramblestar didn't let it bother him.

"ThunderClan is thriving," he went on. "Prey is running well in our territory, and we have four new apprentices. Stempaw has been apprenticed to Rosepetal, Plumpaw to Mousewhisker, Shellpaw to Bumblestripe, and Eaglepaw to Ambermoon."

Yowls of congratulations erupted in the clearing as the cats called out the new apprentices' names. The four young cats sat with eyes shining, embarrassed and happy at the same time.

Twigpaw felt a sudden stab of envy, remembering their apprentice ceremony a few days before. She wished she could feel the same eager energy, but her own apprenticeship had dragged out so long that it was hard to be enthusiastic about training anymore. Still, she was happy for her young Clanmates, and yowled out their names along with the rest.

As the sound died down, Bramblestar dipped his head and sat on his branch once again, waving his tail for Harestar to step forward.

"Prey is plentiful on the moor," the WindClan leader reported, "and we have made two new warriors. Brindlepaw and Smokepaw are now Brindlewing and Smokehaze."

"Brindlewing! Smokehaze!"

As the two new warriors were acclaimed, Harestar gave up his place to Leafstar, who waited for quiet before she began to speak. "SkyClan also has two new warriors," she announced. "Dewpaw and Reedpaw are now Dewspring and Reedclaw."

Twigpaw felt an even sharper pang at the SkyClan leader's news. *They've been apprentices as long as I have!* Then she felt Finpaw pressing affectionately against her side.

"It's okay," he whispered. "It'll be our turn soon."

Instantly Twigpaw's pelt grew hot with shame. Even though she hadn't put her ungenerous thoughts into words, her face must have given her away. If Finpaw wasn't upset, when the new warriors were his littermates, then she had no business griping either.

I chose this, she reminded herself. *I will be a ThunderClan warrior, one day.*

"It's fine," she murmured, giving Finpaw a grateful lick around the ear.

Meanwhile Mistystar had come forward, balancing gracefully on the end of a branch, to give news of RiverClan.

"We thank you all for the help you gave us in escaping the fire," she meowed, "and for the shelter you offered when our camp was destroyed. We are now ready to return and take part in the full life of the Clans, and we'll be grateful for any help you can give us in rebuilding our camp."

"Oh, that's great!" Twigpaw exclaimed. "They really are coming back for good."

Sparkpelt let out a skeptical snort; Twigpaw could tell that her mentor didn't share her excitement. Then Crowfeather, the WindClan deputy, rose to his paws from where he sat on the oak roots with the other deputies.

"That's all very well, Mistystar," he began, his voice harsh, and an irritated look in his eyes. "But it's beginning to feel like you're using the other Clans. You wanted nothing to do with us until we came and saved your tails, and now that you need help, you want to be a Clan again."

"Yeah, what a coincidence!" Scorchfur called out from SkyClan.

Mistystar didn't seem angry at Crowfeather's challenge. Instead she gave him a respectful dip of her head. "There's some truth in what you say, Crowfeather," she meowed. "The timing is awkward, I admit. But before the fire we had already made the decision to rejoin the rest of you."

"Yeah, right!" Sparkpelt muttered.

Twigpaw cast an impatient glance at her mentor. *There's too much arguing at this Gathering already,* she thought. *You don't have to make it worse!*

"After the damage inflicted on us by Darktail and his Kin, we needed time to turn inward and strengthen ourselves," Mistystar continued, apparently having not heard Sparkpelt's comment, or having decided to ignore it. "But now we're ready to contribute again. And the time alone has reminded us of how important it is to be part of something bigger than one Clan."

The RiverClan leader's measured words evidently

impressed Crowfeather, who gave her a nod and sat down again. But the hostile muttering still went on.

"What if we don't want you back?" a former ShadowClan cat called out, his words followed by a scattered chorus of agreement.

Twigpaw could understand why some cats were annoyed by RiverClan's withdrawal and sudden return, but she thought it was mouse-brained even to consider not letting them back in.

StarClan wants there to be five Clans—every cat knows that, she thought. *So why can't the other Clans let it go?*

Bramblestar stepped forward again and raised his tail for silence, but the unrest in the clearing didn't die down. Twigpaw glanced up at the moon, half expecting StarClan to show their anger by covering it with cloud, but it still sailed serenely above the trees.

Then the angry murmuring turned to surprise; Twigpaw turned her head to see Tree rising to his paws. "The timing *is* awkward," he began, completely confident in addressing the whole Gathering of cats, some of whom hardly knew him. "But would the rest of you rather not have RiverClan back at all? Doesn't StarClan want all the Clans to work together? And someday, when the other Clans need them, RiverClan will return the favor."

"We will indeed," Mistystar agreed.

Many of the cats had fallen silent; Twigpaw couldn't tell whether they saw sense in what Tree said, or whether they were too shocked by his sudden intervention to respond.

But there were still others who weren't impressed at all.

"Who is this cat?" Breezepelt of WindClan demanded. "Wasn't he a rogue?"

"He was. And he isn't even a real Clan cat now!" Thornclaw added. "Who is he to tell us what to do?"

Twigpaw saw Violetshine leap to her paws as if she was about to plunge into the argument, but before she could speak, Leafstar raised her voice from her place in the Great Oak.

"Tree is not exactly a rogue," she explained, "or even a loner. He has been living with SkyClan for more than a moon now. Remember how he helped ShadowClan's cats speak with their dead Clanmates?" She took a deep breath, her gaze raking around the clearing, and the remaining cats grew quiet under her authority.

"Now I have more news. Tree and I have discussed his staying with us in SkyClan, and creating a new Clan role," she continued. "He will be a mediator—just as the medicine cats cure wounds and illnesses, Tree's job will be to cure disagreements."

The brief silence in the clearing broke up again into confused questioning.

"But he's not a Clan cat!"

"Yeah, he doesn't know how Clans work. What's his advice worth?"

"True, he's not a Clan cat," Leafstar agreed calmly. "But I believe that might actually *help* him work out differences. He sees to the heart of an issue, without the fixed ideas we Clan cats have about one another."

"I've seen him in action," Hawkwing added from his place among the deputies. "He's good at working out problems. He sees solutions Clan cats might not."

"That's true!" Tawnypelt called out, surprising Twigpaw by her defense of Tree.

"I have an idea," Bramblestar announced, coming to stand beside Leafstar. "Suppose we give Tree a trial period, a bit like an apprenticeship? Tree can try to resolve disputes as they come up, and when we see how he copes, the Clan leaders can decide if we want him to continue."

Tree looked up at the ThunderClan leader, flexing his muscular shoulders. "No pressure, then," he commented.

Silence fell over the Gathering. Every cat's gaze was trained on Tree, and Twigpaw wondered whether or not he had said the right thing.

Then Cloudtail let out a *mrrow* of laughter, and the tension in the clearing suddenly faded. Cats curled their tails up in amusement. Twigpaw breathed a sigh of relief as she saw that there was a chance Tree could become very popular. *I suppose we could use a cat like Tree around.*

"That makes sense to me," Leafstar meowed in response to Bramblestar's suggestion. "I'm happy for Tree to become a SkyClan cat under those conditions. Tree, I can't make you a warrior, but I welcome you to our Clan. Would you like a warrior name?"

"No, I'll stick with Tree, thanks," the yellow tom replied. "It's nice and simple, like me."

"Tree! Tree!"

Not every cat in the clearing was acclaiming Tree and his new position, but enough of them joined in to make it clear he would be accepted among the Clans. Twigpaw spotted Violetshine jumping up and down, waving her tail as she yowled, her eyes alight with enthusiasm.

Alderheart rose to his paws and padded over to stand beside Tree as the noise died down. "I agree with what Tree said," he began. "Remember, the prophecy says there should be five Clans. Letting RiverClan back in would at least make us four again."

Twigpaw noticed some cats shooting annoyed glances at Rowanclaw as Alderheart spoke, as if they were blaming him for the loss of the fifth Clan. But Rowanclaw and the rest of the former ShadowClan cats ignored them.

"So, RiverClan comes back," Tree declared briskly. "Now, Mistystar, what do you need from the other Clans?"

"We need help in clearing the burned debris out of our camp," Mistystar replied. "We've made a start, but it's hard with so many of us injured."

"I'll send a patrol tomorrow," Bramblestar promised. "Harestar, can you send cats the day after, and Leafstar the day after that?"

Mistystar blinked gratefully as both leaders agreed. "Mothwing is still badly hurt from trying to save our herb stores," she continued, "and Willowshine is overwhelmed, trying to care for all the injured cats. Could one of your medicine cats—"

"I'll come," Leafpool offered immediately. "And I'll bring some herbs with me." She paused, gazing around the clearing, her eyes shimmering in thought. "And may StarClan light our path," she added. "Now and always."

As the cats settled down and the last of the hostility faded, Twigpaw spotted her sister sitting close beside Tree. Violetshine's eyes were wide with admiration as she gazed at the yellow tom.

Oh, Twigpaw thought. *So it's like that, is it?*

CHAPTER 16

Carefully Alderheart peeled the poultice off Velvet's burn, then gave the wound a good sniff. "That's healing really well," he mewed. "I think we'll leave it uncovered, to let the fresh air get at it."

"It hardly hurts at all now," Velvet purred. "You're a great medicine cat, Alderheart."

Alderheart wasn't sure that was true. Embarrassed, he tried to think of a way to change the subject, but in the end it was Velvet who spoke first.

"Every cat was so surprised when Ivypool had her kits on the night of the Gathering. None of us thought she was due."

Alderheart nodded, remembering how he had returned to camp to discover Jayfeather cleaning himself up after delivering the kits.

"Of course it had to happen tonight," the blind medicine cat had grumbled. "I had to do it, and I'm not over the sickness yet."

Alderheart knew that Jayfeather wasn't thinking about himself, but whether he might have passed on the sickness to Ivypool or, even worse, to the new kits. *Or Daisy, or Briarlight . . . ,* he thought. Cinderheart had taken her litter to spend the night in the elders' den, but the other two she-cats had insisted on staying to help.

So far, every cat seems to be healthy, Alderheart thought. *But I'll have to keep an eye on them all.*

He started out of his memories as he realized that Velvet was speaking again.

"Clan life is really different from how I imagined it," she mewed. "Fuzzball made me think it was all fighting and hunting, but you do so much more! You heal cats, and you make sure every cat is cared for, especially the kits and elders...."

"That's the warrior code," Alderheart responded.

Velvet's words made him realize that she was fitting into ThunderClan much better than any cat had expected. *We have so much in common,* he thought. *Wouldn't it be great if she decided to stay, and then we could spend more time together?*

Alarm jolted through Alderheart. *What am I thinking?* He knew seeing more of Velvet would be a really bad idea. He could already feel his heart being pulled toward her, and for a medicine cat, that was forbidden.

And we already have Jayfeather hanging over us all the time.

The blind medicine cat was slow to recover from the belly sickness. Alderheart was aware of him now, curled up in his nest, his eyes closed but his ears pricked as though he was listening to every word Alderheart and Velvet said.

It's okay, Jayfeather, Alderheart thought. *I'm not going to do anything you won't approve of.*

Paw steps outside the den distracted him, and a moment later Fuzzball, who slept in the apprentices' den, bounced in through the bramble screen. He was carrying a vole in his jaws.

"Look, Jayfeather," he meowed cheerfully, setting his prey down in front of Jayfeather's nose. "The first hunting patrols are coming back, and I picked out this vole for you. Voles are your favorite, aren't they? Come on, sit up now, and while you're eating it, I'll fluff up your nest so you can have a nice nap."

While Fuzzball was chattering on, Jayfeather let out a long groan. He sat up, irritably shaking scraps of moss and fern from his pelt. "I'm cured," he announced.

"Are you sure?" Alderheart asked, trying to hide his amusement. "I think your belly is still a bit tender. You might do better with another day of rest."

"No, I'm completely cured," Jayfeather insisted, shooting a glare at Alderheart before bending down to take hungry bites of the vole. "I'd better get back to my duties, and that means I can't chat right now."

"That's great, Jayfeather!" Fuzzball exclaimed. "Now I can help you with medicine-cat stuff."

"StarClan give me strength!" Jayfeather muttered through his teeth. "Alderheart, stop sitting there like a frozen rabbit and get over to the nursery. It's only been three days since Ivypool had her kits, and you need to check on her."

Like I haven't been doing that, Alderheart thought, trying to stifle a slight feeling of resentment. *I know he's only saying that to get me away from Velvet.*

But Alderheart knew he had no right to protest. Hauling

himself to his paws, he dipped his head to the gray she-cat and headed out of the den. Behind him he heard Fuzzball's excited squeak.

"Can we go into the forest and look for herbs, Jayfeather? Can we? I know I'll find lots!"

When Alderheart reached the nursery, now securely patched after the damage from the storm, Ivypool was curled up with her three kits snuggled into her belly. Fernsong sat beside them, gazing down proudly at his litter.

"We've named them," Ivypool told Alderheart. "The pale gray she-kit is Bristlekit, the dark gray she-cat is Thriftkit, and the little tabby tom is Flipkit."

"They're beautiful," Alderheart purred, his resentment vanishing as the milky scent of the nursery flowed over him and he gave the three tiny bodies a quick check. "And they seem to be thriving," he continued. "Are they feeding well?"

"They hardly ever stop!" Ivypool responded, her eyes glimmering with loving amusement.

"And we couldn't be happier," Fernsong added.

Ivypool blinked reflectively. "You know," she confided to Alderheart, "I was so angry when Dovewing left, and I missed her so much. I felt betrayed. But now, seeing my own kits . . . I think I'm learning what's really important."

"I'm sure Dovewing had good reasons for what she did," Alderheart meowed.

"I know. I think she had to be with Tigerheart. And if that's true, I think I can accept it, now that she's been gone so long."

"You must still miss her, though," Alderheart suggested.

"Yes," Ivypool responded with a thoughtful sigh. "But it's strange. I've been dreaming about her so much. . . . I have the feeling that we'll see each other again someday."

"I hope so," Alderheart mewed, then moved on to Cinderheart, who was curled up nearby with her own kits, who were much older and bigger than Ivypool's. She was watching Ivypool's kits affectionately. *It must be sweet,* Alderheart thought, *to get to spend time with her kit's kits at the same time she tends her own.*

"Don't disturb them!" Cinderheart begged Alderheart. "The only time I get any rest is when they're asleep." She stroked her tail affectionately over her kits. "But I wouldn't have them any different."

"They're strong young cats," Daisy put in from her nest at the far side of the nursery. "They'll be apprenticed sooner than you know it."

"We'll need to make the apprentices' den bigger," Alderheart agreed.

He padded over to Briarlight, who lay stretched out among the moss and fern not far from Daisy. When he bent his head to sniff at her, he picked up a familiar sour scent.

Alderheart couldn't restrain a gasp of dismay. The sound disturbed Briarlight, who opened her eyes.

Immediately Alderheart's uneasiness grew. Briarlight's eyes were glazed and her movements sluggish as she tried to prop herself up on her forelegs. Her scent had soured too; Alderheart felt his heart thumping uncomfortably as he guessed what was wrong. *She escaped the sickness when she was in the tunnel with Sorrelstripe,* he thought, *but she has it now.*

"How are you feeling, Briarlight?" he asked.

Briarlight hesitated before she replied. "Not so good," she admitted at last. "My belly has been aching terribly for the last couple of days."

"And you didn't tell me?"

"I didn't want to bother you," Briarlight replied. "I hoped it was just something I ate."

"I'm a medicine cat. I'm here to be bothered," Alderheart pointed out. "We'll get you back into the medicine-cat den right away."

He popped his head out of the nursery and beckoned to Thornclaw and Poppyfrost, who were the first cats he spotted. "Briarlight's not well," he told them. "We need to move her back to my den."

Leaving the two warriors to carry Briarlight, Alderheart bounded across the camp. *Briarlight must have caught the sickness from Jayfeather when he delivered Ivypool's litter,* he thought. *We need to get her away from the kits.*

When Alderheart brushed past the bramble screen, Velvet was drowsing in her nest, while Jayfeather was at the back of the den, sorting the herbs stored in the cleft in the rock. Fuzzball was helping him.

"This one's dock leaf, isn't it? Oh . . . no . . . tansy. And this is—don't tell me—catmint!"

"Sorrel," Jayfeather hissed.

He turned at the sound of Alderheart entering the den, looking relieved to be distracted from Fuzzball's constant questioning. But his expression changed to concern when

Alderheart told him that Briarlight had the belly sickness.

"It's a good thing you spotted it before Cinderheart, Ivy-pool, or their kits got sick," Jayfeather mewed. He sounded uneasy; he must have known very well that if Briarlight was ill, she had caught it from him when he delivered Ivypool's kits.

"Yes," Alderheart responded, "but I'll keep a close eye on them for the next day or two, just to be sure."

As Thornclaw and Poppyfrost maneuvered Briarlight past the brambles and into the den, Velvet sprang to her paws and quickly pulled together some dry ferns and moss to make a nest for her.

"Settle down here," she mewed kindly. "Are you comfortable? Is the bedding thick enough?"

"It's great, thanks," Briarlight replied, sinking into the nest with a sigh. "I'm really sorry to be giving all of you so much trouble."

"It's no trouble," Alderheart told her. "It's what we're here for. Now let me fetch you some watermint. You'll soon feel better."

"I'll get it!" Fuzzball plunged into the herb store and emerged with a sprig of leaves in his jaws. To Alderheart's surprise, it actually was watermint.

"Thanks, Fuzzball." Velvet took the sprig from him and stripped off the leaves before laying them in front of Briarlight. "Chew them up small before you swallow them," she instructed.

Velvet gave Briarlight a soothing stroke as she licked up the leaves.

What a great cat she is, Alderheart thought. *She may be a kittypet, but she really cares about other cats.*

As if she had caught his thoughts, Velvet looked up at him and gave him a shy, friendly glance. Warmed through and through, Alderheart found himself returning it, even though he knew he shouldn't.

Dawn light was filtering through the bramble screen when Alderheart struggled out of his nest and went to check on Briarlight. Even before he reached her, he knew that something was badly wrong. He could hear her irregular, rasping breaths, interspersed with spasmodic retching sounds.

"Briarlight, why didn't you call me?" he asked as he reached her side.

Briarlight fought to raise her head and look at him, and with a pang of fear Alderheart realized how weak she was—much worse than when her Clanmates had carried her into the den the day before.

"I didn't want . . . to be a nuisance," she gasped, every word an effort.

She's dying . . . , Alderheart thought.

Briarlight seemed to know what was happening. Her face was peaceful; her eyes were shining as if she was already gazing into the sunlit glades of StarClan's territory.

"It's . . . okay, Alderheart," she gasped. "But I'd like to say good-bye."

Alderheart nodded swiftly and went to wake Velvet, shaking her urgently by the shoulder.

Velvet started up immediately. "What is it?" she asked.

"Briarlight is dying," Alderheart murmured. "Please go and find a Clan cat to fetch her kin."

Velvet's eyes widened in horror. "Oh, no . . ." Then she rose to her paws and slipped silently out of the den.

Alderheart went on to wake Jayfeather and gave him the same terrible news. For a few heartbeats Jayfeather sat frozen, as if he hadn't taken in what Alderheart was telling him.

"She's dying, Jayfeather," Alderheart repeated.

"Nonsense. I won't allow her to die," Jayfeather snapped.

Rising to his paws, he blundered to the back of the den. *So clumsy . . . ,* Alderheart thought, reflecting how ordinarily no cat would even think that Jayfeather was blind, his movements were so neat. *He knows we're losing her, even if he won't admit it.*

He watched Jayfeather soak some moss in the water that trickled down the rock and take it to Briarlight to drink. Then in his turn he slipped out into the open and headed for the tumbled rocks that led to Bramblestar's den.

In the gray dawn light the camp was rousing; Squirrelflight stood outside the warriors' den as if she had begun to arrange the dawn patrols, but all the warriors were clustered around Velvet as she passed on the news. Alderheart heard Millie let out a heartrending cry that echoed around the stone hollow, and saw Graystripe press himself close to her side.

Bramblestar was awake when Alderheart reached his den. Alderheart thought Millie's cry must have roused him. At once he leaped to his paws, alert and sliding out his claws. "Is there trouble?" he asked.

"Not the kind you mean," Alderheart replied. "It's Briar-light. She has the sickness, and she's dying."

Bramblestar's amber eyes filled with sorrow. "I knew this would happen someday. She's lived a long time with terrible injuries," he mewed. "But that doesn't make it any easier."

He led the way down into the camp and moved among the huddled groups of his warriors, listening to their grief. Glancing around, he spotted Larksong and beckoned him over with his tail.

"Leafpool should be here," he told the young warrior. "Fetch her, please—try the ShadowClan camp first. It's closer than RiverClan."

Larksong nodded and hurried off, pausing at the apprentices' den to collect Finpaw.

Alderheart left Bramblestar to talk with his Clanmates and returned to the medicine cats' den. Graystripe, Millie, Blossomfall, and Bumblestripe were already there. Millie was crouching beside her daughter, gently licking her ears, while the rest of the family clustered around them.

"I can't believe this is happening," Graystripe murmured to Alderheart. "She was always so strong, so brave . . ."

"I'm surprised she weakened so quickly," Alderheart responded. "I think she must have been hiding how bad she felt."

She hasn't been eating enough, he added to himself, seeing Briar-light's ribs sliding beneath her fur as she struggled to breathe. *And it's harder for her to fight the sickness because she can't move.*

Alderheart wasn't sure how long he sat in the medicine cats' den, listening to Briarlight's gradually fading breath. At one point Leafpool slipped in quietly and sat beside Jayfeather, wrapping her tail around her son's shoulders.

Later Twigpaw appeared, meowing, "Alderheart, do you—" as she brushed past the bramble screen, then falling silent as she realized how weak Briarlight had become. She crept closer to the dying cat.

"Oh, Briarlight. Good-bye," she whispered. "You were so kind to me when I was a kit."

Briarlight's eyes fluttered open, and she blinked affectionately at Twigpaw. "We had . . . some good times," she rasped.

Millie pressed even closer to her daughter. "Oh, precious one, don't leave us," she mewed, her voice quivering. "Please don't leave us."

Briarlight looked up at her mother. "Don't . . . worry about me, Millie. I shall . . . run and hunt again . . . in StarClan."

Then her eyes closed once more and she sighed out a long, final breath. Millie let out a terrible wail; Graystripe and her two remaining kits huddled around her.

Alderheart couldn't bear to watch them trying to comfort one another. He stumbled out of the den, shocked to see that the sun was already going down, casting dark shadows across the hollow. His legs gave way under him and he crouched with his head on his paws and gave himself up to grief.

Soon he realized that Jayfeather had followed him out and was crouching beside him, his breath coming in short, shallow gasps. "This is my fault," he snarled. "I must have given her the sickness when I went into the nursery to deliver Ivypool's kits. I should never have gone near her."

His guilt and regret struck Alderheart like a massive claw, driving him a little way out of his own sorrow. "It's *not* your fault," he meowed firmly. "Ivypool and her kits might have died without a medicine cat to help. Besides, you could just as well say that Leafpool and I were responsible. We shouldn't have left you as the only medicine cat in camp."

Jayfeather turned his head toward him with an intense blind stare. "We all thought Ivypool had a few more days to go," he admitted. "But that doesn't change the fact that Briarlight got the sickness from me. And I couldn't help her," he added. "No cat could help her. Oh, StarClan, what good are we?"

"You did your best," Alderheart told him, beginning to recover in his need to comfort Jayfeather. "You gave her seasons of life with the routines and the exercises you worked out for her."

He half expected Jayfeather to snap at him, but to his surprise his Clanmate gave a grunt of agreement. "I wish I could have healed her," he meowed.

"So do I," Alderheart responded. "I blame myself. . . . I should have realized how weak she was getting."

"No." Jayfeather shook his head emphatically. "You're a fine medicine cat. None of us saw this coming."

Movement behind Alderheart made him turn, to see Leafpool leading the way out of the medicine cats' den, followed by Graystripe and Millie carrying Briarlight. They laid her body in the center of the camp, and the rest of the Clan began to gather around to keep vigil for her.

Jayfeather rose and padded over to join Leafpool at Briarlight's head. Alderheart stayed where he was for a few heartbeats, pulling himself together to face his Clan. His heart ached, but Jayfeather's unexpected words had comforted him a little.

Jayfeather has praised me before—once or twice—but this is the first time he's made me really believe I might one day be a good medicine cat.

The cats of ThunderClan gathered in a ragged circle around Briarlight's body to keep vigil for her. Alderheart joined them, and he listened as many of his Clanmates rose to share their memories of her.

"She was good to me when I was a kit," Twigpaw declared. "I was scared, and missing my sister, and everything here was strange. But Briarlight made me feel I was helping her, so it was like I belonged."

When she had finished speaking, Graystripe and Millie rose to their paws. Millie's voice failed her, and it was Graystripe who spoke for both of them. "We were so proud of her. She was strong and brave, and even though she couldn't walk, she always had the heart of a warrior."

"That's true," Blossomfall added, standing beside her mother and father. "I only hope my kits will inherit some of Briarlight's optimism and determination."

As they sat down again, Jayfeather rose to his paws. "She never gave up," he began. "She never—" His voice choked, and he couldn't go on.

"She never lost her courage or her sense of humor,"

Alderheart continued, springing up to stand beside Jay-feather. "She was a very special cat, and we'll both miss her. Not because we looked after her, but because she was our friend."

Jayfeather nodded. To Alderheart's surprise, Fuzzball crept up and sat quietly beside him. He was even more aston-ished to see Jayfeather reach out with his tail and touch the little ginger tom lightly on his shoulder.

At last the sky above the hollow began to grow pale with dawn, and the warriors of StarClan winked out one by one. Leafpool rose to her paws.

"May StarClan light your path, Briarlight," she meowed, using the words that medicine cats had spoken over the bodies of the dead for season upon season. "May you find good hunt-ing, swift running, and shelter when you sleep."

Her words gave Alderheart a tiny measure of comfort, like a thin ray of sunlight striking through dark branches. For a moment he seemed to see Briarlight, swift and beautiful, rac-ing through the lush grass and trees of StarClan.

After Leafpool had spoken, Graystripe and Millie took up Briarlight's body and carried it out of camp for burial. Grief caught in Alderheart's throat again as he watched them: this was the traditional task of the Clan elders, but it seemed to hurt so much more since the elders were also Briarlight's par-ents.

When they were gone, Alderheart rose to his paws and stumbled back to his den, feeling cold and stiff after the long vigil. He knew there were tasks he should be doing, but he was too exhausted even to remember what they were.

Then Velvet appeared at his shoulder, guiding him toward his nest. "Lie down and sleep," she mewed, gently pushing him down into the moss and fern. "I'll watch the den until Leafpool and Jayfeather come back. If any cat needs you, I'll wake you, but I can take care of any minor ailments or wounds."

"But I should—" Alderheart began to protest.

Velvet interrupted him by laying her tail across his mouth. "Let me take care of you," she murmured.

That feels so good, Alderheart thought muzzily as he sank into sleep. *Someone to take care of me . . . That hardly ever happens.*

The last thing he was aware of was Velvet's sweet scent wreathing around him.

CHAPTER 17

♣

Violetshine slid through the fern tunnel into the SkyClan camp, a couple of mice dangling from her jaws. Rowanclaw and Macgyver followed her, both of them laden with their own prey. The hunting had been good.

The camp was almost deserted: this was the day it was SkyClan's turn to go and help RiverClan restore their camp after the fire. The only cat Violetshine could see was Yarrowleaf, curled up asleep on a sunlit rock not far from the nursery.

Something about that looks odd, Violetshine thought as she padded across the camp to deposit her prey on the fresh-kill pile. A moment later, she realized what it was.

Where are Yarrowleaf's kits?

Uneasiness stirred in Violetshine's belly. She poked her head inside the nursery to check if the kits were there. Tinycloud and Snowbird were both drowsing in furry heaps with their own kits, but there was no sign of Hopkit or Flaxkit.

Violetshine withdrew again and glanced around, but she still couldn't see the kits anywhere outside. *Oh, StarClan, don't let them have wandered off!*

Rapidly, Violetshine bounded across the camp, leaped the

small stream, and jumped up onto the rock where Yarrowleaf was sleeping. She gave the ginger she-cat a sharp prod in the side.

"Yarrowleaf—"

Violetshine broke off. Lying on the rock beside Yarrowleaf was a half-eaten mouse. Tiny black spots were clearly visible in the torn flesh.

Poppy seeds! Violetshine suppressed a shudder. Once, she had tried to drug Darktail and his Kin with poppy seeds, but she had been unaware that Sleekwhisker had watched her do it. Violetshine's failure had almost led to her death.

And Needletail was killed because of it. . . .

For a few heartbeats Violetshine stood frozen, staring at the seeds. Who could have given the drugged prey to Yarrowleaf? Sleekwhisker and she were often together, but now the yellow she-cat was nowhere in sight. Could she have gotten the idea from Violetshine's failed attempt to drug Darktail? Violetshine remembered the time she had seen Sleekwhisker heading away from the camp on the day of the storm.

She's up to something . . . but what? I should have remembered to report her to Leafstar!

Cold fear drenched Violetshine, and she prodded Yarrowleaf again until the she-cat raised her head and gazed at Violetshine with bleary eyes. "What's the matter?" she asked, her voice slurring.

"Yarrowleaf, where are your kits?" Violetshine demanded urgently.

Yarrowleaf sat up and looked around. Then her eyes

suddenly widened with alarm, and she seemed to throw off the worst of the drug.

"My kits!" she yowled in a panic. "Where are my kits?" She sprang to her paws, staggering a little as she spun around, trying to locate the kits. "Hopkit! Flaxkit!"

"Yarrowleaf, listen!" Violetshine meowed. "Was Sleekwhisker here?"

"Yes, we were watching the kits play." Yarrowleaf looked confused.

"And she brought you this mouse?"

Yarrowleaf nodded. "Are you saying Sleekwhisker took my kits?" she asked. "She would never do that. She's my friend."

"Are you sure of that?" Violetshine asked. "Remember how loyal Sleekwhisker was to Darktail? Is it possible she's working with the remains of his Kin to take revenge on ShadowClan?"

I never trusted Sleekwhisker. She helped kill Needletail. Has she been lying to us all this time?

Yarrowleaf stared at her, dazed, until the horrible idea began to sink in. "Oh, StarClan!" she wailed. "Sleekwhisker has my kits! Where is she taking them?"

"I don't know, but we'll find out," Violetshine mewed grimly. Glancing around, she spotted Rowanclaw and Macgyver, who were sharing a squirrel beside the fresh-kill pile, and beckoned them over with a whisk of her tail.

"What's going on?" Rowanclaw asked. "Why is Yarrowleaf so upset?"

Violetshine explained how Yarrowleaf had been put to sleep with poppy seeds, and how Sleekwhisker and the kits were missing. "We have to find them," she finished.

"We will," Rowanclaw meowed. "We'll follow their scent trail."

He led the way out of camp, with Violetshine and Macgyver just behind him. Yarrowleaf came too, still a bit unsteady on her paws, but determined to keep going until her kits were safe again.

Violetshine was first to pick up Sleekwhisker's scent, heading off in the direction of the old ShadowClan camp. The kits' scent was there, too.

"That proves she took them," Rowanclaw meowed as they began to follow. "She must have told them some sort of story to make them go with her."

"They were both eager to get out into the forest," Yarrowleaf responded. "If Sleekwhisker suggested going, they'd think it was okay. Oh, StarClan," she continued, "I hope she doesn't hurt them!"

"She hasn't yet," Violetshine comforted her. "There's no fear-scent at all." *And no blood, or tiny limp bodies,* she added to herself. *Why did we ever trust Sleekwhisker? She was one of the worst of Darktail's Kin! I should have known!*

After a little while the trail veered away from the direct route to ShadowClan, heading toward the Twolegplace where Loki and Zelda lived.

They can't be going there, Violetshine thought. *They won't want to mess with Twolegs, and anyway, it's too far for the kits.*

Then Macgyver, who had been padding along to the side

of the scent trail, suddenly halted. "I can smell other cats!" he announced.

Violetshine bounded across to him, and picked up the new scent trail he had discovered. "You're right," she mewed. "There are two . . . no, three cats. I don't recognize two of them, but the third . . . oh, Rowanclaw, it's Tawnypelt!"

"What?" Rowanclaw hurried to join Violetshine and Macgyver, worry and confusion in his eyes. "You're right," he muttered, beginning to follow the new trail with his nose close to the forest floor.

The trail joined up with Sleekwhisker's trail a few fox-lengths ahead. From there all the cats went on together.

"Tawnypelt!" Yarrowleaf spat, pure hatred in her eyes. "She never wanted to let us back into the Clan."

"No," Rowanclaw meowed hoarsely. "I don't believe it. Whatever she thought about you and Sleekwhisker, she would never hurt kits."

"I'm sure she wouldn't," Violetshine agreed. "Tawnypelt is an honorable warrior. She would never do anything against the warrior code." *So what is she doing here?*

Violetshine wished desperately that Tree were with them, but he had gone with Leafstar to RiverClan, in case any trouble arose between the two Clans. *He would know what to do now,* she thought miserably.

"You know," Rowanclaw went on when they had followed the trail for several more fox-lengths, "I feel I ought to know the scent of these two other cats, but I just can't place it."

"They're not two of Darktail's rogues, are they?" Macgyver asked. "I heard they weren't all killed."

Violetshine took another deep sniff of the two scents, then shook her head. "No. I would know them," she replied with a shudder, remembering the terrible time she had spent living with Darktail and his Kin.

She had noticed a tang of blood mingled with the scents, and hoped desperately it hadn't come from the kits. *It's cat blood, not prey,* she thought. *Maybe these strange cats fought. Or maybe Tawnypelt . . .*

Her pondering broke off as Rowanclaw suddenly halted, staring into the trees. "*Now* I get it!" he exclaimed.

"Get what?" Yarrowleaf asked.

"I get where we're going. This is the way to the Twoleg nest in the old ShadowClan territory. And now I recognize those scents. They come from those two crow-food-eating kitty-pets!"

Macgyver looked puzzled. "Sleekwhisker is taking the kits to Twolegs?"

Yarrowleaf let out a wail, only for Rowanclaw to slap his tail over her mouth.

"Quiet, mouse-brain!" he hissed. "Do you want them to know we're here?"

"Oh, I'm sure you don't." An amused voice came from somewhere overhead. "That would be a *really* bad idea."

Violetshine looked up to see a huge black-and-white tom sprawled on the lowest branch of a pine tree. He had a torn ear and a fresh scratch over his nose, and powerful claws that dug into the tree bark.

"That's a *kittypet?*" she breathed out.

"Didn't your mother tell you about us?" the huge tom rasped, the amusement vanishing from his tone. "Behave yourself or the big fierce kittypets will get you?"

"Jacques! We've had trouble with Jacques and his friend, Susan, in the past," Rowanclaw told Violetshine. "But I guess by the time you came to the forest we had enough to worry about with Darktail."

"Have you got my kits?" Yarrowleaf asked tremulously. "Oh, please give them back!"

"No, I haven't got your kits, flea-brain," the tom sneered. "But I know where they are. Do you want me to show you?"

"Oh, *please!*" Yarrowleaf begged.

"Okay." The black-and-white tom rose to his paws on the branch and arched his back in a good long stretch. "But lay one claw on me and you'll never see your kits again." He jumped down from the branch and landed with a soft thump at Rowanclaw's side. Violetshine wrinkled her nose at his unfamiliar scent.

"This way," the tom meowed, with a wave of his tail.

Violetshine and the other Clan cats followed him around a bramble thicket and along a path that wound through banks of ferns. At one point a gap in the undergrowth showed her a Twoleg den surrounded by a rough stone wall, and she remembered passing it a few times when she was on patrol.

But the huge tom wasn't going to the den. He veered away, leading the Clan cats downward until he came to a rocky hollow overshadowed by gorse bushes. Water dripped slowly from a gap in the rocks, forming a tiny pool at the bottom of the hollow.

Beside the pool, Tawnypelt was crouched between two other cats. One was a light brown tabby Violetshine had never seen before; she assumed this must be the dreaded Susan. The second cat was all too familiar: Raven, the black she-cat of Darktail's Kin, who had held Violetshine back when Darktail and Sleekwhisker had tried to drown Needletail in the lake.

On the other side of the pool Violetshine spotted Sleek-whisker with Nettle, another of Darktail's rogues, who had mated with Yarrowleaf. Two tiny kits were huddled together beside them, looking up at him with wide, frightened eyes.

"My kits!" Yarrowleaf gasped.

"Yarrowleaf!" Flaxkit wailed, springing up to run to her, only to be batted to the ground with a careless swipe of Nettle's paw.

Yarrowleaf let out a screech and sprang down into the hollow, gathering the trembling kits close to her. Violetshine braced her muscles, ready for a fight to break out, but Nettle simply gave her a contemptuous glance.

"These are my kits," he told Yarrowleaf. "They're staying with me."

Yarrowleaf glared at him, while Violetshine wondered how any she-cat could bear to mate with the obnoxious Nettle, let alone have kits with him.

The black-and-white kittypet strolled down into the hollow and sat beside his denmate, while Rowanclaw and the rest of the patrol remained at the top of the slope.

"Tawnypelt, what's going on?" Rowanclaw demanded.

"I wish I knew," Tawnypelt growled, her green eyes narrowing in a look of fury. "When Leafstar and the others left for RiverClan, Sleekwhisker asked me if I wanted to go hunting with her. But when we got out into the forest, she disappeared, and then these two bee-brains jumped me." She flicked her tail at the kittypets. "At least I gave them something to remember me by."

Violetshine had already noticed the fresh scratch on the black-and-white tom's nose. Now she saw that the tabby kittypet was missing several clumps of fur down one side, and Tawnypelt had a trickle of drying blood on one shoulder.

Thank StarClan! Violetshine thought. *Tawnypelt is a prisoner, not a traitor!*

"I see." There was the first hint of a growl in Rowanclaw's voice. "And then I suppose Sleekwhisker doubled back to camp and took the kits. Very neat. But I still don't see what you want with Tawnypelt."

"Oh, she's especially for you, Rowanclaw." Sleekwhisker rose to her paws and faced her former leader, gazing up at him with triumph in her eyes. "You were a weak leader of Shadow-Clan. I was miserable growing up, and many cats I cared about died because you failed to deal with Darktail."

Rowanclaw bowed his head. "All true," he admitted. "But I have paid for it."

"Not enough!" Sleekwhisker's voice was savage. "Now I'm going to have my revenge, because I've taken the thing you love most—Tawnypelt!

Rowanclaw suddenly stiffened, flexing his claws into the leaf-mold on the forest floor. "You may have taken her, but you won't keep her," he snarled.

"No—I won't keep her. I'm going to kill her," Sleekwhisker meowed. "And you're going to watch."

"I'd like to see you try!" Tawnypelt spat at her.

"Oh, I'll do more than *try*," Sleekwhisker assured her. "Because if any other cat twitches a whisker, the kits will never see another sunrise."

"No!" Yarrowleaf yowled.

She tried to gather her kits closer, but Nettle thrust her away and stood over the two shivering scraps, blocking them from any other cat.

"He'd kill his own kits?" Macgyver murmured, horror and disbelief in his voice. "I knew Darktail's rogues were evil, but this is even worse than I imagined."

For a moment Nettle stood silent; then Violetshine saw him turn his head slowly toward Rowanclaw.

"There is one thing you could do," he told the former leader, his eyes gleaming with mockery. "We'll accept your life in exchange for Tawnypelt's . . . except that we know you're too weak to sacrifice yourself for her."

Rowanclaw drew himself up, quickly and firmly, and Violetshine held her breath in expectation of what he would do or say. But for a moment Rowanclaw didn't respond.

Violetshine let her gaze travel over the cats in the hollow, wondering what would happen if it came to a fight. They were a match for the rogues in numbers, except that Yarrowleaf's first duty would be to protect the kits. And all their opponents, even the kittypets, were formidable fighters.

And what can we do, if Nettle is prepared to kill the kits?

Then Violetshine heard a swift command from Rowanclaw, muttered from the side of his mouth. "Be ready."

Heartened to think that her former leader had a plan, Violetshine tensed, ready to spring, though she tried not to give any outward sign that she might be a threat to the rogues in the hollow.

"Very well," Rowanclaw meowed. "I will sacrifice myself, Nettle, provided that you release Tawnypelt and let Yarrowleaf take her kits."

"Do you think I'm mouse-brained?" Nettle's eyes were insolent. "Tawnypelt can go, but the kits are *mine*. Yarrowleaf will never see them again."

"Nettle, I beg you," Rowanclaw began, taking a pace or two down into the hollow. "I know I was a weak leader . . . I let Darktail and his Kin destroy my Clan, and I alone should bear their suffering. I deserve everything you can do to me."

His head was drooping submissively and his tail trailed on the ground. He was the exact image of a weak and defeated cat. Violetshine could see the contempt and anticipation in Nettle's and Sleekwhisker's eyes.

"Grab the kits! Run!"

Rowanclaw's yowl split the quiet air. At the same moment,

he exploded upward in a massive leap that brought him down on top of Nettle, thrusting him away from the kits. Nettle let out a screech, and the two cats rolled across the hollow in a tight knot of slashing claws and teeth. Sleekwhisker dived in and attacked Rowanclaw from behind.

At the same moment Yarrowleaf snatched up Hopkit by the scruff, while Tawnypelt leaped across the pool to grab Flaxkit. Together the two she-cats raced up the side of the hollow and vanished into the undergrowth.

Raven and the tabby kittypet streaked in pursuit, but Violetshine sprang in front of them, with Macgyver at her side.

"This is for Needletail!" Violetshine hissed as she flung herself at Raven, digging her claws into the black she-cat's shoulders. Raven's paws skidded under her onslaught, and the two of them slid back down the slope. Violetshine's breath was driven out of her as she landed hard on a rock that jutted out of the ground.

Raven's eyes gleamed close to her own. "Darktail should have killed you when he had the chance," she snarled.

In answer, Violetshine lashed out with one forepaw and felt her claws rake across Raven's shoulder. The black she-cat let out a shriek of pain and jerked her head forward, her teeth snapping at Violetshine's throat.

Violetshine thrust herself back, bringing up her hind paws to batter Raven in the belly. She felt a surge of triumph as her enemy scrabbled at the ground to get away. She was starting to rise to her paws to chase Raven off when something struck her hard from behind and a heavy weight landed on her, blotting out the light as she fell to the ground.

The huge tom's voice spoke in her ear. "Get ready to die, flea-pelt!"

Violetshine squirmed helplessly under his weight. She had a mouthful of fur and couldn't breathe. Sharp pain clawed through her hindquarters. Darkness welled up around her as if she were being whirled downward into a bottomless pool.

Suddenly the weight vanished. Gasping, spitting out fur, Violetshine tottered to her paws to see Tawnypelt fighting with the black-and-white kittypet.

She came back! Violetshine realized with relief.

The kittypet's hulking body and powerful but random blows were no match for Tawnypelt's swift battle skills. She darted in and landed blows on his muzzle and his shoulders, then jumped back out of range before he could retaliate. Within a few heartbeats he turned and fled in the direction of the nearby Twoleg den.

Violetshine drew deep, panting breaths as she gazed around. Macgyver was chasing off the tabby kittypet. Raven and Sleekwhisker were limping up the far side of the hollow, to disappear into the undergrowth.

"You've betrayed the Clans for the last time!" Violetshine yowled after them. "Don't show your faces here again!"

At the bottom of the hollow Nettle lay dead, his body half in and half out of the pool, his blood slowly spreading into the water. And beside him . . .

Violetshine let out a choking sound. "Oh, no! Rowanclaw!"

The former leader lay stretched out close to Nettle's body. He still lived, but blood was pulsing steadily from a gash in his throat. His eyes were glazed, and his chest heaved as he struggled to breathe.

Tawnypelt flashed past Violetshine and flung herself down beside her dying mate. "Rowanclaw . . . oh, Rowanclaw," she whispered. "Stay with me!"

Rowanclaw blinked up at her. "No, this is for the best," he murmured. "It was my fault that ShadowClan was destroyed. But don't worry," he added reassuringly, reaching out a paw to touch Tawnypelt's shoulder. "Tigerheart will return. I've seen him in my dreams. . . ."

Violetshine wasn't sure she could believe that, and she guessed that Tawnypelt didn't, either.

"Good-bye, Tawnypelt," Rowanclaw mewed. He let out one last breath and his body went limp. His eyes closed. The flow of blood from his throat slowed, then stopped.

"No . . ." Tawnypelt nuzzled his shoulder. "Rowanclaw, you had nine lives. You *must* come back."

For a few moments Violetshine watched, hardly daring to breathe. *Is it possible that StarClan refused to take back his lives?* she asked herself. *Could he have been Rowanstar all along?*

But as the heartbeats passed and Rowanclaw didn't move, Violetshine realized that the hope was vain. The former leader was truly dead.

"Come on," Violetshine mewed gently, bending over to touch her nose to Tawnypelt's head. "Let's carry him back to camp for his vigil. He gave back his lives," she added, struggling to keep her voice steady. "But he died like a Clan leader."

Macgyver padded down the slope to join them and help them lift Rowanclaw's body. "What do you think, Tawnypelt?" he asked. "Will you be able to lead ShadowClan now?"

Tawnypelt stared at him as if for a moment she didn't understand the question. Then she shook her head. "Not after this," she replied. "Not without Rowanclaw. ShadowClan is dead."

CHAPTER 18

Alderheart watched Velvet carefully as she padded in front of him around the camp. He stood beside her as she paused to watch Ivypool's kits tumbling and playing in front of the nursery, and joined in with her soft *mrrows* of laughter at the little creatures' antics. The sun was going down, and every cat was enjoying the last of the warmth before shadows filled the stone hollow.

A quarter moon had passed since Briarlight's death, and Alderheart could finally think without pain about how much she would have enjoyed watching the kits.

She gave so much to the Clan, he thought, *and we'll all miss her, but I know she'll be able to run again in StarClan.*

"Your leg is much better," Alderheart told Velvet as they resumed their walk. "You're hardly limping at all now."

He was glad she was better, but he suppressed a wistful sigh at the thought that she didn't need his help anymore, and soon she would go back to the Twolegplace.

We'll still be friends, though, won't we?

As they turned back before they reached the thorn tunnel, Alderheart spotted Sparkpelt and Larksong talking to

Bramblestar in the middle of the camp.

"They all look pleased about something," Velvet mewed.

"Maybe there's some good news," Alderheart responded. "We could certainly do with some. I'd better get back," he added. "There'll be herbs to sort, even if no sick cats come by."

Reluctantly he began leading Velvet back to the medicine cats' den. After her brief visit when Briarlight died, Leafpool had returned to RiverClan, and Jayfeather would shred Alderheart's fur if he thought that he was shirking his duties.

"I can help you," Velvet offered. "I've learned even more about herbs since I've been with you in the medicine-cat den. I can be useful!"

When they slipped past the bramble screen into the den, Alderheart saw that Jayfeather was peering down Rosepetal's throat, while Fuzzball bounced around at his paws.

"What's wrong with her, Jayfeather?" he asked. "Can I fetch the herb for her? I know lots now!"

Jayfeather muttered something between his teeth, of which Alderheart caught the words *annoying little furball*. Suddenly worried about what he had done, Alderheart beckoned the little ginger tom with a twitch of his ears.

"Are you okay with Jayfeather?" he asked in an undertone. "I know he can be difficult—"

"Oh, *no!*" Fuzzball exclaimed, blinking up adoringly at the skinny gray tabby. "Jayfeather is so cool! I know he's strict, but that's because he's so important."

Alderheart exchanged an amused glance with Velvet. *There's no accounting for tastes. . . .*

"Hi, Jayfeather," he meowed. "Can I do anything to help?"

Jayfeather's only reply was a slight shake of his head. He straightened up from examining Rosepetal. "It's only a sore throat," he told her. "I'll give you some tansy for it, but you can go back to your warrior duties." Then his glance fell on Alderheart and Velvet. "On second thought," he added to Rosepetal, "maybe you'd better spend the night here."

"Oh, come on, Jayfeather!" Rosepetal meowed. "It's not that bad."

"I still don't want you passing the sickness on to other cats," Jayfeather retorted. "We had enough of that with the belly-ache. Velvet, how's your leg doing?"

"It's much better, thanks," Velvet replied, clearly confused by the abrupt change of subject.

Jayfeather bent his head and gave the injury—barely visible now among Velvet's long gray fur—a good sniff. "You're right, it is," he mewed. "Now that Rosepetal's here, you'd better move into the apprentices' den with Fuzzball. We need the space, and I don't want to send you back to the Twolegplace sick."

So that's what it's all about! Alderheart felt his shoulder fur beginning to bristle. He sensed that Jayfeather felt threatened because he and Velvet were so close, but he didn't have to make her feel so unwelcome. *He's only fussing over Rosepetal because he wants Velvet out of our den.*

"I don't know when I'll be able to go back to the Twoleg-place," Velvet responded sadly. "I don't know whether my housefolk will ever come home. But you're right, Jayfeather.

I shouldn't take up space in the medicine-cat den now that I'm better."

With a huge effort Alderheart made his pelt lie flat again. *I don't like this, but I have to admit that Jayfeather has a point. Velvet doesn't need to be here anymore.*

While Jayfeather was fetching the honey for Rosepetal, the bramble screen swayed back, and Twigpaw barreled into the den. "Guess what, Alderheart!" she exclaimed. "Sparkpelt and Bramblestar say that I'm ready for my warrior assessment."

"That's great news!" Alderheart told her.

"Larksong's going to assess Finpaw, too," Twigpaw continued, her eyes sparkling. "And I'm *finally* going to be a ThunderClan warrior!"

"I'm glad you've *finally* decided to settle down," Jayfeather mewed waspishly.

"Pay no attention to him," Rosepetal put in, with a flick of her tail at Jayfeather. "We're all really pleased for you, Twigpaw."

"Yes, congratulations," Velvet added.

Alderheart could feel a purr surging through his whole body. He thought that he would burst with pride. *I can't believe that the tiny little kit Needletail and I found will be a warrior tomorrow!*

"Come on," he meowed to Velvet. "I'll help you get settled into the apprentices' den."

"Oh, are you joining us, Velvet?" Twigpaw asked. "I'll help you make a nest. It's pretty crowded in there just now: there's me and Finpaw, Eaglepaw, Shellpaw, Stempaw, and Plumpaw, as well as Fuzzball. But there'll be two less after tomorrow!"

Still fizzing with excitement, she headed out of the den again.

Alderheart and Velvet followed more slowly. "I'll miss having you around all the time," Alderheart murmured as they padded across the camp. "You'll still come and help in the medicine-cat den during the day, won't you?"

Velvet's reply was cut off by a disturbance at the mouth of the thorn tunnel. Poppyfrost, Shellpaw, and Bumblestripe were returning from a border patrol, but they weren't alone. A strange cat was with them: a powerful tom who, for all his size and strength, looked very nervous to be entering a Clan camp. More of the ThunderClan cats were gathering around to find out who the stranger was.

"That's Ajax!" Velvet exclaimed. "He's a kittypet like me. He lives with his housefolk just a few dens away from mine."

She veered aside to greet her friend, but before she reached him, Squirrelflight raced past and confronted the newcomer. "What's going on?" she asked.

"We found this kittypet on ThunderClan territory," Poppyfrost reported.

"We were going to chase him off," Bumblestripe added, "but he said he was looking for Velvet and Fuzzball, so we thought we should bring him to camp."

"And why are you looking for them?" Bramblestar asked, padding up to stand beside his deputy.

"I hope we're not planning to take in *more* kittypets," Sparkpelt put in, with an unfriendly look at Ajax.

"Right," Thornclaw meowed. "We have too many as it is."

Several other cats were murmuring agreement.

Squirrelflight whirled around, her gaze raking over them. "We'll respect Bramblestar's decision, whatever it is," she snapped.

"But I don't *want* to stay with you," Ajax protested. "I like my housefolk just fine, thanks. I only want to talk to Velvet and Fuzzball."

Velvet slipped through the crowd to stand in front of him, and Alderheart followed, along with Fuzzball, who scurried across from the medicine cats' den. Jayfeather followed with a curious look on his face.

"Hi, Ajax," Velvet mewed, dipping her head toward him.

"Hi!" Fuzzball added, with an excited little bounce. "It's great to see you, Ajax."

"Thank goodness I've found you," Ajax responded. "I thought I'd be wandering around this creepy forest all night. I've come to tell you that your housefolk are back, and they've fixed their dens after the fire. Won't you come home where it's safe?"

"Oh, we're fine here!" Fuzzball exclaimed. "I've had such a great time with these wild cats, and now I can hunt and fight just like they can. And I've learned about all sorts of herbs."

Alderheart spotted several cats exchanging amused glances at the little tom's enthusiastic boasting.

"But I've *really* missed my housefolk," Fuzzball went on. "And they'll be so happy to see me." Blinking happily, he gazed around at the cats gathered around him. "Thanks for being such great friends. Especially you, Jayfeather."

Alderheart gave Velvet a long look. *I'm really going to miss her,* he thought.

"That's good news, that you can go home now," Bramblestar meowed firmly. "But since it's getting dark, you're welcome to stay the night and leave in the morning." His brisk tone made it quite clear that the two kittypets weren't invited to think about staying any longer with the Clan.

"I'm not sure about this," Ajax muttered as Velvet and Fuzzball led him over to the apprentices' den. "It's dark and crowded in there," he added as he peered through the ferns, wrinkling his nose at the scent of Clan cats. "I don't want to get fleas."

"We offer him a bed for the night, and he fusses about fleas," Sparkpelt murmured to Alderheart. "Does he think we're *rogues?*"

Fuzzball had dashed over to the fresh-kill pile and returned with a large thrush. "Look," he mewed to Ajax, "I've brought you some prey."

Ajax stared at the bird, clearly struggling to stay polite. "It's got feathers," he choked out after a moment.

"Well, yes, it's a bird," Fuzzball responded. "Don't you want it?"

"Er . . . no, I'll pass, thanks," Ajax told him. "I had a big meal earlier, so I'm not really hungry."

"Your friend is a bit . . . strange," Alderheart meowed to

Velvet. He had fetched a vole to share with her, and they crouched side by side to eat in the gathering twilight.

"I know," Velvet replied. "But he's a good friend to come so far to find us. I know he doesn't like to stray too far from his housefolk."

"Do you want to get back to *your* housefolk?" Alderheart asked her.

For a moment Velvet hesitated, and Alderheart felt his heart lift in the hope that she would stay. *I know that would be a really bad idea, but still . . .*

"Yes," Velvet finally responded with a sigh. "But there are some parts of Clan life that I'm going to miss."

As she spoke, she gave Alderheart a shy, sideways glance, and he realized that she was talking about him. Not sure how to react to her, he concentrated on gulping down his share of the vole.

Later that night, Alderheart couldn't sleep. The den seemed empty without Velvet sleeping close by him. He tossed and turned in his bedding, feeling hotter and more uncomfortable with every heartbeat. He was fearful of disturbing Jayfeather and Rosepetal, but finally he couldn't stand being in the den any longer. Rising to his paws, he slipped stealthily past the bramble screen. Out in the open, he stood drinking in the cool night air and gazing up at the frosty glitter of Silverpelt splashed across the sky.

A quiver in his whiskers told Alderheart that some cat was standing beside him; he turned his head to see Jayfeather.

"You may think it would be better, easier, outside of the medicine cats' den," his fellow medicine cat meowed. "But it won't."

"What do you mean?" Alderheart asked, his eyes widening in confusion.

"I know you and Velvet are starting to care for each other." Jayfeather's tone was dry and unemotional. "And I know how that story usually ends."

"But I—" Alderheart began.

"I understand," Jayfeather interrupted. "Your *feelings* aren't wrong, but acting on them would be wrong. A mate and kits can't be part of a medicine cat's life. Your responsibilities to the Clan mean that you stand as a father to them, and they need to be your focus. You know Leafpool's my mother, right? You've heard that story?"

Alderheart nodded, and tried once more to speak, but Jayfeather forestalled him.

"Leafpool decided to fall in love and have kits," he went on. "Then she had to pretend that they were Squirrelflight's, and Squirrelflight went along with that because she loved her sister. That decision ruined part of my life, and my littermates'—especially my sister's life, because Hollyleaf killed Ashfur to keep the secret."

Jayfeather fixed his blind gaze on Alderheart, sounding unusually serious. "We need you in ThunderClan, Alderheart. You're a *good* medicine cat. You work hard to keep your Clan healthy, and you have a real connection to StarClan. And you're young: you'll take care of the next generation of ThunderClan cats, just as you looked after Twigpaw. If ThunderClan had to lose you, it would be like a wound that wouldn't heal."

For a few heartbeats Alderheart was too stunned and flattered to speak. *Is this really* Jayfeather *telling me this?*

"It's true, I like Velvet," he mewed at last. "And I do feel a pull toward her. But you don't have to worry, Jayfeather. I would never leave ThunderClan. I don't doubt any longer that my place is here. It's just . . . well, it's nice to have a cat to talk to who doesn't need my help. I'll miss that."

"Really?" Jayfeather sounded surprised and relieved. "You weren't thinking you might go with Velvet to the Twolegplace?"

"No," Alderheart responded. "I was thinking about how to say good-bye."

Jayfeather gave his shoulder fur a couple of awkward licks, clearly finding it hard to respond. "Thanks, Alderheart," he meowed with a clumsy dip of his head. "That's good to hear." He took a pace backward and disappeared into the den.

Alderheart watched him go, letting out a purr of affection. *I know where I belong,* he thought. *It's with you, you grouchy, difficult, dedicated furball. And with ThunderClan.*

Dawn had turned the sky above the hollow to a soft rose color as Alderheart hovered in the entrance to the medicine cat den. Across the camp, Velvet and Fuzzball were saying good-bye to some of the other cats, while Ajax waited impatiently beside the mouth of the thorn tunnel.

The cowardly part of Alderheart wanted to hide in his den until Velvet was gone, but he saw her glancing around, her nostrils flaring to catch his scent, and he knew she would be hurt if he didn't appear.

Bracing himself, Alderheart emerged from his den and padded across the camp. Velvet left the group of cats around her and came to meet him.

"I'm going to miss having you around camp," he mewed.

"I'll miss you, too," Velvet responded, a slight quiver in her voice. "But I know there's no way we could be together. We lead such different lives. I can't stay here, and I know you have responsibilities and can't leave your Clan."

Alderheart nodded. "Thanks for understanding, Velvet. I'll never forget you."

Velvet stretched out her neck, and the two cats touched noses briefly. "Good-bye, Alderheart," she mewed.

"Hey, Velvet!" Ajax's raucous yowl came from the camp entrance. "Are we standing around here all day?"

"I have to go." Velvet blinked sadly at Alderheart, then turned and trotted briskly toward the other kittypets.

"Good-bye," Alderheart called after her.

Velvet's sweet scent drifted in the air for a few moments. Then she was gone.

CHAPTER 19

❧

Twigpaw's heart was pounding uncomfortably as she left the camp and padded into the forest with Sparkpelt by her side.

I know I'm ready to become a warrior, she thought. *I don't think I can bear it if it doesn't happen today. Suppose something goes wrong? I'm so tired of waiting!*

She knew that somewhere in the forest Finpaw was doing his assessment under Larksong's watchful gaze, but there was no sign of them now, only a fading scent trail from when they had headed out shortly before.

To begin with, Sparkpelt took the old Twoleg path that led to the abandoned den, but before they reached it, she veered off into the undergrowth and halted beside a bramble thicket.

"Right," she meowed. "I want you to catch as much prey as you can by sunhigh. You won't see me, but I'll be watching you."

This is it! Twigpaw struggled to keep her voice steady as she replied. "Okay, Sparkpelt."

Her mentor's stern gaze suddenly softened. "No need to be nervous," she meowed cheerfully. "You're an excellent hunter, and hedgehogs will fly if you don't pass this assessment." With that she turned and rapidly disappeared among the ferns.

Twigpaw stared after her. Since her return to Thunder-Clan, she had felt that Sparkpelt didn't like her much, and hadn't wanted to be her mentor. Now she was heartened by Sparkpelt's praise, and her confidence flowed back like a stream released from the ice of leaf-bare.

I can do this!

Parting her jaws to taste the air, Twigpaw picked up the scent of vole, and located it underneath a nearby holly bush. She fell into the hunter's crouch, then crept forward until she was close enough to pounce, and she killed the vole with a swift bite to its neck.

"Thank you, StarClan, for this prey," she murmured.

The easy catch made Twigpaw feel even more confident. Gazing around her at the sunlit forest, glowing with the reds and golds of leaf-fall, she felt energy filling her like rain filling up a dip in the ground.

"I'm going to enjoy this," she mewed aloud.

Sunhigh was approaching, and as Twigpaw waited for her mentor to return, she felt satisfied with her hunt. She had caught several more pieces of prey, scratching earth over them until she was ready to carry them back to camp.

Now Twigpaw spotted a blackbird that had alighted on an ivy-covered tree stump in a clearing just ahead of her. Making sure that her tail was low and still, she stalked carefully toward it.

At the last moment, the blackbird took off. Twigpaw

leaped, remembering the trick Sparkpelt had shown her for hunting birds, and aimed her body above where she could see the blackbird. She intercepted it easily, and landed with the bird in her jaws.

Just as Twigpaw turned, carrying the blackbird, she heard the rustling sound of something racing through the undergrowth. Dropping her prey, she picked up the scent of rabbit, and not just that.

There's something else. Twigpaw drew in a deep breath to taste the air. *Finpaw's scent, too!*

A heartbeat later, the rabbit shot out of a bank of ferns and raced across the clearing toward Twigpaw. Finpaw was hard on its paws. The rabbit let out a squeal of terror as it spotted Twigpaw right in front of it, and it veered aside, but Twigpaw was too fast for it. With a massive leap, she slammed a paw down on its hind legs, while Finpaw pounced on its shoulders and bit its throat to kill it.

"Great catch!" A voice came from behind Twigpaw.

She turned to see Larksong emerging from the undergrowth with Sparkpelt just behind him.

"You've both hunted very well," Larksong continued.

Sparkpelt nodded. "We're especially impressed by your teamwork, catching that rabbit," she meowed. "And, Larksong, did you see the way Twigpaw caught that bird? I couldn't have done better myself."

Twigpaw felt almost embarrassed at the gleam of approval in her mentor's eyes. Pride warmed her from ears to tail-tip, particularly when she remembered how she and Sparkpelt had gotten off on the wrong paw.

Sparkpelt thinks much better of me now. I must really be doing well!

As Twigpaw and her Clanmates returned to the camp, laden with the prey the two apprentices had caught, Lilyheart and Ivypool came bounding up to them.

"We were watching for you," Lilyheart meowed. "It looks as if you had a good hunt."

"We knew you'd do well," Ivypool added.

Twigpaw was purring so hard she had to let her prey drop. It meant a lot to her, to be praised by the cat who had mothered her and her first mentor in ThunderClan. *She left her kits in camp, just so she could wait to congratulate me!*

"Let me take that." Ivypool collected her catch and carried it off to the fresh-kill pile. Lilyheart laid her tail over Twigpaw's shoulders and guided her toward the medicine cats' den.

Alderheart was waiting there, and Twigpaw's eyes widened in disbelief as she saw the two cats who were with him.

"Hawkwing! Violetshine!" she exclaimed. "I didn't expect to see you here."

"Alderheart arranged it," Hawkwing meowed.

"Yes, I talked Bramblestar into letting them come," Alderheart added, obviously pleased with himself. "I didn't want them to miss your warrior ceremony."

"It's really going to happen, after so long!" Violetshine purred, pressing her muzzle into Twigpaw's shoulder.

"Thank you, Alderheart," Twigpaw mewed, blinking at him gratefully. "This means so much to me."

A scurry of paw steps announced Finpaw's arrival; he threw himself on Hawkwing, butting him in the side with his head.

"Take it easy," Hawkwing protested with a *mrrow* of amusement. "Show a bit of respect."

Twigpaw remembered Finpaw telling her that Hawkwing had helped take care of him when he was a kit and his father, Sandynose, was missing. It was good to see that they were still close.

"I'm so glad you're here to see me become a warrior," Finpaw declared. "It's almost as good as having my own family here. Are they all okay?" he added, suddenly sounding a little nervous.

"They're fine," Hawkwing assured him.

"And they don't mind that I came to ThunderClan?"

"Oh, they *mind*," Hawkwing replied. "They didn't want to lose you, and they think you should have stayed with SkyClan. But I think they'll come around after some time has passed. You can always talk to them at Gatherings."

"Thanks, Hawkwing," Finpaw mewed fervently.

"It's all my fault," Twigpaw murmured, her pelt prickling with guilt at the thought that she had dragged Finpaw away from his family and his Clan.

"No, it's not, you daft furball," Finpaw whispered back. "I'd rather be here with you anyway."

Twigpaw's heart swelled with happiness. *I've had so many challenges, these last few moons, but I'm so lucky to have found Finpaw and to have him in my life.*

"Come here," Lilyheart meowed to her, stepping forward

again. "I think you've got half the forest in your pelt."

"Yes, you can't be made a warrior looking like that," Violet-shine agreed, combing a dead leaf out of Twigpaw's fur.

Twigpaw ducked away. "Paws off!" she protested. "I'm not a kit!" She gave her pelt a shake and her chest fur a couple of quick licks. "There. Happy now?"

"I think you look fine," Hawkwing purred.

"Let all cats old enough to catch their own prey join here beneath the Highledge for a Clan meeting!"

The yowl startled Twigpaw. While she had been talking to her kin, she hadn't realized that her Clanmates had begun to gather around. Now she looked up to see Bramblestar leave the Highledge and leap down the tumbled rocks into the camp. Sparkpelt and Larksong followed close behind him.

"I hear that I have to make two new warriors," Bramblestar meowed.

He padded forward to take his place at the center of the circle of cats and beckoned with his tail for Twigpaw to join him.

Twigpaw felt her paws tingling with excitement as she joined her Clan leader. She was finding it hard to breathe. She had heard the words of the warrior ceremony so many times, and now, at last, they were to be spoken for her.

"I, Bramblestar, leader of ThunderClan, call upon my warrior ancestors to look down on this apprentice. She has trained hard to understand the ways of your noble code, and I commend her to you as a warrior in her turn."

Now Bramblestar rested his amber gaze on Twigpaw; she raised her head to look at him without blinking.

"Twigpaw," the Clan leader continued, "do you promise to uphold the warrior code and to protect and defend this Clan, even at the cost of your life?"

All Twigpaw's heart was in her words as she replied. "I do."

"Then by the powers of StarClan," Bramblestar declared, "I give you your warrior name. Twigpaw, from this moment you will be known as Twigbranch. StarClan honors your energy and the way you have carefully thought out where you belong. You have proven over and over that your heart is in ThunderClan, but I'm also impressed by the way you care for all the Clans, and for how they function together. Having such a wide view will make you a stronger warrior.

"I give you the name Twigbranch in memory of the way you came to our Clan as a small, fragile kit, and have grown into a strong warrior, just as a twig grows into a branch. We welcome you as a warrior of ThunderClan."

Twigbranch shivered with happiness as Bramblestar rested his muzzle on her head. She gave his shoulder a respectful lick, then withdrew to stand again beside her kin and Finpaw.

"Twigbranch! Twigbranch!"

As the rest of her Clan acclaimed her, Twigbranch looked around at their shining eyes and waving tails and knew that, at last, she belonged.

She watched as Finpaw had his warrior ceremony, nodding in agreement as Bramblestar praised his courage and his dedication to his new Clan, and joined in joyfully to chant his warrior name, Finleap.

The clamor was still continuing when a sharp cry rang out over the camp from Brightheart, who was standing guard at the mouth of the thorn tunnel.

"Bramblestar!"

Every cat whirled to face the camp entrance. A jolt of alarm ran through Twigpaw as she recognized Grassheart and Strikestone, who had burst into the camp and were racing across to the crowd of ThunderClan warriors. Their eyes were wild and their fur bristling.

Brightheart bounded after them. "I couldn't stop them!" she gasped.

Bramblestar thrust himself to the front of the crowd, sliding out his claws and letting his shoulder fur bristle up. "What does this mean?" he demanded with a lash of his tail. "What are you doing here?"

Grassheart and Strikestone skidded to a halt in front of him. "I'm sorry, Bramblestar," Grassheart panted. "We haven't come to attack you. But the missing ShadowClan cats are back—along with Tigerheart. We need Hawkwing."

Shocked caterwauls rose up from the assembled Thunder-Clan cats.

"Tigerheart!"

"Where has he been?"

"Is Dovewing with him?" That was Ivypool, pushing her way through the crowd to face the two intruders with anxiety in her blue eyes.

The intruders didn't seem to be listening to the questions of the cats who were pressing around them.

"Hawkwing, you have to come now," Strikestone meowed urgently. "Tigerheart is dead!"

CHAPTER 20

Violetshine whisked out of the thorn tunnel behind her father and the two ShadowClan warriors. Alderheart brought up the rear; after Strikestone's shattering news that Tigerheart was dead, he had insisted on coming with them—with Bramblestar's permission—to see if he could help.

I can't believe Tigerheart is dead, Violetshine thought, *especially so soon after Rowanclaw died.* Tigerheart had always been so strong, so full of life, and so kind to her when she was a kit, bewildered in her new Clan, and missing her sister.

Violetshine knew it wasn't the same for Hawkwing and Alderheart, who hadn't known Tigerheart that well, but she could see her own shock and horror reflected in the faces of the ShadowClan cats.

"I wonder what this means for the prophecy," Alderheart meowed, catching Violetshine up to bound along beside her. "Is Tigerheart the shadow that must not be dispelled? But if he's dead . . . ?"

He let his voice trail off with a confused shake of his head.

Violetshine felt just as confused. She hadn't even realized

the direction they were heading until, a moment later, Alderheart halted.

"Hang on!" he exclaimed. "This isn't the way to the SkyClan camp. Why are we going toward WindClan?"

"We're not," Grassheart told him. "We're going to the Moonpool. The cats with Tigerheart insisted on taking his body there."

"Puddleshine and Frecklewish are with him," Strikestone added.

Alderheart shook his head sadly. "If Tigerheart is truly dead," he mewed quietly, "then I don't think StarClan can help him."

Violetshine's legs and paws were aching by the time she and the other cats reached the last steep slope that led to the Moonpool. The sun had started to go down, casting a red light over the rocks.

Her jaws gaped with astonishment as she saw the crowd of cats waiting at the foot of the slope. The first cat she spotted was Dovewing, her claws flexing, scraping anxiously at the stones. Three kits huddled beside her.

"Dovewing!" Alderheart exclaimed, rushing over to her. "You're here—you're safe! Oh, thank StarClan!"

Dovewing leaned forward briefly to touch noses with the ThunderClan medicine cat. "It's not the homecoming I wanted," she responded. "But I have to be brave for our kits."

"Yours and Tigerheart's?" Alderheart mewed, looking down at the three young cats. "The dark brown tabby looks exactly like him."

"That's Lightkit," Dovewing told him. "The gray striped tom is Shadowkit, and the gray she-cat is Pouncekit."

While Alderheart admired the kits, Violetshine was staring at the other cats who stood with Dovewing. Four of them were ShadowClan warriors.

"Berryheart, Sparrowtail, Cloverfoot, and Slatefur," she breathed out, hardly able to believe what she was seeing. "We all thought you were dead!"

Three even smaller kits were clustered around Berryheart. And beyond them were three cats Violetshine had never set eyes on before: two full-grown and one younger, the age to be an apprentice.

"Where have you all come from?" Violetshine asked.

It was Dovewing who replied. "I was living in a huge Two-legplace with Tigerheart and our kits. That's where we met Ant, Cinnamon, and Blaze." She flicked her tail toward the three strange cats. "But in the end, we knew we wanted to return. And on our way back we found Berryheart and the others."

Dovewing fell silent, and Violetshine was aware of the tension among the cats as they waited, breathless with fear and anticipation. *What are they waiting for? What is there to hope for? Tigerheart is dead!*

Movement in the shadow of the rocks alerted Violetshine, and she realized that still more cats stood with them, sharing in the anxious vigil. All the other ShadowClan cats were there, along with Leafstar and Frecklewish. She took a pace forward and dipped her head to her Clan leader.

Leafstar returned her nod. "Violetshine. Hawkwing. This is all so strange. . . . What are these cats expecting to happen?"

No cat replied to her.

Just behind Leafstar, Tawnypelt was standing, her head bowed as she stared at her paws. She seemed numb with grief.

I'm so sorry for her, Violetshine thought. *Dawnpelt, Rowanclaw, and now Tigerheart. Tawnypelt is so brave—but how can any cat bear so much loss?*

Violetshine wondered too what this would mean for the remaining ShadowClan cats.

Trying to shake off her worries and the overwhelming feeling of strangeness, Violetshine padded over to the newly returned ShadowClan warriors.

"It's so good to see you again," she meowed to Berryheart. "We'd all given you up for lost."

"It's good to see you, too, Violetpaw," Berryheart replied. "Kits, say hi to Violetpaw."

"Hi, kits." Violetshine touched noses with each of the tiny cats. "But my name is Violetshine. I'm a warrior now."

"That's great news," Berryheart purred. "And these are Hollowkit, Spirekit, and Sunkit. Maybe one of them will be your apprentice."

"Me!" Sunkit squeaked, bouncing up and down.

"No, me!"

"Me!"

Violetshine found that the ache in her heart was eased by the antics of the kits. But she knew it would be hard for Berryheart to learn that her kits would be raised in SkyClan—that

ShadowClan was gone. "That will be for the Clan leader to decide," she mewed. "So what happened to you?" she added to Berryheart. "Where have you been all this time?"

"We were all so terrified by the way Darktail took over ShadowClan," Berryheart explained. "We ran away and found a place of our own, in a tumbledown Twoleg den. Then we met Tigerheart and Dovewing traveling home, and they told us Darktail was gone, and it was safe to come back." Her expression darkened. "We were traveling back to ShadowClan when Hollowkit was attacked by an owl." She rested her tail on the kit's shoulder, and Violetshine noticed for the first time that Hollowkit had lost a few clumps of fur, and had a healing scratch on one shoulder. "Tigerheart saved Hollowkit," Berryheart went on, "but the owl injured him so badly that he didn't recover. If only we could have made it back to where he could see a medicine cat before he died. . . ."

"But he's *not* dead!" The shrill assertion startled Violetshine. She turned to see where it had come from and saw Dovewing and Tigerheart's little gray tom, Shadowkit. "I know he's not!"

A pang of sorrow clawed through Violetshine as she gazed at the kit, who faced them with wide eyes. *He's too young to understand,* she thought.

"I had a dream," Shadowkit went on. "I was playing with my father, in a place not far from here, and I *know* it was a true dream."

Violetshine stroked her tail gently down the kit's side,

noticing the dark stripes, so like his father's. "What makes you think so, little one?" she asked.

"I just do. We were in this big hollow, with boulders and bushes at the top and pine trees all around. Their branches hung down really low. At the bottom of the hollow there were ferns and bramble thickets, and I lived in one of them with Dovewing and Pouncekit and Lightkit. We all played moss-ball with Tigerheart."

Violetshine exchanged a puzzled look with Berryheart. "That sounds like the ShadowClan camp."

"But he's never been there!" Berryheart protested.

A shiver passed through Violetshine as if she had been lapping at icy water. "One of his parents must have told him about it," she murmured to Berryheart, but all the same, Shadowkit's words had woken a tiny spark of hope inside her.

Suppose it was a vision?

Time crawled past until the last streaks of sunlight disappeared, far away over ShadowClan territory. Violetshine was finding it harder and harder to keep her spark of hope alive, while the cats huddled together in the gathering shadows. The first warriors of StarClan appeared in the sky, and a pale moon rose above the summit of the hill.

"Whatever happens," Cloverfoot whispered after a while, "it will be good to go back to the ShadowClan camp. It never stopped being home, no matter what happened."

"But ShadowClan doesn't live there anymore," Violetshine

told her miserably. "There were so few of them left, and they didn't have a leader, so they joined SkyClan in their new camp."

The returning ShadowClan cats stared at her, horror in their eyes, their ears lying flat as their shoulder fur began to bristle.

"What do you mean?" Sparrowtail demanded. "No leader? What happened to Rowanstar?"

Violetshine swallowed, wishing that she didn't have to be the bearer of such terrible news. "Rowanstar is dead," she replied. "But before he died, he . . . he gave his nine lives back to StarClan. He didn't think he was worthy to be a leader because he had let Darktail destroy his Clan."

Stunned, the ShadowClan cats gazed at one another. Violetshine could see that they didn't want to believe what she had told them.

"I didn't know . . . that a leader could do that," Berryheart rasped.

"No cat knew, until it happened," Violetshine meowed. "And since then, StarClan hasn't sent a sign to say which cat should be ShadowClan leader in Rowanclaw's place."

"So all our Clanmates joined SkyClan?" Cloverfoot's eyes were full of pleading, as if she wanted some cat to tell her it wasn't true.

Violetshine nodded.

"Fox dung to all that!" Slatefur exclaimed loudly. "I don't *want* to be a SkyClan cat! I've always been ShadowClan, and I always will be."

His strident tones had caught the attention of Leafstar and Hawkwing, a couple of fox-lengths away. Violetshine noticed them giving him an annoyed look.

Neither cat said anything, though Leafstar was rising to her paws when the sound of paw steps came from the top of the slope, followed by the rustling sound of a cat pushing their way through the bushes that surrounded the hollow of the Moonpool.

Leafstar sat back down as Puddleshine emerged into the open. His eyes were wide, his fur bristling with shock, and his breathing came fast and shallow.

He's given up on Tigerheart at last, Violetshine thought despairingly as a murmur of sadness arose from all the cats around her.

But then there was a second sound of rustling. Puddleshine stepped aside, and a cat stepped into the open. His muscles rippled under his brown tabby fur, which gleamed in the silver wash of moonlight, and his eyes were shining.

For a heartbeat Violetshine didn't recognize him, because she had never imagined that she would ever see him again.

It can't be . . . yes, it is Tigerheart!

For a moment Tigerheart remained motionless; then, with a sudden leap, he launched himself down the rocks to land in the middle of the ShadowClan cats.

Yowls of amazement broke out as Tigerheart's Clanmates clustered around him, eagerly questioning him. Dovewing pushed through the crowd until she stood beside him.

"You're alive!" she gasped.

Violetshine withdrew to the edge of the group, beside her father and the other SkyClan cats, not wanting to disturb Tigerheart's reunion with his family and his Clanmates. She caught only snatches of what they were saying as she stared in confusion at the strong, healthy cat. "Maybe—maybe he wasn't dead after all," she stammered to Berryheart.

"Oh, yes, he was," Berryheart responded. "I know what a dead cat looks like."

Violetshine had to believe her. Even if Puddleshine had managed to revive Tigerheart, he should have been weak and wounded, not standing there as if he was ready to leap down the hills and run all the way around the lake.

The first joy of the ShadowClan cats was dying away, and Violetshine spotted uneasiness in their eyes, as if they were asking themselves the same question. Then Tigerheart seemed to stand taller, his gaze sweeping around his Clan.

"I left you," he meowed evenly. "But now I've returned. I bring with me cats who will make our Clan strong again. Accept them as I accept you. Give them your loyalty as I give you mine. I am ready to lead you."

Lead you? Violetshine could hardly believe what she was hearing.

For a moment there was a frozen silence among the ShadowClan cats. Then Juniperclaw's voice rose up to the glittering stars. "Tigerstar!"

"Tigerstar! Tigerstar!" The rest of the Clan joined in, their voices echoing around the rocks.

As the clamor died away, Tawnypelt pushed her way

through the crowd to her son's side and pressed herself against him, purring as if she was going to burst. "Tigerstar, tell us what happened," she begged at last.

It was Puddleshine who replied. "StarClan brought him back and gave him nine lives. He is the new leader of ShadowClan!"

"Yes, it was . . . amazing." Tigerstar's voice was full of wonder. "I found myself on a grassy slope, with the sun shining and a stream running around the bottom of the hill. I thought I was in StarClan—and I was, but I didn't expect what happened next."

"Go on . . . ," some cat breathed out.

"I was transported to a different place," Tigerstar began. "Rocks beneath a night sky. Rowanclaw and Dawnpelt appeared, and . . . oh, many more cats. Their fur was shining so brightly I could hardly bear to look at them. Rowanclaw told me I was being sent back to become leader of my Clan. And then they gave me nine lives."

Standing beside Leafstar and Frecklewish, Violetshine thought that the SkyClan medicine cat looked troubled, and Leafstar's eyes narrowed as she addressed the ShadowClan cats.

"I'm not going to cross the will of StarClan," she announced. "But I'm tired of ShadowClan cats treating the SkyClan camp like some sort of temporary nest. RiverClan has gone home, so your old camp is waiting for you. From now on, you need to stay out of SkyClan's camp for good. You are not welcome there—and we *will* be patrolling our borders."

Tigerstar dipped his head to the SkyClan leader with chilly politeness. "You're right, Leafstar," he meowed. "It is time for ShadowClan to go home—to the ShadowClan camp."

Beckoning with his tail, he headed down the steep moorland, and his Clan streamed after him. As she passed Violetshine, Tawnypelt paused.

"Are you coming with us?" she asked. "I know Tigerstar will be glad to have you."

"No, I'm SkyClan now," Violetshine replied, with a glance at her father. "I want to stay with Hawkwing. But thank you for asking me."

She watched sadly as the ShadowClan cats walked away. Tigerstar had been kind to her when she was a kit. And she had admired Tawnypelt for her strength, and for her commitment to her Clan despite everything she had suffered. The cats of ShadowClan had been Violetshine's Clanmates for a long time. For the first time, Violetshine thought she understood a little of what Twigbranch had felt, torn between two Clans.

Something moved uneasily in Violetshine's belly as she wondered what would become of ShadowClan now. *Tigerstar is a great cat, but so many bad things have happened. . . .*

Violetshine saw that Dovewing was leaving, too, guiding her kits down the slope with sweeps of her tail.

"Hey, Dovewing," Alderheart called out to her, surprise in his voice. "Aren't you coming back to ThunderClan?"

Dovewing halted and looked back at him, then shook her head. Her eyes were sad, but her voice was firm. "No, I belong with Tigerstar now. I've chosen a mate and kits over Thunder-Clan. I'm sorry."

Alderheart blinked in shock, and Violetshine saw his claws extend, scraping on the rock. "But we all thought you were dead," he protested. "And Ivypool will want to see you. She has kits now, too."

For a moment Dovewing hesitated, her indecision clear in her eyes. Then, leaving the kits, she bounded down the slope until she had caught up with Tigerstar. They spoke together for a few moments; then Dovewing leaped back up the slope to Alderheart.

"I'll come and visit ThunderClan before I go to Shadow-Clan," she mewed hesitantly, "if you think they'd like to see me. I've missed you all terribly. Come on, kits."

She and Alderheart headed down the slope side by side, both of them helping the kits over the uneven places.

"Well, Violetshine?" Leafstar came to stand beside her, a challenge in her voice. "Are you sure about coming back with us? You can't be like Twigpaw, or the other ShadowClan cats, and come and go as you please. Either you're a SkyClan warrior forever, or you need to leave now."

Violetshine drew herself up proudly. "I don't have the slightest doubt, Leafstar," she responded. "I'm a SkyClan cat."

CHAPTER 21

♣

A cool dawn breeze swept through the forest, and the warriors of StarClan were winking out one by one, by the time Alderheart reached the ThunderClan camp with Dovewing and her kits. He was so exhausted that he could barely put one paw in front of another, and his head was still spinning with wonder.

I can hardly believe that Tigerstar has been brought back from the dead, he thought. *Surely it's a sign that he's something special.*

Relief flowed over Alderheart like a cooling breeze as he reflected that now there were five Clans again. *I'm sure we were on the edge of disaster, but now, thank StarClan, I'm starting to think that everything will be all right.*

On the long trek from the Moonpool, Dovewing had questioned Alderheart about what had been happening since she left ThunderClan. She listened eagerly as he told her about Ivypool's and Cinderheart's kits, and grieved at the news of Briarlight's death.

"She was such an amazing cat," Dovewing meowed. "I sometimes think she had more courage than the rest of the Clan put together. I'll never forget her. I just wish I could have been there to say good-bye to her."

All the while the three kits were bouncing around their mother's paws, demanding to know all about Clan life and their kin.

"Will we be made warriors?" Pouncekit asked.

"Not right away," Dovewing told them. "You have to be apprentices first, and you're not quite old enough for that yet."

That drew a groan of protest from all three kits, but soon they were chasing around again, extending their tiny claws and bushing up their soft fur.

"I'm a warrior! Get off our territory!"

"No, you get off, mange-pelt!"

"I don't know where they get their energy from," Dovewing sighed.

Now, with the camp entrance in sight, she halted and faced Alderheart. Even in the faint light of the waning moon, he could see how nervous she looked.

"Do you think ThunderClan will forgive me?" she asked. "I ran away, and now I'm leaving to join another Clan. How can they see it as anything but a betrayal?"

Alderheart had an uneasy feeling that she might be right, but he tried to reassure her. "Every cat has been worried about you," he mewed. "They'll be so relieved to see you that they'll understand."

Dovewing didn't look as if she entirely believed him, but she said no more, and let Alderheart lead the way through the thorn tunnel and into the camp.

Inside the stone hollow the Clan hadn't yet begun to stir,

and at first Alderheart thought that no cats at all were outside their dens. Then two figures loomed up beside him: Twigbranch and Finleap, keeping their warrior vigil.

At first Twigbranch simply dipped her head to Alderheart as he entered, but when she saw Dovewing and her kits following him, she let out an excited squeal, completely forgetting the rule that she should stay silent.

"Dovewing!"

Her cry echoed around the camp. For a moment it was followed by silence; then cats came bundling out of the warriors' den, racing across the camp to surround Dovewing and the kits. Graystripe and Millie bounded over from their nests under the hazel bush, while Jayfeather and Leafpool appeared, blinking, at the entrance to the medicine cats' den.

So Leafpool is home from RiverClan, Alderheart thought, pleased to see her again.

Fastest of all, Ivypool shot out of the nursery and skidded to a halt beside her sister, pressing up against her and drinking in her scent. For a few moments she was unable to speak, she was purring so hard.

"Where have you been?" Dovewing's father, Birchfall, thrust his way through the crowd, with her mother, Whitewing, hard on his paws. "We thought you were dead."

"It's so wonderful to see you again!" Whitewing exclaimed.

Dovewing seemed almost overwhelmed at first, trying to answer every question at once, until Ivypool's kits came wriggling their way through the crowd, sniffing inquisitively at the newcomers.

"Are these yours, Ivypool?" Dovewing asked. "What lovely kits!"

"Yes, they're mine and Fernsong's," Ivypool replied proudly. "This is Bristlekit, this is Thriftkit, and this is Flipkit."

"They're kind of small," Lightkit remarked, stepping up warily to touch noses with Bristlekit. "Not like us!"

"They're only a few days old," Ivypool explained. "Their eyes only opened this morning."

"They're beautiful!" Dovewing introduced her own kits, explaining to them, "These kits are your kin. Their mother is my sister, Ivypool—you remember I told you about her."

The two sets of kits examined each other with wide-open eyes. "It's great to have kin," Pouncekit mewed with a purr of satisfaction.

Bumblestripe, who had been Dovewing's mate for a brief time, padded up and dipped his head stiffly to her. "I'm glad you're okay," he told her.

Alderheart could tell that he really meant it, but at the same time he recognized the hurt in Bumblestripe's voice. *It can't be easy, knowing she chose to be with a cat from another Clan.*

"And there's more to tell you," Alderheart meowed. "Tigerstar is alive."

His news caused barely a ripple among the Clan; they were all too focused on Dovewing's unexpected return.

"Yes, these are Tigerstar's kits," Dovewing added. "He's my mate now. I had to leave, because I was afraid I wouldn't be welcome here anymore, carrying kits with a father in ShadowClan."

For a moment there was an awkward pause, the Thunder-Clan cats exchanging doubtful glances. Alderheart supposed it was asking a bit much for them to be thrilled with the news that Tigerstar was the father of Dovewing's kits.

"Well, a lot of things have changed between the Clans," Squirrelflight declared at last. "Anyway, Dovewing, we're just happy that you're back."

"And there was another reason I left," Dovewing went on. "I was having terrible dreams where our nursery was destroyed and my kits died."

A murmur of sympathy rose from the surrounding cats.

"I wish you'd let me know," Daisy mewed, stroking Dove-wing's shoulder with her tail-tip. "I could have told you that all she-cats have weird dreams when they're expecting kits."

Dovewing flicked her tail, looking irritated. "I did what I thought was best."

Alderheart wasn't so sure that they had just been the weird dreams of a queen expecting kits. He remembered that the nursery had been damaged in the storm, though Cinder-heart's and Blossomfall's kits had been safely bedded down with the elders. *But who knows what might have happened to Dove-wing's kits, if they'd been here?* "Just a moment." Bramblestar, who had listened to all this in thoughtful silence, took a pace for-ward. "Did I hear you say Tiger*star*? What *did* happen at the Moonpool?"

Alderheart launched into the explanation of how StarClan had sent Tigerstar back to be the leader of a newly revived ShadowClan. Bramblestar pressed him with questions, his gaze intent and his tail-tip flicking to and fro. Alderheart could tell that something was disturbing him deeply.

"I don't like this," he meowed when Alderheart had finished. "There's something ominous about a Tigerstar leading ShadowClan again."

Shock jolted through Alderheart as he remembered that once there had been another Tigerstar, the infamous cat who nearly tore the Clans apart in his efforts to control the whole forest.

He was Bramblestar's father, and this new Tigerstar is his kin as well. No wonder Bramblestar has his doubts!

"Yes, I remember those days well," Graystripe put in with a shiver. "No cat wants to go through that again. What will ShadowClan be now?"

"Honestly, you don't need to worry," Dovewing responded with an irritable twitch of her whiskers. "Tigerstar is the same reasonable, good-hearted cat you've known all along. And StarClan *chose* him and brought him back to life to revive ShadowClan. He must have a great destiny."

Her eyes glowed as she spoke of her mate, and Alderheart could understand how badly she wanted to reassure her former Clanmates. But he could see she realized that the first happiness at her return had faded.

"Well, kits," Dovewing mewed, gathering them closer to her with a sweep of her tail. "It's time to go. We need to get back to your father and ShadowClan."

For a heartbeat a frozen silence settled on the cats of ThunderClan. Alderheart's belly clenched as he realized that they had all thought Dovewing was returning for good.

"You're going to *ShadowClan*?" Sparkpelt exclaimed. "You traitor!"

Ivypool said nothing, only turning her back on her sister and gathering her kits away from her.

"I'll come back to visit." Dovewing's voice was pleading. "I had to make this choice. I couldn't be torn between my Clan and the cat I love."

Her words did nothing to soothe the outrage that rose like a powerful scent from the cats who surrounded her. Even Whitewing and Birchfall looked deeply disappointed as they gazed at her.

Eventually Bramblestar stepped forward. "You need some protection for those young kits," he mewed. "I'll send a patrol with you to the ShadowClan border."

"We'll go," Birchfall offered, taking a pace that brought him to his daughter's side.

Bramblestar nodded. "Good. Fernsong, you can go too. Once you see Dovewing safely onto ShadowClan territory, you can do the dawn patrol along the border." Turning to Dovewing, he added, "We look forward to seeing you at the next Gathering. But if you're not part of the Clan anymore, you can't just drop by the camp whenever you feel like it."

For a moment Dovewing looked taken aback, as if she hadn't realized quite what her choice would mean. Then she dipped her head in acceptance. With a last glance at Ivypool, who was still refusing to look at her, she gathered her kits together and headed out of camp, escorted by Birchfall, Whitewing, and Fernsong.

As the dawn light strengthened, Squirrelflight began to arrange the remaining patrols, while some cats moved away to pick over the remains of the fresh-kill pile.

Alderheart felt so tired that his paws seemed to have turned to rocks. He dragged himself over to the medicine cats' den, muttered greetings to Leafpool and Jayfeather, and collapsed into his nest.

His wonder at the return of Tigerstar had faded into sadness. *I thought everything would be fine now. We listened to StarClan's warnings, and the missing ShadowClan cats have found their way home.*

But things hadn't worked out like that. Instead of relief that the storm had passed, there was still so much tension between the Clans and within ThunderClan itself.

Please, StarClan, show me the way forward, he prayed as he sank into the darkness of sleep.

Sunlight striking through the bramble screen woke Alderheart, and he realized that the morning was well advanced. Neither Leafpool nor Jayfeather was there. Rising from his nest, Alderheart shook scraps of debris from his pelt and gave himself a quick grooming. Then he slipped out between the brambles and into the camp.

The sky above the hollow showed a clear blue, with not a cloud in sight. There was a tang of frost in the air, but the sun was shining. Alderheart's worries of the night before seemed distant, less urgent. Now he felt fresh and invigorated.

Maybe this beautiful weather is a sign from StarClan that all will be well, now that there are five Clans again.

Wandering aimlessly around the camp, enjoying the feeling of sunlight on his fur, Alderheart reached the apprentices' den, where Velvet had stayed briefly before she went home. On the ground outside the den, in the shadow of the ferns, he spotted what he thought at first was a dead mouse. But when he hooked it out with one paw, he realized it was the scrap of fur Velvet had brought with her from the Twolegplace.

Her favorite toy, he thought. *Did she leave it behind on purpose, or did she drop it as she left?*

A little way away, outside the nursery, Ivypool was questioning Fernsong about everything that Dovewing had said when he escorted her to the ShadowClan border.

"Did she send me a message? Did she say anything about leaving ThunderClan?"

Fernsong was shifting his paws uncomfortably, obviously finding it hard to deal with his mate's persistent questioning.

On the other side of the camp, at the bottom of the tumbled rocks, Bramblestar and Squirrelflight had their heads together in some intense, worried discussion.

Suddenly Alderheart didn't want to deal with the tensions in camp. He wanted to hold on to the hopeful feeling he'd had when he first woke. Picking up the scrap of fur, he headed out of the camp, reflecting that ThunderClan could spare him long enough to take a walk.

It surely can't do any harm to return Velvet's toy to her . . . and see her one more time. . . .

* * *

Alderheart knew the general direction of the Twolegplace, across the unknown territory beyond the ThunderClan border. After a while, he was able to pick up the scent trail of the cats who had returned the night before.

But when he reached the Twolegplace, it was far bigger and louder than he had anticipated. His fur bristled as he crept along a narrow Thunderpath between two rows of Twoleg dens, and his heart thumped painfully in his chest. Somewhere close by he could hear the shouts and thumping paw steps of Twoleg kits, and farther away a dog was barking.

Monsters were sleeping in front of some of the Twoleg dens. Alderheart was scared of waking them, so he slunk past, trying to keep out of their sight and stay well away from their round black paws. He didn't know where he might find Velvet, and when he tasted the air in an attempt to pick up her scent, he was assailed by so many weird, competing smells that he couldn't distinguish any of them.

Maybe I should go back, he thought, hesitating at a spot where another Thunderpath crossed the one he was following.

Then Alderheart heard a voice. "It was so cool, living with the wild cats! I became an *amazing* hunter. And I know *all* about herbs!"

Fuzzball!

Following the sound of the voice, Alderheart leaped up onto a fence that surrounded a Twoleg den. On the other side, short, smooth grass stretched from the fence up to the den, edged by bushes covered in bright, unfamiliar flowers.

Fuzzball stood in the middle of the stretch of grass. He was talking to another cat: a white tom. Alderheart stared in astonishment as he recognized him.

That's Rippletail, one of the missing ShadowClan cats!

"Rippletail!" Alderheart called out, leaping from the fence into the garden.

Rippletail whirled around and gave Alderheart one stunned look. Then he dashed across the grass and thrust his way into the Twoleg den through a small gap in the bottom of the den door. With a whisk of his white tail, he disappeared.

"Hey, Rippletail!" Alderheart yowled after him, dropping Velvet's toy. "It's me, Alderheart from ThunderClan!"

Rippletail didn't reappear.

Fuzzball trotted up to Alderheart and touched noses with him. "Hi, Alderheart," he meowed. "It's good to see you. What did you call that cat?"

"Rippletail," Alderheart replied. "He's a ShadowClan warrior."

Fuzzball looked puzzled. "No, I think you've got it wrong. That cat's name is Buster. And I've told him *all* about life with the Clans," he added. "He would have mentioned if he knew them."

"Has he been here long?" Alderheart asked, certain that he wasn't making a mistake.

"A while." Fuzzball shrugged. "He seems very happy with his Twolegs."

Alderheart wasn't sure what to do. *If Rippletail is happy, maybe I should leave him alone.*

"Fuzzball, when you see him next, could you give him a message?" he mewed at last.

"Sure. What message?"

"Tell Buster that ShadowClan is whole again." Alderheart spoke slowly, thinking what would be best to say. "Darktail is dead and the rogues are gone, and Rippletail's littermates, Cloverfoot and Berryheart, have come back. Can you remember all that, Fuzzball?"

For once the little tom looked uncertain. "I'll try. Let's see . . . 'Tell Buster that ShadowClan is down a hole . . .'"

Alderheart suppressed a sigh. "Repeat it after me."

It took several repetitions before Fuzzball got it right and Alderheart was reasonably sure that he would remember it.

"Okay, I'll tell him," Fuzzball promised at last. "But even if he's who you think he is, I don't think he'll want to leave."

Alderheart guessed that he was right, if the way Rippletail had fled revealed how he felt. "Well, it's up to him," he declared. "Now, can you show me where Velvet lives?"

Fuzzball's eyes shone. "She'll be so glad to see you! She misses you."

Alderheart retrieved Velvet's scrap of fur and followed Fuzzball through a gap in the Twoleg fence and down another narrow Thunderpath until they stood outside a second Twoleg den. This one had a wall of red, square-cut stones around a bigger garden with small paths leading through clumps of bright flowers.

"This is Velvet's den," Fuzzball told Alderheart. "And I'd better be getting back. My housefolk's kit sometimes cries if

I'm away too long." He flicked his tail at Alderheart and padded off down the Thunderpath, pausing at the corner to look back and call out, "Tell Jayfeather hi from me. And come and see me anytime!"

Alderheart leaped up onto the top of the wall and examined the den. Almost at once he spotted Velvet, looking out through the hard, transparent stuff that blocked the gaps in the den walls.

"Velvet!" he yowled.

Velvet looked up and to Alderheart's dismay immediately disappeared.

What's wrong with me today? Alderheart wondered. *First Rippletail flees at the sight of me, and now Velvet.* A cold, hollow place opened up inside him. *Doesn't she want to see me?*

Then Alderheart saw a Twoleg open the door of the den and Velvet slip past it into the garden. He leaped down from the wall and bounded forward to meet her beside one of the clumps of flowers.

"I'm sorry I took so long," Velvet mewed, stretching forward to touch noses with Alderheart. "I had to get my housefolk to let me out, and *honestly!* They don't understand anything. A newborn kit has more sense!"

"It's okay." Privately Alderheart was appalled. *It's a good thing I didn't come with her. I wouldn't want a Twoleg telling me when I could go out and when I had to come in.* "You're here now. Look," he added, pushing the scrap of fur over to her with one paw. "I brought you this."

"My toy!" Velvet's eyes stretched wide with delight. "Oh,

thank you, Alderheart! I completely forgot it when we were leaving your camp." She let out a purr, then continued, "In the Clan, I didn't need it as much as I thought I would. I suppose it shows how different life is there."

Alderheart nodded sadly. *Yes, our lives are so different. . . .*

"It's wonderful to see you," Velvet went on softly. "Would you like me to show you around a bit?"

It can't hurt to linger a while, Alderheart thought, hoping to convince himself. "Yes," he replied. "I would like that a lot."

The sun was going down by the time Velvet led Alderheart back to her own den. "I suppose it's time for you to go," she mewed regretfully.

"Yes, I must be getting back," Alderheart responded. "Good-bye, Velvet."

"Good-bye." Velvet gave Alderheart a quick lick around his ear. "I'm glad you came," she went on. "I've missed you. But I'm not sure we can be friends. You've chosen one life, and I've chosen another."

Her amber eyes were full of sadness, but there was wisdom there too, and Alderheart knew she was right. He had been sure all along, deep down, that this was the last time he would see her.

"I'll always be grateful to ThunderClan for taking me and Fuzzball in," Velvet told him. "I want to give you something, to say thank you. Come with me."

Velvet led Alderheart around the back of the Twoleg den. The garden was different here: there weren't so many flowers.

Instead leafy green plants grew in neat rows.

"Over here," Velvet mewed, showing Alderheart a corner where some small bushes were growing.

Alderheart examined the woody stems and sniffed the broad, pointed leaves. "Is that thyme?" he asked. "It looks a bit like it, but it's different from the thyme that grows in the forest."

"Yes, it's a different kind of thyme," Velvet explained. "Twolegs plant it, and I think it's stronger than the kind you have. It's good for coughs and colds and indigestion." She began scratching at the soil until she had uprooted one of the small bushes. "There. I'd like ThunderClan to have it."

"Thank you," Alderheart responded, touched that Velvet had been so thoughtful. "I'll plant it and take care of it."

Velvet leaned into his shoulder, and for the last time he drank in her sweet scent. "Good-bye, Velvet," he murmured. "I'll never forget you."

"Good-bye, Alderheart." Velvet gazed at him for a moment longer, blinking affectionately, then whisked away around the side of the Twoleg den.

For a moment more, Alderheart stared after her. He tried to imagine a life for himself here, eating kittypet food, sleeping in a Twoleg nest, and waiting beside the door for a Twoleg to let him in or out.

No, I can't. Jayfeather was right. I'm a medicine cat, and a good one.

Yet he could not deny the pain in his heart as he remembered Velvet's beautiful eyes and soft gray fur, and more than that, her gentleness and care for every cat. *But I can't let myself think about that.*

Picking up the thyme bush, Alderheart leaped up onto the garden wall. In the sky in front of him he could see a pale half-moon rising.

Alarm clawed through him. *Oh, no . . . I'd better hurry if I'm going to make it to the Moonpool for the half-moon medicine-cat meeting!*

Night had fallen, and the half-moon floated high in the sky by the time Alderheart reached the Moonpool. He had raced there straight from the Twolegplace without returning to the ThunderClan camp, and as he climbed the last rocky slope, his spine prickled with nervousness.

Jayfeather will have something to say to me about this!

The water cascading down the rocks into the Moonpool looked like liquid starshine, and the surface of the water reflected the silver light of the moon. The beauty calmed Alderheart and made him feel that this was the place, above all others, where he belonged.

As Alderheart pushed his way through the bushes and began to follow the spiral path down to the Moonpool, he could see the other medicine cats waiting for him at the water's edge. Satisfaction warmed his pelt when he saw that Mothwing and Willowshine were there, reunited with their fellow medicine cats for the first time since Darktail had attacked their Clan.

"Greetings, Mothwing, Willowshine," he meowed as he reached the bottom of the path. "It's good to have you back."

The two RiverClan medicine cats dipped their heads in response.

"Never mind *greetings*," Jayfeather snapped. "Where have you been? We're wasting moonlight here."

"Yes, we were worried about you," Leafpool added.

"I'm sorry," Alderheart explained. "I went to the Twolegplace to see how Velvet and Fuzzball were doing."

Jayfeather gave him a scorching look from his sightless blue eyes.

"They're fine," Alderheart went on, meeting his gaze levelly. "I won't need to go there again. And look at this." He set down the thyme that Velvet had given him.

Jayfeather gave it a sniff. "It's thyme."

"Yes, but it's a different sort of thyme," Alderheart mewed. "Velvet says her Twolegs planted it, and it's stronger than the kind that grows in the forest. There's not enough to divide between the Clans," he added to the others, "but I'll plant it, and when it grows, we'll share it with you if you need it."

Jayfeather grunted, obviously unwilling to admit he was pleased. "We can give it a try, I suppose."

"There's something else," Alderheart confessed. He felt bad, because the ShadowClan tom clearly wanted to be left alone, but it wasn't a secret he felt he could keep. "I saw Rippletail, living as a kittypet in the Twolegplace. I called out to him, but he bolted into his Twoleg den and wouldn't come out."

The other medicine cats exchanged shocked glances.

"It's good to know that he's okay, at least," Puddleshine mewed at last. "I'll tell Tigerstar and Tawnypelt, and they'll decide if they want to send some cat to talk to him."

The mention of Tigerstar brought the previous night's events back into Alderheart's mind, and he felt a renewed touch of wonder at the way Tigerstar had been sent back to his Clan. He could tell that the other medicine cats felt the same.

"What exactly happened?" Kestrelflight asked, curiosity alight in his eyes.

"StarClan appeared," Puddleshine replied. "They brought Tigerstar back and gave him nine lives."

And that doesn't really tell us anything, Alderheart thought. *But then, it's always been forbidden to tell other cats what happens at nine-lives ceremonies.*

Frecklewish let out an irritated snort. "It's certainly convenient that StarClan gave ShadowClan the chance to rebuild itself," she mewed. "But you'd better not be planning on reclaiming the territory you ceded to SkyClan. We'll be patrolling our borders, you can be sure of that!"

Puddleshine looked taken aback at the SkyClan medicine cat's waspish tone. But Alderheart could understand Frecklewish's irritation. Clearly, she shared Leafstar's opinion that the ShadowClan cats who had joined SkyClan and then left had taken advantage of SkyClan's generosity.

"Of course," Puddleshine meowed after a moment. "I'm sure all the ShadowClan cats value their friendship with Sky-Clan."

"And now, can we *please* get started?" Jayfeather's tail-tip twitched irritably. "Are we going to meet with StarClan tonight, or aren't we?"

At his words, all the medicine cats took their places at the water's edge and leaned over to touch their noses to the surface of the Moonpool. Alderheart felt the familiar rush of darkness and icy cold, and opened his eyes to find himself sitting in dappled sunlight and shade. The scent of fresh, growing things filled his nose; he could hear birds singing in the branches and, a little way away, the gurgle of a stream.

Rising to his paws, Alderheart looked around him. At first he couldn't see any cat, and he wondered what StarClan meant to show him in this place. Then he saw fronds waving in a nearby bank of fern, and a gray she-cat stepped into the open. Her eyes were a clear, intense blue, and starshine glimmered in her fur and around her paws.

Alderheart couldn't remember ever seeing her before, though she looked familiar. As she approached, he dipped his head to her in a gesture of deepest respect.

"Greetings, Alderheart," the she-cat meowed. "I am Cinderpelt."

Understanding flooded over Alderheart. *She looks so much like Cinderheart. That's who she reminds me of!* He remembered too the story that Leafpool had told him when he was first apprenticed as a medicine cat: how Cinderpelt had died defending her Clan, and how StarClan had sent her spirit back for a while to live another life in Cinderheart's body. *This is a really special cat!*

"I was once Firestar's apprentice," Cinderpelt went on, "but I was injured on the Thunderpath and could never live the life of a warrior. Instead I became ThunderClan's medicine cat." She brushed her tail along Alderheart's side, purring warmly; Alderheart shivered at the touch.

"I loved Firestar," Cinderpelt continued; memories swirled in the depths of her blue eyes. "But I chose my duty over the hope that he would love me, and it was the right choice. ThunderClan needs you, Alderheart, just as it needed me. For the future to remain unclouded, medicine cats must choose their duty to their Clan over anything else."

"I understand," Alderheart murmured. "But it's hard."

"True, but the rewards are great," Cinderpelt assured him. "And now," she went on more briskly, "now that the five Clans are finally united once more, there will be new challenges. The sky has cleared at last, but the Clans must come together to make the forest grow."

Her voice began to fade on the last few words, and the sunlight dazzled Alderheart's eyes. His last sight was of Cinderpelt's gentle, approving gaze. Then he woke beside the Moonpool to see his fellow medicine cats stirring from their own visions.

Happiness warmed Alderheart from ears to tail-tip as he rose to begin the journey home. But he couldn't feel completely at peace. *I wonder what Cinderpelt meant,* he asked himself. *What challenges will we face, now that the five Clans must learn to live together?*

ENTER THE BRAVELANDS

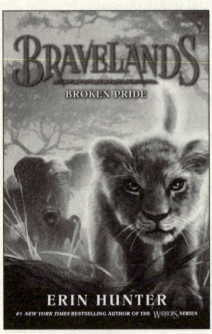

1

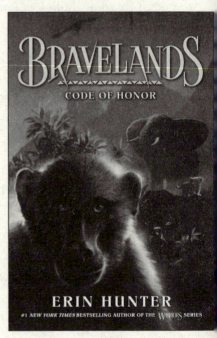

2

Heed the call of the wild in this
action-packed series from **Erin Hunter**.

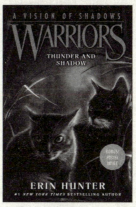

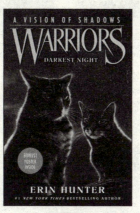

WARRIORS: SUPER EDITIONS

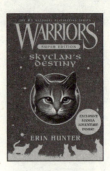

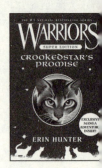

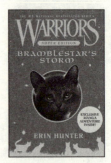

These extra-long, stand-alone adventures will take
you deep inside each of the Clans with thrilling tales
featuring the most legendary warrior cats.

HARPER
An Imprint of HarperCollinsPublishers

www.warriorcats.cor